Books by Alisa Allan

WINDS OF CHANGE - ISBN: 0-9761480-0-5
Release Date: July 29, 2005
Cruise to Bermuda with a young woman who is forced to choose. Rekindle a past?... Or set it free?

AFTER MIDNIGHT – ISBN: 0-9761480-1-3
Release Date: August 31, 2005
Cruise to the Mexican Riviera and the Canada/New England coast with two strangers who marry and clash in a blaze of differences.

THE BEST MAN - ISBN: 0-9761480-2-1
Release Date: September 30, 2005
Cruise to Hawaiian Island paradise with a woman caught up in a tailspin of revenge after a failed wedding attempt, and finds herself in the middle of a bond that could not be broken.

BEYOND THE HORIZON - ISBN: 0-9761480-3-X
Release Date: October 31, 2005
Cruise to the Caribbean with three friends who are taken away by balmy tropical breezes and become vulnerable to its magic, then discover a web of lies and deceit underneath its beauty.

ONE LAST TIME - ISBN: 0-9761480-4-8
Release Date: November 30, 2005
Cruise to the Caribbean with a single mother and her son as they set off on a journey of adventure. Immersed in exotic ambiance, a woman lets go of a battle that threatens to drown her, but must eventually return and face it, and she must risk all she found to face it alone.

ANGEL MIST - ISBN: 0-9761480-5-6
Release Date: December 31, 2005
Cruise to Alaska as a young woman discovers a calm to the haunts of her past, but she finds she would truly have to go home again before she could find real peace.

Visit our website for more details and to join our mailing list:
www.BonVoyageBooks.com
www.TravelTimePress.com
www.AlisaAllan.com

Beyond The Horizon

Alisa Allan

Bon Voyage Books
An Imprint of Travel Time Press

Bon Voyage Books
An Imprint of Travel Time Press

Beyond The Horizon
Copyright © 2005 Alisa Allan, All Rights Reserved

ISBN: 0-9761480-3-X

The reproduction or utilization of this work is strictly prohibited. This includes not only photocopying and recording but by any electronic, mechanical, storage and retrieval system or any other means hereafter invented, in whole or in part without the written permission of our editorial office.

This is a work of fiction. Any names, characters, places or incidents are products of the author's imagination or are used in a fictitious manner. Anyone bearing the same name or names is not to be construed as real. Any resemblance is entirely coincidental.

Visit us
www.BonVoyageBooks.com
www.TravelTimePress.com
www.AlisaAllan.com

Publisher SAN# 2 5 6 – 5 7 9 X

Dedication:

To my Steel Magnolia's

Elizabeth, Lois, Wanda, and one who will always be in my heart, Phyllis, you've all given me memories to cherish and so much more. You were all an inspiration to read, you gave me the encouragement to write, and you instilled in me this wanderlust to go out and see the world.

You've all had the courage to go through things in life I wouldn't feel strong enough for, and I admire you. You've all been through your trials and tribulations and come through with bells on, and I applaud you. You've all managed to keep your hearts close, and at times I've envied you. You've also included me, and I am grateful to you. I thank you for everything you've been to me, but above all, I love you.

CHAPTER ONE

"Maggie, I need to see you in my office sometime today." Wilma tapped long, professionally manicured nails on her desk when she walked by without stopping or turning back around.

Maggie looked up to see her boss, Wilma Hughes, sashay by without waiting for an answer, then she realized she didn't have to wait for an answer because it wasn't really a question, even though it was presented as one. She worked on her own, very seldom did she meet with anyone or discuss her projects. She would complete it, turn it in, and then start on another with very little supervision or anyone looking over her head. Now she had to wonder why Wilma requested the meeting, it was rare to be summoned to her office for anything except maybe a personal chat on occasion.

If she wanted to meet for lunch she'd have said lunch, but she hadn't. And she used her professional 'boss' voice, the business one instead of the friend one. Maggie looked back to her computer and the research she'd been doing but couldn't concentrate any longer so she saved it and closed her program. If she didn't go see her now she'd forget about it later.

"I have a few minutes, what did you need?" Maggie poked her head around the door to Wilma's office and the elegant, dressed to perfection woman, motioned her to come in and sit down.

"We're short, and I have a new assignment I need you for, but I'm afraid you're not going to like it much." Wilma knew her preferences and this was not one of them. "I need you to do a behind the scenes kind of thing."

"Behind what scene?" By the look on Wilma's face, she was already prepared to decline.

"We're sending a few models on a cruise ship for a photo shoot and..."

"You're right, that scene is not mine. No models, no fashion, I could care less whether the purse was made of leather or cardboard and really don't give a rat's ass who's name is on it. The Pope can make a Holy blessed bag and every nitwit in the world would pay fifty grand for the privilege of schlepping it around, with the name on the outside of course, so everyone would know what kind of bag it was and how much they paid for it. Never mind the fact they charged it and will pay for it the rest of their lives." Maggie took a deep sigh and a breath to continue her exaggerated rampage. "But they'll blame me, they'll say they read an article and it was something they had to have and..."

"Get off your soapbox, I need you for this."

"You know me, no models, no fashion bull crap, I won't help to promote the latest name, no contribution whatsoever. I know journalist sometimes don't have morals, but I do. It's menial and I've placed myself above that, even if nobody else has." She quickly went to leave but Wilma screamed for her.

"Maggie Pace, get back here!" Wilma raised her voice with all the authority she could muster for a friend.

She returned slowly and sighed. "This isn't me, this is Marsha's thing."

"She's sick, had to have emergency gall bladder surgery, and she isn't happy about it."

"And I'm even unhappier. Tell her to be a trouper, I traveled across country for a story when I had a broken foot, tell her to muster up some guts and get on with it." Maggie had no sympathy for Marsha when it would involve her taking over a stupid assignment she cared nothing about.

"She's bed ridden for at least a month."

"They have beds on cruise ships."

"I need you for this one Maggie." Wilma sighed and looked at her. "I know you don't like it, and I wouldn't ask you if it wasn't important."

"Why me? Can't that new girl..." Maggie began to protest more but was stopped immediately with every excuse her boss could counter with.

They bantered for at least ten minutes back and forth as to why Maggie was the one she needed for the assignment. The main one being she had nothing else but male writers available, and she could only imagine what kind of article it would end up being. Also, since it was on a cruise, rather than send a supervisor to oversee everything, she trusted Maggie to act in that capacity.

"Not only do you want me to write about this whole stupid thing you want me to supervise the entire job?" She almost screeched the words.

"It makes sense. You're the only one I trust to do both." Wilma placed her chin on her hand and looked pleadingly, as if Maggie had a choice when they both knew she didn't. "Just this once? Do it as a favor for me and I'll let you run whatever you want for the next issue. Whatever piece you give me, I won't change a thing, won't question it, nothing, you'll have free reign."

"I normally do have free reign anyway, my pieces don't have to be altered."

Wilma looked up with one eyebrow raised in her playful threat. "Then I'll change things. I'll change everything and you'll have to do it all over. Come on, Maggie, the next issue you get to submit whatever you want. I know you have those stories I wouldn't let you put in before, you've been waiting for an opportunity for me to approve them."

"The next four issues," Maggie pushed.

"Two," she countered.

"Three." Maggie knew by the look in her eyes she should take the offer of two before it was reduced, but she pressed.

"Three," Wilma gave in, "But I didn't even have to do that, all I had to do was use the fact that one of the stops on the cruise is Roatan."

"Aren't you sweet?" Maggie finally smiled for the first time in their conversation, excited at the prospect of Roatan, it was one of her favorite places. "That's all you had to say from the beginning and you gave me the three issues as a bonus, even if the assignment will still stink."

"It won't be as bad as you make it out to be. You can even take your boyfriend if you want, hell, take three more people but they'll have to pay for themselves. The room actually sleeps four, so take some friends and consider it a paid vacation."

"So when do I leave?" All she saw then was the vision of Roatan, and it made her feel better.

"Don't you want to know the details?"

Maggie shrugged her shoulders and Wilma went on to explain. Since Marsha was sick, instead of going with her usual fashion section they would send a few models for a photo shoot and Maggie would write a behind the scenes piece to go along with it, a day in the life of a model so to speak. Maggie openly cringed, it wasn't her type of story because her pieces had substance, much more than what this would entail.

She wrote about medical stories, people who overcame great obstacles, she'd even had a few of her war pieces go national in reprints. She thought of the assignment before her as being demoted when she'd done nothing to deserve it, any other writer would jump on it just to have the vacation aspect of it, but Maggie had more important things to do, and she could always book a trip to Roatan herself, she didn't need the assignment to visit.

Maggie hated the fluff stuff, as she called it. Menial articles on the right things to wear, the things not to wear, it was all fashion trend that made people want to go out and blow their money to look hip, only to spend more hard earned dollars the next year on that years latest trend. It reminded her of a bunch of stupid mice on a wheel that never stopped. Maggie never thought it was important who was wearing what, or the latest five hundred dollar purse everyone had to have because it had a certain name and logo on it. It wasn't Maggie. And she really didn't like contributing in the least little bit, made her feel like she'd bought into the game.

When Wilma explained the cruise, she almost laughed at the thought of models with eating disorders on an all you can eat cruise vacation, and then cringed at the thought of spending a week with women who honed themselves to perfection. She'd been around her share of models at various parties and functions and hadn't found one yet that could carry on a conversation. Except if you counted tedious, mind-numbing jargon, interspersed with fits of giggles and the batting of lashes as they flashed a bright white smile that could give a blind man back his sight.

It wasn't jealousy. Although they were breathtakingly gorgeous, Maggie never put much emphasis on a persons looks. She based judgments on character and moral values. As for her own looks, she was pleased when she looked in the mirror, she wasn't as lovely as the flawless women splattered on their magazine covers and every other page inside, but she didn't scare little children either.

Her task would be not only model interviews but she would also talk to the photographer and the crew during the weeklong shooting schedule. A piece about how it looks like a dream job to travel for a week to exotic places, but to get the hard work that it took to actually make it a success.

Wilma tried to make it sound as good as possible. "So as you can see, it isn't all fashion trend, it's an inside story about the process. Of course our readers want to know how they look so good for an early morning shoot and how they protect their hair from salt water."

"Of course, how could anyone possibly live their lives and not know those things?" Maggie's voice was filled with sarcasm. "I can't believe I've waited all my life and not known the right way to apply foundation so I don't look tired at 5 a.m."

Already in her head she imagined she certainly wouldn't be having dinner with the models, they seldom ate, but they did lie on beaches and lounge in hot tubs. Besides, a week on a cruise ship would be a major benefit over sitting at her desk and she couldn't remember the last time she made time to get out of town for awhile. Not even for a long weekend.

Wilma smiled with the satisfaction she talked her into it. "As I said, you can take three other people if you want, your room sleeps a total of four, and I'll need their information and they'll have to pay for themselves but it's at a discount. Maybe your boyfriend, what's his name, Jerry?"

"Where have you been? I haven't seen Jerry in months."

Wilma raised her eyes in question. "How could I not have known that? I thought he was serious?"

"Serious about taming me, he didn't like the fact I had my own brain. I haven't found one secure enough in himself to not be intimidated because I have a mind of my own."

Wilma laughed. "Why do you think I've been divorced twice?"

"Guys don't want strong independent women, they want someone to take care of them. Fix their dinner, do their laundry, I don't do that shit for myself half the time, and I'm certainly not going to do it for anyone else."

"Mothers don't do their sons any favors by taking care of them so well. They can't fend for themselves as adults."

"Jerry actually had the nerve to tell me we were having problems because I didn't do things the way his mother did. And he had a way of trying to make me feel guilty for not giving a shit. Why does demeaning a woman make a man feel superior? For some reason they have to feel superior still. I thought that went out with clubbing wildlife for dinner and dragging it back to the cave." Maggie pictured it in her mind and almost laughed out loud. She should have known he'd be that kind of guy the first time they'd met when he jokingly asked her to pick up his dry cleaning after their first date then said he'd come by the next day and pick it up at her place. Maggie told him to 'go to hell' but she should have taken it as a sign of things to come.

Wilma simply listened to her rave with understanding. "Sounds like you've had some pent up emotions you had to let out."

"I'm just tired of the dating crap, I think Jerry was the last straw."

"Maybe you're just dating the wrong kind of man?"

"So tell me where to find the right one," Maggie laughed. "If I had the inside on that I could sell a blockbuster non-fiction. It's the million-dollar question every single woman in America wants to know. Or should I say, the one's who are still looking, I've decided I can do without altogether."

"Oh, I don't know about that."

"I can take out the trash and hook up a DVD player, men can't even do that. I'm serious, I can do without."

"That's what I thought before my first marriage, then before my second, and then for a while again before I found my third husband. The third time was a charm. We just have to sift through some rocks to find the diamonds." Wilma thought Maggie too young and pretty to be so cynical about men.

"Well the only rocks I've come across couldn't shine if you put them in one of those rock tumblers I used to have as a kid."

"The way you push yourself, you don't have time for men." Wilma smiled. "Make time, Maggie."

Maggie picked up the folder Wilma had closed for her new assignment. "I can't find a man that can get my mind off work. Guess if that happens, which I highly doubt, I'll know he at least would have potential."

"That's quite a job to give a man, you don't want much, do you?" Wilma sighed as she leaned back in her soft leather chair, knowing where she was, she'd been there herself before, but there was hope. "Don't give up, Maggie, there's always something around the corner when you least expect it."

Maggie laughed. "I find them around every corner all the time, but everything I find is quite scary. It's like Halloween in my life all year long."

Her feelings were affirmed that evening when she went out for a few drinks with a friend after work. They'd been enjoying some appetizers and a few glasses of wine when a man approached. He was certainly good looking, tall, blond, dressed to GQ perfection, but he should have kept his mouth closed, Maggie was turned off the moment he spoke.

"Hey, girls, I didn't think you'd mind a little company, especially not when it's someone like me. My name's Al," he smiled.

"Well, Al," Maggie said with a bland tone and saw the surprise on his face that she hadn't immediately jumped in his lap. "Tell you the truth, we do mind, especially when it's someone like you."

"Oh. You two are together, huh?" He leered at them.

"If it makes you feel better to think that."

"What else could it be?" He couldn't possibly comprehend he was an idiot asshole.

Maggie continued as her friend sat quiet, not as outspoken as she was. "I don't think I need to explain. As I said, we do mind. Your interruption was rude, and we're not interested."

"Oh come on, ladies. Let me buy you a drink, anything you want."

"I'm not so desperate that I go out and pray to meet a man so I can get a drink. I'm drinking what I want and I can afford to buy another." Maggie thought it a shame, maybe if he'd kept his mouth shut she would have enjoyed looking at him. "I'll ask you to leave just once more. I'm sure you'll find what you're looking for elsewhere."

Her friend laughed when he left. "Every time I meet someone like that, I so appreciate what I've got at home. How do you do it being single and dealing with his kind?"

"I've decided I won't anymore. I'm even thinking of wearing a fake wedding ring."

"I used to do that, and even that doesn't work with some of them. You know, Jason has a friend that..."

"Don't even go there." Maggie almost choked on her drink. "I'm happy that you're happy in your wonderful, committed, relationship, but it's not for everyone. I'm one of those people who've come to the conclusion it has no place in my life."

"But he's..."

"Probably a great guy, I'm sure," Maggie was insistent with her words. "End of conversation."

That evening, as Maggie sat in her apartment alone, she knew she could live the rest of her life that way. Men complicated things, didn't do things the way she did, left the toilet seat up, waited for her to put it down, left clothes piled everywhere, waited for her to pick them up. It just didn't work. Most men wanted the docile creature that complimented them and made their worlds perfect. Not someone like Maggie who was much too independent and head strong in her opinions and the way she lead her life.

It was something her mother couldn't understand. Being an only daughter, her mother waited daily for a phone call to tell her news of an engagement and Maggie disappointed her every time. When she called her mother to tell her of the trip, of course she had to listen to complaints of her single status, it was as if the entire world waited for her to get married, according to her mother it was that way.

"Mom, I just called to tell you I'd be going on a trip in a few weeks. Not to discuss my love life, which there is none."

Her mother sighed, "I'm sorry, dear."

Maggie rolled her eyes. "It's nothing to be sorry about. Can't you understand that? All those brothers I have, and all older than me. Let's pretend its law it has to go in birth order, I'm the youngest and I can't get married till they're all married."

"Nonsense dear, I just worry about you by yourself. Sandra Billings keeps asking me, and I'm almost embarrassed to tell her you don't have anyone yet. Honey, do you," she paused, unsure of the exact words to say. "If you like something other than men, you can..."

"Mother." Maggie screamed in shock into the telephone.

"Well you could tell us."

"You'll be the first to know," Maggie rubbed her forehead, it gave her a headache to talk to her mother about this all the time. And it irritated her more to think her mother had given her statement any thought, just because she didn't have a man in her life. It frustrated her she couldn't make her mother understand that she didn't need one.

In the beginning of being on her own, Maggie even stooped so low as to lie to her a few times, just to make her feel better. Told her about some made up person she was seeing, never embellished it, the simple statement she was seeing someone would make her happy for awhile. Then when she'd ask about him later, Maggie would say it hadn't developed further, even told her one time she discovered the guy was married. Had even planned to milk it for sympathy, tell her she couldn't get over him so didn't want to date, but her mother surprised her with her reaction.

"Oh, dear. Is he getting divorced?"

She'd even suggested Maggie meet someone on the Internet once. "I saw a program the other day. They had a dating site online and..."

Her mother made her feel like she was a desperate woman no matter how many times Maggie told her it was by choice. So lying didn't work, now she just told her the truth, even if she had to endure the disappointing sighs. Knew her mother didn't need to hear the list of losers she actually had dated. And her mother couldn't understand that it wasn't that she couldn't get a date, there were tons of offers, but she had a problem with thinking Maggie didn't want to and couldn't comprehend that.

That evening's phone call went smoothly once she finally got her off the subject and asked about all of her brothers, sister-in-laws, nieces and nephews. That was enough to have a few hours of conversation because Maggie had seven older brothers.

Afterwards, she flipped open the folder and glanced through the notes about the trip. Now that she committed herself to it, she did begin to get excited at the prospect of cruising for a week and visiting the Caribbean, especially Roatan. She'd been there often, had made the little island a second home and it would be the highlight of her trip, the only thing to look forward to. That and spending the week with her best friends she hadn't seen in quite some time, because of course there was no question she would invite Kyla and Nicole to come along and enjoy it with her.

What Maggie didn't know at that moment in time, was the impact the carefree trip would have on her life. She would find much more than she'd bargained for along tropical shores edged with turquoise sea.

CHAPTER TWO

"My client is willing to settle for one million even and nothing less. We all know she could get millions but she just wants to move on." Kyla Reeves moved a piece of paper across the table. "This is the settlement agreement, look it over and have it returned to my office by tomorrow morning. If I don't receive it by 9:00 a.m. we go to court."

"I don't need to give her anything, she's nothing but..." The almost ex-husband began to rant but Kyla stopped him.

"Mr. Kerry, no one will be interested in your opinions of your wife and what you think she is."

"I'm not forking over a dime, and I'll tell anyone what she is."

"Will you tell them you've sent her to the hospital numerous times, threatened her life just about every day, and almost succeeded in killing her once in a drug induced stupor?"

"She knows that's her fault." He glared across the table at her client, his wife, a threatening, menacing look. "You're not getting a dime bitch."

Kyla's voice became more aggressive. "She'll get more than that. I wanted her to push for at least ten million, with confidence that I could rake you through the coals and by the time I was done, the only thing I'd have left in my hand would be the top of your skull. Now I'm not sure what your lawyer is going to advise you to do, but I can tell you one thing, if I don't have an answer tomorrow morning, you'll be millions of dollars poorer by the weekend."

"Can she talk to me like that?" He looked to his own attorney in rage, his eyes wild in anger. "I bet I'll..."

Kyla leaned across the perfectly waxed and shiny conference table of dark wood. With no fear she faced the man who was prone to abuse, her eyes cold and unforgiving. "What? What do you want to do, Mr. Kerry? Beat me? Like you did your wife?"

He said nothing more when his attorney placed his hand on his arm to try as best he could to calm him, possibly stop him from doing something stupid as Kyla suggested. "Calm down, Mr. Kerry."

"Nine o'clock in the morning is the deadline for this settlement. If not, get your suit cleaned Mr. Kerry, we'll see you in court," she pulled back and without another word escorted her client from the room. Like Ellen Kerry, she couldn't stand the sight of him.

"You okay?" She asked the frail looking woman beside her.

"Better than I used to be in front of him. He doesn't scare me anymore."

"Therapy is working well then?" Kyla was sincere in her concern. The woman had come to her six months previous broken and tattered like a rag doll. She'd set her up with the right kind of help, could see she was much stronger now but still had a long road ahead.

"I can't live without therapy right now. If I hadn't of found you and the right kind of help, I'd still be with him, Kyla, and that scares me. I could never do it before, I could never leave him for good, and I can't thank you enough for everything. You've helped me get a life back."

Kyla put her arm around the woman. "No thanks needed. I'm just glad you had the sense enough to get away from him, but more important, to get your daughter away from him. How are her sessions going? How is Jamie?"

"Like me she's a changed girl too. It took her awhile, but I think she's confident now that we're not going back. We did so many times before, but she knows it won't happen this time."

They'd lived the roller coaster life before of leaving him, going back, only to leave him again several times over the years. She'd never mustered the strength needed to leave him for good. Frightened, as well she should have been, from threats and actions by a physically abusive man, one who stopped at nothing to control her. Many outsiders thought it was his money that kept her there. They didn't know it was her fear of death that prevented her from running as far away from him as she could get, and never look back.

Kyla walked outside with her and continued to Ellen's car as she unlocked and opened the door then as Ellen sat in the driver's seat they chatted casually through the open car door. Neither saw her husband who pulled his car behind hers, pulled out a gun, and fired several shots, and then glass shattered all around them. Kyla felt a bullet pierce her leg just as she pushed Ellen down in the seat to protect her. Bullets hit the car, came through the back window, the side window, and all around them until he was out.

When she realized he'd finished and pulled off, Kyla ran to the end of the car but all she saw were the taillights and heard the screech of tires then the sound of metal against metal as he hit several cars. Then his tires screeched again as he managed to get out of the parking lot and speed down the road.

"Ellen, you okay?" Kyla hollered but she didn't answer. She turned to go back to check and searing pain shot through her leg as she looked to see blood already soaked into her stocking and now rolling down her leg. She limped, rather hopped, lightly but quickly.

"I'm okay. I wasn't hit." Ellen was huddled in a ball shaking as shards of glass lay both in and outside of the car. "I just... oh my God, he really would kill me. Thank God Jamie wasn't here."

"Kyla! Was she hit?" James Robertson, Mr. Kerry's attorney and a frequent opponent of Kyla's rounded the corner quickly.

"No, she wasn't hit." She answered as she leaned her back against the car and sighed. The shock of it began to take affect, along with the pain.

"Shit, Kyla, you were." He reached down and pulled her skirt up to see the bullet wound and handed her his cell phone as he took off his jacket. "Call 911, you've already lost quite a bit of blood. Lay down and..." But he couldn't get the words out quick enough.

"It isn't that bad, is it?" The next she saw was blackness that enveloped her as she passed out.

But it was only momentary and James was quick enough to catch her before she fell, and then he laid her gently on the pavement of the dirty, greasy parking lot. When she came to, James had taken his coat off and pressed hard on her leg to stop the bleeding and Ellen was talking to her.

"You'll be okay, Kyla, the ambulance is on the way, it's just your leg but it's bleeding quite a bit. You'll be fine."

She glanced down to James who pressed hard with his expensive suit coat that was now ruined, saturated with her blood. "You're not going to let me bleed to death, James? Not like there's any love lost between us."

He laughed, "It crossed my mind, but I'd rather win fair and square in a courtroom settlement."

"I think it's safe to say we call this one early. My win." She closed her eyes as if it would stop the pain she could now feel.

"Off the record, you'll get no argument from me, counselor," he looked at his jacket and thought it was doing a pretty good job of stopping the blood, but if help didn't arrive soon he'd have to search for something else, as he wasn't sure how much more it would hold.

"How does it look?" She asked, not quite sure she wanted to know and couldn't look down to see.

"I'm not a doctor, but I'm sure you'll be fine." He looked to the back to see if he had to stop blood there, but there was no hole, the bullet hadn't come out.

"Damn. A brand new pair of pantyhose too," she cursed.

Kyla would be fine as Ellen promised. But they had to operate to remove the bullet and she would remain in the hospital for a few days. When she called her husband she thought maybe they'd given her too many drugs because the conversation was not what she expected. Certainly not one she ever thought she'd be having from a hospital bed.

"Ted, where have you been?" She almost screamed into the phone. "I haven't been able to reach you at home and when I called your cell, the number's been changed. I had to call your partner to get your new number."

"Kyla." He spoke with a soft hesitation of shock that she didn't know. "I left two weeks ago."

"You went out of town, but..."

"No, Kyla, I left two weeks ago. Left the house, left you. I want a divorce. Didn't you notice my empty drawers? My things missing from the bathroom? I took everything with me."

She thought about his words, had to take a moment and let them sink in, her husband left her and she hadn't even known. She didn't tell him the reason for her call, didn't tell him she'd been wounded and lay in a hospital bed. They chatted a few moments about a divorce being the right thing to do. It wasn't working anymore and neither held any bad feelings for the other, both knew it was best, and she thought the drugs did help in keeping her calm and in control. Then again, the shock of it hadn't really sunk in and she hung up the phone in a daze.

When she returned to her empty house she looked for any sign of him, but he'd been right. He'd taken everything and it was as if he'd never lived there at all. As if their life together was simply erased and never really happened. How could she have not seen how empty it now was?

She'd lived without him for two weeks and hadn't noticed his shaving cream and deodorant no longer sat on the bathroom shelf. Hadn't noticed the top of his dresser was completely bare of anything, wiped clean. She had her own space, so there was never any reason for her to go inside his dresser drawers, or into his closet, so she hadn't noticed there were no clothes there. Until now as she opened the closet door where his meticulously cared for suits used to hang. Now there were only the hangers they used to hang on.

When Maggie called a week later to invite her on a cruise, it took her two seconds to say yes.

Maggie laughed, "I thought I'd have to spend days talking you into it."

"I just got out of the hospital because a crazed husband wanted me and his wife dead. And my own husband up and left me, and I didn't even know he was gone. How pathetic is that life?"

"Are you okay?" Maggie gasped.

"With what? The gunshot wound or the empty house?" Kyla sighed. "I'm fine with both, that makes it even more pathetic."

"First, what kind of gunshot wound?"

"It was in the leg, the top of the thigh, but they had to cut the bullet out. It's fine though, still a little sore but I lost a lot of blood. Good thing is, the husband of my client was caught and arrested of course, and he's given her everything, millions of dollars. He won't need it anyway, he'll be in jail for attempted murder and I laugh thinking about him being beat up and bullied, just like he used to do to his wife. That's my justice."

"And the marriage?" Maggie asked more cautiously.

"It hasn't been right for a long time. I knew it was coming, I just thought I'd know about it when it happened. He left on a business trip a few weeks ago and I didn't think anything of it until I called him from the hospital and he told me when he left, he'd taken everything with him. His clothes, his personal things, how could I have not noticed that?"

"Now will you believe me when I tell you that you work too hard?"

They laughed at the situation, Kyla could easily laugh now that the shock of it had worn off, and talking to Maggie, and the invitation, gave her something else to think about other than her life that was nothing but work. And her house, that was nothing but empty.

Kyla smiled at the prospect of the upcoming trip. She hadn't had a vacation or been away in so long she'd forgotten what it was like to leave everything behind, she'd forgotten how to relax. But after she hung up the phone with Maggie she propped her leg up on the end of the sofa and decided it would be fun to learn again.

She didn't know what fate had in store for her, it never crossed her mind that it would be a trip that would change her life forever.

****

Nicole pulled her car into the drive and approached the door, which was opened before she got there.

"I thought I heard you pull in." Janice opened the door wide and revealed a bottle of wine. "I've been chilling it all day. You're not going to take the kids and run, are you?"

"I have no place to run but home and the only thing waiting for me there is dust. And it's Friday, I'll have all weekend to get to it."

She appreciated Janice's help not only as a sitter, but a friend. Nicole was a single mother with two kids, Anthony was thirteen, Elizabeth eleven, and an insurance adjuster who worked her hours to make ends meet, but couldn't wait until the end of the day to get home to her children. She noticed the older they got, the more excited she was to see them. But their excitement had faded over the years after the divorce and they'd gotten used to her working, it was their normal life now.

"Hey, Mom," Anthony greeted her quickly as he ran back upstairs to Janice's son's room with another video game. He'd long passed the kissing welcome stage.

"Mom," Elizabeth screamed before she was about to rush downstairs. "I have a team cookout tomorrow and need hotdogs."

"At least you're glad to see me," she said sarcastically and laughed at Janice who smiled with understanding.

"How was your day on the outside?" Janice said. As a stay at home mom, she often envied Nicole going out to work everyday.

"A rough one, I need the wine this evening."

They sat on the outside deck and Nicole took her heels off and rested her feet atop the empty chair across from her. "This feels so good, just to sit. I've been running around all day today. At least when I used to stay home and run the roads all day, it was in tennis shoes."

"But they didn't look nearly as nice as those. Great shoes, are they new?"

"Brand new. I had to buy them today when my heel got stuck in a grate and broke right off in the street. Should have seen me hobbling down the sidewalk," Nicole sipped the wine appreciatively. "This is great wine."

"Jimmy brought it home last night. By the way, he mentioned maybe doing dinner or something, that guy that works with him wants to go out with you again."

Nicole moaned, "No way. How old was he anyway? Twelve? He had more fun with Anthony playing video games while he waited for me to finish getting ready. I have two children, I don't need another."

"What about that guy from work you were seeing for awhile."

"I told him I had kids and I haven't heard from him since."

"Well..."

Nicole wouldn't let her finish. "Well nothing. Not interested. Don't want to. Would rather sit on a porch and knit if that's how I'm to spend the rest of my life. But it will just be me and me alone, only room for one rocking chair."

Janice knew even though it had been five years since her divorce she was still a little distrustful and bitter. Her husband left her for another woman, and that was always a hard one to overcome and gain self confidence again. And she knew it must be difficult to live a single life with children. So Nicole was happy to simply live the life of the mother she was, one who put her children first, anything else came second.

"You can't rock alone forever."

Nicole cocked one eyebrow up. "Why not? When I get too old and weak, my kids will feel obligated to pay me back for all the years I gave them, and they'll rock me. Anthony will probably rock so hard I'll fall off the porch, but I can trust Elizabeth."

"What about when they go off to college and get their own lives? It will happen one day."

"One day far, far away. I don't need anyone else, I have my kids and that's enough. That's my life." Nicole certainly didn't want to think about that, didn't want to imagine it would one day happen that her kids would be old enough to go off to college, even though it couldn't be avoided. But she would deal with it when that time came. For now, there was nothing else she needed.

Nothing but the hot bath with soothing eucalyptus oil she dove into after the kids were settled in bed that evening. The wine and time spent relaxing was followed with a trip to the store for the hotdogs Elizabeth needed at the last minute, then the video place for movies. When they returned home she washed Anthony's uniform needed for the next day, cleaned up the shredded newspaper the dog scattered all over the house, and opened all the windows because a bird had gotten down the fireplace chimney and perched himself on a plant in the living room.

The hot soak was just what she needed as she closed her eyes and laid limp in the warm water, instantly felt the day escape from her every pore. As if it washed it away so she could renew herself for morning. It was followed by a few pages of reading her novel she'd been trying to get through for the last month, and just as she put it down to go to sleep the phone rang.

"Hello?" She asked, concerned with the late night call. It was close to midnight.

"Nicole, this is Ken."

"I know your voice, Ken, we were married once remember? Oh, but you couldn't remember that when we were married, how do I expect you to remember it when we're not."

She couldn't help but lash out, hated to hear his voice, even after five years of being divorced. Nicole still felt the betrayal of trust just as she had when she found out he'd been having an affair the final two years of their union. And then he left her for a woman whose nails were always perfect, firm toned body, long silky hair, and ten years her junior. She still felt the sting like a slap in the face, although the initial sting was finally beginning to get a little numb. Where were the men in the world who appreciated maturity? Were there any of those left?

"I didn't call this late to argue."

"What the hell did you call for then?" Nicole's voice was sharp and hostile. He could have at least had the courtesy to pretend she was probably on a date. Or with a man and shouldn't be disturbed at this late hour. It angered her more to think he hadn't even taken that into consideration.

Ken sighed, wondered if they would ever get to a nice place. "We're planning a vacation to take Missy to Disney World and I wanted to include Anthony and Elizabeth."

It angered her he planned it for his new little girl, and his older children were the after thought to take along while they were going anyway. Why couldn't he have planned it for them first?

"Certainly you're not leaving tonight, couldn't you have waited to call in the morning?" She didn't wait for an answer, knew he probably waited to call when he thought she was sleeping, just to piss her off. "When are you going?"

He gave her all the details and she knew she couldn't deny them the opportunity. Time wise it would work for them. Anthony would be over his games and Elizabeth would be through with her activities and have the summer free. Ken was the one who could afford to take them, not her. Even though it still angered her he'd never thought to take them on a family vacation to Disney World. With no reason not to, she agreed.

It worked perfectly when Maggie called her the next day, as if it were pre-planned in destiny.

"Nicole Cates, I've been trying to reach you for days, I was about to send the police to your house to see if the kids had tied you up and escaped," Maggie joked and laughed. "How are you?"

"Missing you, please tell me you're coming to town soon," Nicole smiled, it was good to hear her voice. Other than her children, Maggie and Kyla were the most important people in her life. They were childhood friends whose bond lasted the years of age and change for all of them.

"You sound desperate, everything okay?" Maggie noticed the tone of her voice that held a slight edge.

"The normal life, running around with work, running around with the kids, running with the dog, and all with no relief in sight. It's a good thing I can still afford a decent pair of tennis shoes." Nicole reached across the counter and grabbed the plate with the hamburgers on it before the dog managed to plop his face in it. "Tell me you're coming to visit. You haven't been to town in decades it seems, and you're due."

"Even better, I've called to invite you to come out of town with me." Maggie smiled to herself on the other end of the line. Knew it would be a wonderful surprise and opportunity for Nicole to be able to get away.

"Where and when? But you know it has to be a short trip. I don't enjoy the freedoms you and Kyla do."

"It's a week long cruise."

Maggie went on to explain the details of how the trip came about. How she'd already called Kyla who agreed and whatever arrangements Nicole would need to make for the kids, they would help somehow. Do whatever they could, even if it meant pitching in and paying for someone to take care of them if her ex wasn't agreeable. Maggie loved her kids, would love for them to go, but she only had one room. When she told her the date Nicole screamed.

"Maggie, that's perfect! Ken is taking the kids to Disney World that same week." Nicole beamed at her good fortune.

The timing couldn't have been better. She wouldn't have been able to afford to take the kids with her on a cruise and she would have passed on the invitation, would have felt guilty leaving them at home while she went alone. But with them going to Disney World she didn't have to feel guilty and could afford to take only herself.

"I can't believe this," Nicole still beamed. "For once, Ken managed to get his timing right. Where are we going anyway?"

Nicole knew it didn't matter because it would be wonderful wherever it was. She'd enjoy just sitting on the dock for a week and not have to worry about hot dogs, arranging the kid's transportation, picking up after the dog and the numerous other things that consumed her time and life, what little life she had. Heaven was just around the corner.

"We sail out of Houston and the ports are Cozumel, Roatan, Belize and Cancun."

Nicole's voice was ecstatic, "I have to go pack!"

She didn't actually begin to pack, but she mentally made notes, mentally it was all she could think of, getting away to the Caribbean with friends. The freedoms she would have somewhere warm and sunny, time for herself, time she never took at home when so many other things consumed her day.

There was no reason for her to think the trip wouldn't be anything but wonderful, and there was no reason for her to think anything could go wrong. Nicole would find herself looking back later and realizing how naïve a woman she actually was. Life wasn't all fairytales and little girl dreams hardly ever came true.

CHAPTER THREE

Even if the assignment itself was not to her liking, Maggie would make the best of it with her friends. She packed lightly, skilled at squeezing in the most in the smallest amount of space, and headed off to the airport with Wilma's gratitude and a company credit card. The company credit card also served to cheer her up, and she had it with full blessing to use as she saw fit.

"This could be a lot more fun than I thought," she commented to her boss.

"Yes, and I'm afraid you'll get down to the Caribbean and never come home. It does expire in a few years."

"A few years is enough time."

"At least you have a smile on her face." Wilma commented on her attitude, she knew as much as Maggie didn't like it, she was the best and she would come back with a great article.

Maggie tried to keep the smile on her face when she met the models but it was difficult, they weren't the most talkative group, but she excused them since it was early in the morning. She'd introduced herself but they were cranky, still half asleep.

"Want to give me some of your background?" Maggie asked one politely.

"Not now. All I can think about is sleep. This is crazy, flying out at this hour."

Another one began to talk but fell asleep in the middle of a sentence. She knew the crew would have been much more cooperative, but they'd gone a few days previous to secure equipment they would need in Houston. So there was nothing to write about for the moment and she wouldn't be getting anything out of the girls so she busied herself on her laptop at the boarding gate.

Maggie worked on what she would submit for the next edition when she had free reign. There were so many stories she wanted published. They would need to be fine tuned to make them perfect for submission, and the one she set her first sights on, was one she wanted published desperately. Maggie didn't want to, but was just about to freelance it elsewhere, now she wouldn't have to and she'd have the large distribution of her own magazine.

Two separate mothers who both lost their sons in the Iraq war and each of them had two very distinct opinions. One had decided to make it her mission to raise her voice and oppose the war. The other supported it, just as her son had. At a political function, the two of them actually almost came to blows over their differences. Then, with shared tragedy, they became the best of friends, even if they still opposed each other.

Through them, she'd gotten to know their sons, their lives, Maggie was pulled into their torment and pain and her story didn't focus on political views, but gave the reader a glimpse to the people they'd been. Made it more than the name of a deceased soldier that flashed across the news screen, Maggie's article made the reader feel the men's loss as well, just as the mothers did, and at the same time, made the reader understand the soldier's devotion to a cause they believed in. A military life they'd chosen and served.

She was sure when the reader finished, no matter their opinion on whether they opposed or supported the war, they'd want to thank the men who served them well. They would have gratitude for two strange young men in a far off country that had made the ultimate sacrifice for something they believed in.

Those were the stories Maggie concentrated on. That's why it was so frustrating to do something as trivial as a model shoot. She often thought of leaving the magazine, had offers from newspapers, but she'd always felt she was reaching people at the magazine she wouldn't have otherwise reached. Plus, most newspapers she picked up contained so many biased articles and she viewed them as nothing but a reporters opinions.

Not only would she have the current assignment finished before she got back, she would be set for the next two editions and ahead of the game. Maybe she'd use some of her vacation time and visit her family.

"Maggie Pace?"

"Yes," she answered, without looking up immediately, still typed away on her computer.

He didn't say anything else and she did finally look up. He was a tall man she didn't recognize, but assumed he'd be the photographer as it was the only person missing. She'd been so into her story it even took her mind a few moments to notice how attractive he was.

"I was told to introduce myself, I'm the photographer." He stood directly in front of her but made no attempt to shake her hand and there was not one hint of a smile. He looked peeved, as if he was forced to check in with a room mother or something.

Maggie didn't smile either. "Do you have a name?"

"Yeah," Was all he said before he walked away.

She glanced up discreetly as he picked a seat alone. When a few of the models saw him they approached him but spoke only briefly, then left him. His name hadn't been on her list of people that would be working for the week and Wilma told her not to worry, she was trying to get a specific photographer, and if she did he would be there. If she didn't, another photographer would be there. Maggie wondered if this was first choice or second.

He remained to himself reading the morning paper as they waited to board, and it didn't make it any more pleasant they were seated next to each other on the small cramped plane.

"Since we'll be working together for the week, it would help if I knew your name." Maggie finally asked him even though she knew he wanted to be left alone, maybe that was why she asked.

"Jackson Turner," he said, and then proceeded to fall asleep.

Or pretend to sleep, Maggie wasn't sure, it was probably a ploy to avoid any conversation. But he needn't have worried, she wasn't prepared to converse with someone who's attitude made it known he wanted nothing to do with anyone so she continued on her computer until the flight landed.

As they were walking off the plane the stewardesses and Captain stood at the door. The stewardess was a perky woman with a much too bright smile. "I hope you enjoyed the flight," she said grandly.

Lovely, Maggie thought to herself, but only smiled at the woman and then watched as the photographer quickly passed her as soon as they stepped off the plane and he disappeared into the crowd ahead. Obviously she would be on her own with the still cranky models. This trip was just getting better and better and she wondered what happened to the good attitude she'd come with. These people just seemed to suck it right out of her.

"How far is the hotel from here? Can we sleep for the day?" One of them whined in a tone that hit a nerve and actually made Maggie's eye twitch.

Like a leader of a whiny, petulant brownie troop of much younger girls, Maggie looked to her schedule. "According to the schedule I have, your first shoot is late this afternoon at the Aquarium. Don't you have a schedule to know where you're supposed to be and when?"

"Somewhere. I tried to tell my agent I needed an assistant, and they won't listen to me. I can't keep these things straight." The woman's face did a complete change when a handsome guy walked by and she smiled the big, beautiful smile she was paid for. Afterwards, she sighed as if it had taken the rest of her energy. "I need a shower, those people on the plane were dirty. Why didn't we fly first class?"

Maggie did her best not to scream. No wonder the photographer ran off, he must be used to this but she wasn't. Her first phone call when she checked into the hotel and got to her room was to Wilma.

"How could you do this to me? I was actually excited this morning, but now I don't even think it's worth it if you gave me free reign for my articles for the next year. These women are spoiled brats and the photographer is an arrogant mute."

"Jackson? He's the best in the business. I've never personally met him but I hear he's quite handsome, is it true?" She hadn't planned it, but it crossed Wilma's mind that maybe Jackson would be what Maggie needed to bring her out of the ban she'd placed on men being in her life.

Maggie thought about the handsome face of stone, a statue come to life with chiseled features, his muscular form, and... okay, Maggie, you're getting carried away, so he was handsome. "Handsome doesn't make a man."

"I would have thought you and Jackson would get along."

"Don't think that's going to happen, it took me an hour to get his name, he's not the chatty kind."

"He has control over the shoots."

"So I can't even fire him?" Maggie at least thought it would be an option.

"Absolutely not." Wilma almost screeched the words, feared it was something Maggie would actually do. "Do you know how tough it was to get him?"

"I can only imagine. I'm sure it's his personality that puts him in high demand," she said it with much sarcasm.

"He's the one who set the schedule. If you'll notice there are quite a few sunrise and sunset times. All has to do with the light he needs and all the other things that go along with the great pictures he's famed for taking. But I still want him in the article, an interview."

"How can I interview someone who doesn't talk?" Maggie looked down to her list where she'd scratched his name in as the photographer.

"You've had tougher interviews, I know you'll find a way around him."

"The only reason I'm staying is because I'll at least have friends with me. You planned it well didn't you, Wilma? You knew they'd come and be my salvation. Even made the price so cheap for them, anyone would have been a fool to turn it down. I'd high tail it out of here so fast if I didn't have that."

Wilma laughed on her end. "Yes, maybe it was part bribe, maybe it was just being your friend. Look at it as a big favor I did. If I hadn't gotten you your own room, you'd have bunked with a few of the models."

"I would have thrown myself overboard if I'd ever made it to the ship. They're spoiled brats."

"Yes, but their faces sell magazines, and that magazine pays our large salaries."

"I'm not included in the large salary group, but of course that's something you can take up at the next board meeting if you so choose." Maggie doodled on the paper in front of her. "I'll put up with the spoiled brats, and the mute photographer, but if there are any more surprises I might have to rethink our deal."

She sipped on her third cup of coffee when she replaced the phone and sighed. The shoot wasn't until that afternoon and Kyla and Nicole wouldn't be in until early evening. So she worked for the majority of the morning then arrived at the shoot late, surprised to see a crew member she knew well. John Carob was actually head of the crew and not only had she worked with him before, he was a dear friend and she liked him tremendously. John was an older gentleman in the age proximity of her father and just as kind.

Maggie stepped unnoticed behind him then slipped her hand under his arm, "Hey handsome."

He turned in surprise and hugged her with affection. "Maggie Pace on a fashion shoot? What did you do to get demoted?"

"It isn't by choice, I'm a reluctant replacement."

"So how have you been?"

"No, you're going to tell me about you first, I haven't been able to reach you hardly, haven't you gotten my messages?" She'd worried about him and it showed.

"I'm sorry, by the time I get a chance to call you back it's late."

"I'm up," she countered.

"Okay, I promise I'll be better about it." He looked like a child who'd just been scolded. "But I've really been out of town so much lately."

Maggie seemed to study his face, she could tell he was truly okay and it probably was only a matter of a busy work schedule. She had worried about him often, even though he was quite old enough to take care of himself, he had no children to look out for him.

"I'll let you slide this time, but I at least need to hear from you once a month."

"Yes ma'am," he saluted as if she were a General. "So now about you, did you run off and get married behind my back? Weren't you and…"

"Don't even say the name, we're not anymore. And that was by choice." Maggie looked around. "How's everything going?"

"The setting is great. The models a little testy today, but when are they not?"

They talked of many things. Maggie hadn't seen him in quite some time and there were many things she wanted to know, had been worried about him since his wife passed away. She worried, but whenever she couldn't reach him she ran into people all the time who knew him also and assured her he was doing well.

"I was actually thinking you might have been kicking up your heels when I couldn't get a hold of you, thought maybe you'd taken up ballroom dancing, been out on the town."

"Just staying busy, I'm not home much because the house is too quiet, so I work." He laughed at the thought of himself ballroom dancing.

"Ballroom dancing isn't such a far fetched idea, it would probably do you some good."

John shook his head. "I'll stick to having a few beers with the guys on occasion."

"Just the guys? Surely you plan to join me for a few this week."

He put his arm around her. "I wasn't looking forward to this trip until now."

"And you don't know how much better you've made my day. It started out bad and got worse, but it's looking better now."

"That bad?" He raised his eyebrows.

"You know me, I'm not used to dealing with models, and that photographer certainly isn't pleasant."

Before John could say anything they needed him and he had to go to work so Maggie was left on her own and she stood by quietly, watched and took mental notes of all that went on. The models whined and complained, one was too hot and another too cold. Simone was half asleep with eyes that seemed almost closed, yet looked sexy in the camera, and she noticed Tedi either singing or humming to herself, lost in a world of her own. Maggie had to think about drugs, wondered what she was on and hoped Wilma knew she took no responsibility for their stupid choices or actions.

Jackson took pictures at a constant rate. He emitted a quiet brood, a steady remoteness in a stone expression that never changed once the entire time she stood there. He had patience, she had to admit that. If she had to stand around all day and listen to the complaints these ladies dished out, she'd be arrested for assault and battery.

One thing she had to smile about was a particular fish. Two of the girls stood in front of a huge crystal clear glass tank with tropical colored fish, amazing coral formations and plants. There was one fish in particular, it was a rather ugly one that kept coming up to the window and lingered just over the girl's heads.

Maggie couldn't help but laugh. The fish was quite large, probably a good three feet long, brownish in color and a face that was like a wrinkled old man's with the biggest eyeballs that bulged out. When she spoke, she wasn't thinking that Jackson wouldn't find it as amusing as she did.

"I hope you're getting that fish. He seems adamant about getting in the picture."

He didn't say anything, acknowledged her in no way and his rudeness got under her skin.

"Hello?"

He finally sighed and put his camera down. "That's it for the day."

"Thank you." Tiffany sighed in a long winded release. You'd have thought she'd just run the marathon instead of standing in front of a fish tank smiling.

"Are you always this rude? Or is it me?" Maggie asked directly.

He didn't look at her nor answer, only opened his camera, removed the film, and then placed it in his bag very meticulously and with great care.

Maggie spoke up again, without words he drove her to anger. "I think it must be a combination of both. And rude is being awfully nice. All I asked was if you were getting the fish also, a simple yes or no answer would have done."

"I'm not here to take pictures of fish."

"Well maybe I wanted pictures of fish?" Maggie blurted it out with all the authority she held.

"Then I think the gift shop has some disposable cameras." He didn't say anything else as he continued to pack his equipment and she left him with a huff.

She didn't see him again until later when she left her hotel room on her way to meet Kyla and Nicole at the airport. Maggie had run into the elevator just as the doors were about to close and then wished she hadn't. Jackson was the only one there.

Without a word, she moved to the back and stood silent, refused to say anything even though it was difficult. She could tell he'd just showered, his hair wet, a fresh soap smell and she wondered if he was going out with one of the models, thought it would be a perfect pairing. The model would complain and he wouldn't interrupt while she ranted on about trivial things, because he didn't talk. Yes, Maggie thought to herself, a perfect pair. It was childish and little satisfaction was achieved, but when he stepped out ahead of her, she scrunched her face up behind him and stuck out her tongue. Maggie didn't realize there was a mirror directly across and he'd seen her.

****

They said they'd take a cab and see her at the hotel, but she surprised them by being at the airport. When she saw them in the distance she jumped in the air to wave above the crowd. They saw her head bob up and down and like schoolgirls squealed and ran to hug her, Nicole much faster than Kyla who still limped. Although they talked on the phone several times a week, it had been months since they'd seen each other. They laughed and hugged as people walked around them.

Maggie looked to Kyla. "I saw that hobble, how are you feeling?"

"Still a little sore. Nothing the sand, sun and a margarita won't fix."

"This trip is going to be great, but we don't have to hang around you while you're working, do we?" Nicole joked. "I don't feel so secure and confident standing next to perfect 10 models."

"It's a good thing none of us are looking for men on this trip, the competition is a little rough." Kyla commented, knew all three of them had no interest in the opposite sex.

"Beautiful indeed, and I'm normally not judgmental when it comes to people, but I haven't found anything yet to substantiate anything between the ears other than a face full of makeup to hold the head together."

Back at the hotel, they put their things in the room then found a nice little Mexican restaurant around the corner that served wonderful margaritas. It seemed the crew had found it also and Maggie was surprised to see Jackson among them.

"Hey guys." Maggie smiled and stopped for a moment as they walked to their table. Not all of them hated her, Jackson was the only one.

"Where have you been? I thought you'd be here earlier." One of them asked.

She told them and introduced Nicole and Kyla all around, even to Jackson who she wanted to skip over. If not for him, she probably would have joined them when they asked.

"They all seem nice," Nicole commented when they sat down.

"They are, with one exception. And I'll give you one guess which one that is."

"The gorgeous one who looks so serious? The photographer I think you said?" Kyla discreetly glanced over again.

"Jackson Turner. An arrogant asshole, but that's just my first impression. I don't know him well, rather, I don't know him at all, but my opinion is that with beautiful women fawning all over him it goes to his head. I get the feeling he thinks he has it all, whatever 'all' is."

"He makes good eye candy anyway." Kyla certainly wouldn't have been interested, but he was good to look at. Dressed in a pair of khaki pants and a black shirt, he had a hard edge to him.

"A man has to have some usefulness to prevent it from being a total waste to society," Maggie laughed. "So I guess eye candy is his contribution to the world."

Nicole laughed. "A little harsh, don't you think?"

"I'm so thoroughly over men, I could even do worse than that," Maggie said. "And after this trip, besides you two, I'll probably feel the same about women. The models are driving me insane."

"Already?"

"As early as the airport boarding gate this morning, these girls speak in one syllable words in between giggles if they speak at all. They might be too tired, too hungry, or too cold. The only thing useful I got today was how important waxing is before shoots, and we're talking Brazilian wax. It's the only time as a writer I've never wanted so many details about something."

The atmosphere became noisy, rowdy and fun as the evening wore on. Maggie noticed Jackson talked to the crew, mainly to John, they appeared to be friends and she suspected they too had worked together before. It served to confirm it was only her he had a problem with. And there it was again, that angry feeling. What had she done to him? Then she shrugged it off, refused to be bothered by a stranger.

They sipped margaritas, toasted to bon voyage early, and talked about all the things going on in their lives. Nicole's children, Kyla's tales of her clients and Maggie's love woes and article reprints that went national. Family and other friends always made it into the conversation that never lagged. All of them talked so much and so fast as if they wouldn't have a week to catch up, but not one of them wanted to waste one minute.

When the crew left, most of them came by their table to say goodbye, with Jackson being the exception as he disappeared easily. The women stayed so long they closed the place down and walked back to the hotel with merriment as the margaritas had gone straight to their heads and there was much laughter as they steadily chatted away.

As they were about to enter their room, Maggie saw the photographer going into his room and she wondered if a model waited inside. Or maybe he'd just come from one of their rooms, or several of their rooms. They made eye contact but he didn't make it a point to acknowledge her in any way, so neither did she.

Except after he closed his door, her face scrunched again, her tongue stuck out in some sort of childish silent retaliation.

CHAPTER FOUR

The morning of departure came and Kyla and Nicole went to breakfast while Maggie lagged behind to finish some writing. When she stepped in the elevator she wanted to step back out because Jackson was the only one there, but of course she didn't. Could she not get away from him? Then she decided out of courtesy to ask him if he'd like to join them. After all, they would be traveling and interacting together for a week, whether they wanted to or not.

"I was meeting my friends for coffee, want to join us?"

"No," he answered flatly.

"Did you already eat? Is the breakfast here any good?" Maggie asked with all the politeness she could muster.

"I don't know. I didn't eat here."

"Is the coffee any good?" She continued, just to try and drag him into conversation, or maybe because she knew he didn't want to talk and she just wanted to push him.

"I don't know."

He offered nothing more but short, bland answers. Her irritation began again. "I'll have to interview you some time. Do you think you could come up with a few more words?" When he looked at her, all she saw was distance, gorgeous brown eyes that gave her nothing.

"I'll have nothing to contribute to your article, no point in wasting your time. I'm here to take pictures, not talk to people."

"It's just me you don't talk to."

"And that bothers you?" He stared at her and waited for an answer.

"It's my job to talk. Not only that, it bothers me that I've done nothing to you and you can't even be polite. All I'm asking is for a little..."

Maggie found herself more infuriated when she couldn't finish. The elevator doors opened and with a calm stance, Jackson meandered on his way. She would have run after him in a rage had her cell phone not rang. She looked to the screen and saw it was Wilma and Maggie began talking immediately.

"Are you calling to cancel? Can I tell everyone they can go home?"

Wilma laughed, "Not over your frustration yet?"

"I'm used to working on my own, it's difficult to work with people who don't cooperate, and that photographer is not cooperating. I can tell you now I'll get nothing out of him." Maggie had stopped walking and leaned against a wall to talk as she watched his back when he walked out of the door.

"Get something." Wilma encouraged.

"More frustrated is the only thing I'll get."

"I just called to wish you a good Bon Voyage. Happy sailing, Maggie. For you it won't be hard to write the story, just think of the fun you'll have."

"I am in charge, right? I could just fire everyone before the ship takes off and have the trip to myself. That's the only fun I'll have."

After the call she joined Kyla and Nicole as they lingered over breakfast for as long as they could.

"This is so luxuriant for me," Nicole commented. "I love my children, they're my life, but to be away for a week and not have to worry about carpooling, clean uniforms, cooking dinner. It's absolute heaven, just the thought of it."

Kyla finished her coffee and set her cup down. "For me, it's being with you two for a week. Not that I don't like my independence, but that empty apartment can be awfully quiet at times. And I haven't had any fun in a long time. I didn't even know when my husband left me, I certainly wasn't thinking about how long it's been since I've done something like this."

Both of them noticed Maggie was quiet.

"Hey, you awake yet?" Nicole laughed and waved her hand in front of her face.

"Oh, sorry," she looked apologetic but her mind had been on Jackson, only because she thought about how she would get him to talk to her when he couldn't even be pleasant. "Wilma keeps insisting I have to include that photographer in this article. Apparently he's one of the best in the business. He might be that, but he certainly isn't going to talk about it."

"I don't envy your week. We heard a couple of the models this morning when they were talking," Kyla chuckled and rolled her eyes. "They were talking about how they couldn't believe they didn't have a limo to the port."

"I think in the islands, I might put them on a chicken truck just for spite."

They laughed at the thought. In Maggie's mind it would make a great photograph and it was something she would keep in the back of her mind. Why not? They needed to be brought down to earth a little, along with Jackson Turner.

****

The cab dropped them off at the port and they didn't run into anyone else as they checked in and made their way onboard. Maggie wondered if the models had made it, but she wasn't their babysitter or caretaker, not that day anyway. They were adults and could do things on their own so she didn't worry about it. If they missed the ship it wouldn't be on her head.

It wasn't a large ship, not in enormous proportions anyway, and the amount of people didn't seem overbearing as they made their way to their ocean view room hardly running into anyone once they left the center atrium. One got an immediate sense of comfortable intimacy.

Their room was on the Promenade deck, and although it was small, they knew it would be efficient for their needs. Almost immediately, the room steward was there to introduce himself, in great animated manner as he explained he would take care of them for the week and try his best to grant their every wish.

"I am Bozcovienet. It is on my nametag but no one ever know how to say it, so you call me Bo. Everyone call me Bo. My brother call me Bozo." He threw his hands in the air in exasperation. "Bozcovienet. What kind of name? My mama, she eat the crazy fruit when she name me."

They could do nothing but laugh and he was comical in his seeming familiarity with them.

"You will be the one I will pick up all your shoes everyday, am I right?" He asked Kyla with his funny little accent they couldn't distinguish.

"Why do you say that?" She looked playfully offended.

"Your shoes, you will have the most shoes. You see?" He bent down and touched her shoes. "Shiny, new, no scuff. You bring lot's of shoes, no?"

"A few." Kyla was amazed he'd pegged her correctly, but she didn't actually admit she had an entire bag filled with shoes.

"I know people. I work here long time and I know by looking. And you," he turned to Nicole. "You will have papers. All the papers you can find you will save as souvenirs, but do not worry, I will make them nice and neat for you every evening. You bring back menus, you bring ship plans, you bring brochures for your next cruise, and I will make order."

He turned to Maggie then and seemed to stare for a long time as if he could see something no one else could. When he spoke his voice was softer and he sighed. "Ah, such a pretty one you are, but you? I will pick up the pieces of your heart."

The shock on her face was evident as a chill ran up her spine. How could this stranger tell her something like that? She knew he was wrong but it puzzled her anyway.

"I guess two out of three isn't bad," Maggie laughed it off, but still felt the slight chill up her spine.

Then he continued cheerily as if he hadn't even said the words. "It will be my pleasure and great honor to be of service to you three beautiful women. I am lucky man, the other staff will stare in envy." He bowed gallantly before he left the three of them in silence.

Maggie opened a cabinet and stored her small computer bag inside. "He says that now, wait until he meets the models. I'm afraid we'll lose our beauty status after that. We'll be lucky if we can get him to bring us clean towels."

"That was kind of weird, huh?" Nicole questioned as she picked up the first of the papers she would save. The daily paper that would tell them everything they needed to know about what was going on anywhere on the ship.

"What? Me and my broken heart?" Maggie said lightly. "I certainly don't put stock into something a stranger's going to tell me, even if he did call me pretty one."

"Out of all of us, Maggie is the last one it would happen to," Kyla found a small bottle of lotion in the bathroom and put some on her hands, "Not that it's going to happen to any of us, since we've all come to the conclusion we don't need men in our lives. Have you two realized this is the first time we've ever been together as three single friends since our college days?"

"That's ironic," Maggie said. "The last time we were all single together we were dreaming of weddings and having fantasies about our dream man. We swore he was out there looking for us somewhere. Now we're three old jaded women who would do a hundred yard dash in Olympic record time just to get away from him if he came close to finding us."

"Hey!" Nicole protested quickly. "I may be jaded, but I'm not old. I haven't hit forty yet."

"I hate to tell you Nicole, but Maggie's right. We've passed the young stage. Like everything else in my life, I didn't notice when it happened, but it did. And forty isn't old."

"Okay," Nicole agreed. "So we don't exactly look like the models down the hall, but I think Bo knows what he's talking about. We are beautiful women, mature beautiful women."

"Mature, old, jaded, and now that we've boosted our self esteem, let's all go have a drink," Maggie laughed as she walked out the door and the others followed. She didn't want to think about Bo's strange words of picking up the pieces of her heart, as wrong as she thought he was, it was still odd. It wasn't something she worried about though, Maggie knew herself, she certainly wouldn't be putting her heart out there anywhere to get damaged.

The center hub of the ship seemed to be where everything took place. Several desks were busy as passengers signed up for ship excursions, obtained information, purchased postcards or utilized the purser to place items in a safe deposit box. An enormous crystal piece hung from the ceiling of the large atrium and although glass, one could pretend it was water that flowed through the roof.

Nicole was astonished, "I can't get over this, this is a floating resort, a complete resort on water. I don't even know I'm on a ship unless I look out the window."

They looked over the excursions and talked about a few but Maggie would have to check the shooting schedule first to determine which one's she could partake in. Then they wandered past the gift shops that would open when they were at sea, then through the Casino. It too would open later and Kyla playfully held her wallet over the trash can.

"I might as well make my deposit now, I've never been lucky in a casino."

"I thought you won a bundle when we went to Vegas a few years back?" Nicole questioned.

"That was Maggie."

"No, that was more than a few years back, it was Ken that won all the money." Maggie corrected.

"Oh, no wonder I don't remember," Nicole rolled her eyes. "And he blew it when we got home, not on me of course, I think on his girlfriend."

Maggie felt her pain. It was the ultimate betrayal for a man to pretend to love you and not really care about you at all. Nicole told her once she felt like it had all been a lie, even the good years they had were negated by his cheating.

While exploring the ship they often passed the same staff that always seemed happy to see them and always had a smile or a kind word to make them feel welcome. Each concluded it would do very well as their home away from home for a week and it didn't take long to get a good feel of the layout. Though none of them were so confident to think they would be able to navigate it so quickly without at least a little help for awhile. A trusty plan of the layout would come in handy.

"If we didn't have this map, we'd be walking around in circles."

Maggie looked up and laughed as she saw a few of the models almost doing just that. "Should we give them a map?"

"They probably already have one," Kyla joked.

They didn't bother to help out, Maggie knew it wouldn't have been appreciated anyway, and continued on their tour to see the various restaurants, lounges and bars. Then wandered out to the pool deck that seemed to be where the crowds gathered.

There were also many quiet places if one chose to be alone or wanted a more peaceful setting. They sat for some time and watched people pass. Maggie was fascinated by people, wondered about all their lives, the story behind them. Then when it was time for a mandatory muster drill, they donned their lifejackets in the hopes they'd never have to use them.

"I didn't know we'd be drilled. We won't have a test, will we?" Nicole snapped hers but it was wrong and someone came to help her. "I've already failed."

They were instructed to stand in a straight line. Their assembly stations went by room number and she could hear the models a few lines over complaining. What else did they do? Was there nothing to satisfy them? There was less complaining when another instructor showed up, a handsome one. It was always the good looking men who calmed them.

Maggie also noticed Jackson and a few of the crew among them. As usual, he was talking to them, so there was his voice again, he did have one somewhere. A snob, she concluded. An arrogant snob who was used to women pawning all over him, he didn't need to talk to get attention, didn't have to do anything.

She paid no mind to him and after the muster drill the three women settled at a table on the top deck for sail away. The steel drum music made the party atmosphere and each held a frozen cocktail in their hand as they watched the city fade behind them.

"Look at that vast horizon ahead of us. It looks so empty," Maggie said as they looked out.

Kyla laughed and agreed. "Just like my life. We could look at it as a clean slate. Think of it as literally sailing off into our futures."

"Well, I hope there's something better out there than what's on shore." Nicole commented.

Maggie squinted her eyes and placed her hand over them as if she was seriously searching for the hope she spoke of somewhere beyond that horizon line. "No hope there, still looks pretty empty to me."

The three laughed together and Maggie sighed as she held her head back and closed her eyes. "But it doesn't matter. Not that we're searching for anything anyway. This is perfect, just like this."

"I have to agree." Nicole too smiled. "Along with my kids, you two are everything I need."

"Well," Kyla said hesitantly and the other two looked at her with question. "I have to agree for the most part, but I still need my female toys every now and then. You two can't be everything."

"I don't have the energy or desire for any of it. I think I'll remain celibate for the rest of my life." Nicole would be okay if that were the case. She'd been so hurt by a husband she thought she'd spend the rest of her life with, didn't care about any intimacy at all.

"I don't know about that extreme," Maggie added. "Maybe a happy medium somewhere, is that possible?"

When they returned to their room to change for dinner, Maggie saw Bo with his hands full of fresh towels and extra pillows. He rushed from a linen closet into a room with a worried look on his face. As she passed, she realized it was one of the rooms that held three of the models and they already had him running at their beck and call.

"It is better now, no?" She heard him ask pleasantly but the tone of the answer wasn't as kind.

"If it's the best you can do. If you can perform magic you can make this room at least ten times its size. How am I supposed to live like this for a week? There is only one mirror and one phone in this closet."

Bo shrugged his shoulders, it was an area he could not help in, but he offered what he could. "I can find you other mirror?"

"As quick as you can." She barked as an order.

Maggie thought about the ship to shore calls that would be made since cell phones would be out of service soon. She had to wonder what kind of arrangement Wilma had with the model agency and hoped it was a good one with limits, if not it would cost the price of a small country by the time the week was up.

She also noted to herself to tell Bo not to bend over backwards. It wouldn't be appreciated and they would only expect more from him. He'd be best advised to stick to his normal duties of cleaning the room, turning it down for the evening, then making himself as scarce as possible from the model's rooms, they would never be pleased.

Proof of that was when they'd dressed and left the room again. Poor Bo seemed harried and rushed as he tried to accommodate them still and she wondered if he'd been there the entire time. Kyla and Nicole continued down the narrow hall, and she waited for a few moments for him to return from a room he'd gone into around the corner.

"Bo, don't wear yourself out over these ladies."

"Oh, but it's my job, pretty one."

"They take advantage. Whatever they ask for, tell them you don't have. Unfortunately, they're working with me this week and I know how they can be. Don't do every little thing they ask and if they complain about it, I'll deal with it." Maggie looked in his hands and he held yet more towels. "How many towels have you taken to them?"

"They say they shower every time they come in. They have been in three times now."

"That's ridiculous, no one takes three showers in less than three hours." Maggie was going to go to the room herself and say something but he stopped her.

"Oh no, it's okay, really, I enjoy my job, I enjoy making their stay well."

Maggie knew he only said it out of fear. No one could enjoy running around for a group of demanding women. As she looked at him she could see he possibly feared losing his job if they complained, so she decided against it for the time being.

"If it gets too much, just tell me. I'll take all the blame with your boss if that's what you're worried about."

"You no waste time with worry about me, too much fun to have. You go get dinner and have fun." He smiled and continued with his task of delivering the towels.

As she walked down the hall she heard a door open just ahead of her in the narrow passageway and slowed down. The person turned to close their door and she waited momentarily so as not to bump into him. When he turned, it was Jackson.

"Oh, hi," she said with surprise, didn't know his room was so close to hers. "I didn't expect to see you."

"Who were you expecting to come out of my room?" His eyes looked directly into hers but there was no friendliness to be seen, simply his usual cold glare.

"I wasn't expecting anyone at all. I meant... guess it doesn't matter what I meant, does it? Do you really care what I meant?" She asked stiffly, her irritation evident also. But she had reason to be irritated, he didn't.

"No." Jackson made the simple comment and turned the opposite direction of her.

"Jeez," Maggie sighed, her mouth started going when she caught up with the other two. "I don't think I've ever seen such an arrogant, rude man. I've come across many in my day but he beats them all. And we've probably exchanged less than ten words. Is that possible to dislike someone so much and not have said more than ten words to him?"

"Who are you talking about?" Kyla asked.

"Who else but that non-talking, arrogant, conceited," Maggie couldn't finish as the two laughed at her.

Kyla smiled and teased. "Playing hard to get, is he?"

"Like anyone would want him. I think that's the problem, he thinks everyone does, he gives that impression anyway. What else could it be? Either that or he's just the epitome of a true asshole, the genuine article. He can't even be pleasant, is that so much to ask? The common courtesy of…" Maggie continued her ranting as the other two just smiled and listened to her vent her frustrations.

CHAPTER FIVE

The dining room that evening was their first discovery of impeccable service and pampering that awaited them for meals. It was a magnificent room with crystal chandeliers and they were seated by the window where they could see the moonlight cross the sea.

"I am in heaven, I think this is the first meal I've had without the kids in I don't know how long."

Maggie laughed. "And you can have more than grilled cheese or hot dogs."

"Well I think this is the first meal I've had with other people in I don't know how long, it's usually me sitting at my desk with Chinese take-out," then Kyla looked to Maggie, "What about you? You've given up dating so you don't enjoy meals with men, what are your dinners like?"

"Dinner? If I eat anything it's usually another candy bar out of the vending machine at the office, sometimes a bag of chips." As she looked to the menu the choices were wide and varied that evening, she wouldn't miss the choices she had at home.

Marco and his assistant Danisa introduced themselves as their servers for the evening and they chatted awhile before going into taking their order. Asked about where they were from, if it was their first cruise, were they having a good time, and they sincerely seemed interested in the answers.

Marco helped them decide when they had a hard time on what to choose, and then brought Kyla two appetizers when she debated both of them. During the meal they made sure none of their needs were overlooked and the three women, not used to such luxuries when they were on their own at home, enjoyed every single moment.

Then after the meal they even went to extra lengths when Key Lime Pie wasn't on the dessert menu, but when Nicole mentioned it Marco brought both her choice from the menu, and a select piece of Key Lime pie which Nicole said was delicious. She ate both desserts so as not to let it go wasted.

"Okay, and the fitness center is where again? Didn't we see that?" She laughed after her last bite.

"Like you need it, you're one of those people who can eat anything. It's me you'll be lying in bed watching outside of the window as I jog, or rather hobble, tomorrow morning around the Promenade deck one hundred times." Kyla sighed, knew it wouldn't be so many but probably should be before the week was out. Then she looked at Maggie. "And you'll watch me too."

Maggie probably would watch. She ran sometimes but not often, there was never any time to exercise even though she knew it was probably something she should start making a priority as she got older. Growing up with many brothers, she was more of a tomboy more than the other two, and her exercise seemed to come from interactive games such as racquetball, volleyball, tennis, and sometimes a few games of basketball and football with her brothers. She also knew that age would prohibit her eventually, but for now, it was all she seemed to need to keep in fairly fit shape.

As they sat, some of the others in their group came in and stopped to say hello, except Jackson who didn't notice her existence in his usual arrogant style, even though he walked in with John who stopped at the table. Instead of even pretending to be sociable, Jackson walked on.

"I called your room to see if you wanted to join us for dinner." Maggie hadn't gotten an answer so then left a note on the door.

"I actually ate earlier, just coming in with some of the guys to have coffee while they eat."

Maggie noticed John looked relaxed already and they'd only been on the boat for the day. He'd come up in the ranks over the years and was now supervisor without having to do the hard manual labor involved in lugging and setting up equipment. But most times he didn't take the traveling jobs, preferred to stay home, then again, that was when his wife was alive. She suspected it was lonely at home for him so he'd taken more traveling jobs.

After he left with promises to meet her later so they could spend time together, her thoughts were still on him when Kyla spoke.

"Too bad he's rude and mean. Isn't that what you said about him?"

"Who?" Maggie almost shouted. "John?"

"Oh Heaven's no, he's the sweetest man. That photographer, he's absolutely to die for but he can keep his looks with a personality like that."

"We need to invent some sort of process to match looks and personalities to make the perfect man." Nicole too looked over to his table with discretion and Maggie chuckled.

"There would still be fault somewhere. It was never God's intention to have such a thing. If there were, the amount of guys we've been through, we would have found him by now."

"Speak for yourself." Nicole sounded playfully offended, "Maybe between you and Kyla."

"You had your share before you married."

"And some mighty fine prospects." Kyla added.

Nicole sipped her coffee and smiled. "I remember them well, there were a few winners in there," then her smile faded. "But then I met Ken. I think about it sometimes and a few of them I probably should have kept in touch with at least."

"Like who? Contact them now." Maggie tried to encourage.

"They're all married and bald, probably at least a dozen children. Nah, you can't go back to the past. If that were possible I would have done it a long time ago and certainly would have obliterated my ex husband out of my life."

Afterwards they decided the fun was on the top deck, where the night was filled with stars and a breeze that smelled fresh as the sea, and a calypso band played on a stage overtop the pool. It was as if Nicole's words of going back to the past were fate as they watched the activity and enjoyed the music and through it all Kyla heard familiar laughter.

"What's the matter?" Nicole asked her when she noticed an odd expression on her face.

"Do you hear that?" Kyla answered as she looked towards where it came from, and then as a few people moved away from the bar, she saw him. "It can't be."

Both Maggie and Nicole looked in the direction and knew instantly what had grabbed her attention. They all saw a dear familiar face, an old boyfriend of Kyla's who had been her college sweetheart, and the love of her life.

She walked up behind him with a serious tone. "Excuse me sir, you'll have to quiet down over here, we've been receiving complaints."

Alan turned around with a start, thought the person was really part of the staff for a moment. "I... uh..." He stuttered for a moment, the surprise threw him off and then he realized who it was. "Kyla?" Then his mouth turned into a broad grin across his face as he stood and pulled her into his arms. "Kyla Reeves."

She laughed and gave him a hug. "My God, how long has it been?"

"Too many years to count," he looked at her, studied her face quickly and it was as if a time warp had taken over. She looked exactly the same but more beautiful if that was possible, the years had been kind. Then he looked behind her expecting to see her husband there, instead he was surprised again to see two old friends. "And you two?"

Both women were greeted with hugs as they all laughed at the surprise of it all.

"You look great. What are you doing here?" Maggie asked when she pulled away from him.

"A bachelor party, my little brother is getting married. I came not only as the best man but also as the oldest of the group to keep these young boys in line." His eyes tried to take them all in but they kept returning to Kyla.

"In line? You're the one I heard from across deck, you're probably worse than any of them." Kyla glanced across the bar and saw Randy, his little brother, all grown up. "Is that Randy? Randy's getting married?"

Just then he looked up and saw her too. It took him a few moments but his face lit up and he ran around the bar to get to them, greeted the three with boisterous, shocked, affection. He was a small kid when they'd known him and Kyla couldn't get over how old he'd gotten, how grown up he was. She and Alan had dated through college and she often went home with him to Texas, Maggie and Nicole tagging along for fun when they could. His family became important to her, she knew them as well as her own, Randy like her own little brother.

Kyla often thought about Randy and what he'd grow up to be like. He'd been a surprise to Alan's parents and came much later in life than they expected so he was much younger. He was such a charmer at a young age, it was impossible not to believe he was meant to be on this earth and there wouldn't have been anything they could have done to prevent it.

"Look how handsome you are." Kyla knew he'd be just as handsome as Alan one day.

"This is too weird. What are the chances?" The young man beamed and looked to all for answers. "Did Alan tell you I graduated college this year? And that I'm getting married?" He quickly pulled out a picture of his soon to be bride and she was beautiful.

"Congratulations." Kyla felt like a proud sister. She'd been a part of their family for so long and the feeling of it hadn't changed even though they'd been apart for years.

He introduced them to all his friends, the entire bachelor party, and the group carried on for the rest of the evening. They stayed outside until the band stopped, then later went to the ship's Disco to try and catch up a little on all the years they'd missed.

Kyla was still in shock Randy could be so much older, it was affirmation of how much time had passed, he served as physical proof in the form of a young handsome man that many years had slipped by. But she was glad Alan hadn't changed, he looked the same. He was always handsome with a ruggedness that came from living in Texas, and she supposed always would be.

What surprised her most was that he hadn't even lost the ability to give her a flutter in her stomach every time he smiled, for every time he did, he pulled her in just as in days past.

They had dated from their first year of college until four years after they graduated and often talked of marriage, but both were so busy with other things and hadn't made it a priority. Each assumed it would all come together somehow. But they found themselves trying to survive a long distance relationship when she took a great opportunity with a firm in California and he stayed to operate the family business in Texas. It broke both their hearts when it hadn't worked out.

Most were either dancing or standing as a group talking but Kyla and Alan took a seat together at one of the small tables.

"I can't believe Randy is old enough to get married." Kyla looked over to him as he stood at the bar and waited for the drinks he ordered.

"She's a great girl, you'd love her. What about you? Still married to Rick?" Alan asked without seeming as if he was too interested.

"Divorced him and made the same foolish mistake again with someone else. That didn't work out either. What about you? Surely you're married with a dozen children by now."

Alan glanced away from her as he answered. "Haven't married yet, not even once."

Neither one let the uplifting of their hearts show on their faces. They quickly caught up on their lives, the surface of it anyway, it would take much longer for in depth review. His mother was doing well but she was so sorry to hear his father had passed away a few years previous. Alan had taken over all responsibilities of the family business and it had consumed his life but he couldn't see himself doing anything else, it was a life he'd been born into.

After several hours, Randy eventually went off with his friends and Alan and Kyla continued to talk well into the night after Maggie and Nicole left. They rested on two deck chairs on the top deck in the salty air. It was a clear sky filled with stars and a bright moon that shone a line of light across the sea. The atmosphere made it hard for her not to remember their romance, the feelings of her heart.

"This is the weirdest thing, I still can't believe it." Kyla said as she huddled into his coat jacket he'd given her to ward off the slight chill in the breeze. "I never thought I'd ever see you again."

"And of all places," Alan agreed.

Their relationship remained with her long after it was over. They'd been a vital part of each other's lives, planned a future together that never came. Kyla thought of him and the future that wasn't quite often over the years. Both times she married other men he crossed her mind, and as she sat next to him now, their connecting bond hadn't faded in the least.

They walked around the Promenade deck before he walked her to her cabin where she took off his coat and then leaned against the wall next to the door. The hallways were narrow, it was difficult not to stand close, and the feeling it gave her was something she could only dream about over the years in detailed memory.

"I feel like I did on our first date and I walked you back to your dorm. Should I kiss her? Should I not kiss her? What if she wants me to and I don't?" Alan tried not to stand so close to her.

"Times have changed, Alan, a girl doesn't wait anymore." Kyla leaned in to him and pressed her lips against his, felt the sensation down to her toes just like she had on that first date he spoke of.

****

After they'd left Kyla and Alan alone, Maggie and Nicole ran into John in a quiet section of the atrium area where he sat reading a book and Maggie joined him while Nicole went off for coffee.

"I'm not interrupting, am I? Are you waiting on some hot mama?" She teased him with affection.

"Not a chance. I know it's been awhile since Edith has been gone but I'm not interested, I'll leave that up to the young kids like you."

"Young kids? I'm flattered, but I think I might be past that stage of my life."

"You're certainly not past the dating stage. And you've already warned me so I won't ask about what's his name, but surely there's someone."

"I've banned all men from my life, they only complicate things when they don't see things the way I do."

He chuckled and shook his head. "Strong, independent, opinionated, Edith always loved those qualities about you, but I've been around this world long enough to know you're probably right, and most men see those qualities as a hazard."

Maggie shrugged her shoulders, "It's just as well, no time for that sort of thing anyway."

"Not when you make your life all work. Are you ever going to slow down a little so someone can catch up to you?"

She thought about what she'd told Wilma. That she'd seriously consider the man who could take her mind off work, but she hadn't found that and probably never would. "I shouldn't have to slow down, way I look at it, is if they're fast enough they might stand a little chance."

"But you won't make it easy on them."

"Men have it too easy already."

"Edith always said it would take just the right man for you. That you wouldn't settle down with just anyone, and you shouldn't have to."

Maggie was quiet for a moment, decided to broach the subject he hadn't wanted to talk about before, but it was obvious he was ready to talk about her now. "I miss her too."

"I think I'm finally letting it sink in. For a long time I didn't, but it's hard to spend a lifetime with someone and get over it quickly, and I know how she would want me to live, and it wouldn't be sitting around being miserable."

"Have you thought anymore about moving? I know you've mentioned it a time or two."

"I was actually going to call you for help pretty soon, I think I'm to the point of moving out of that big place, all I need is something simple."

"I think that's a great idea and of course I'll help."

They spent a good few hours together and Maggie enjoyed talking about Edith. The two were her salvation when she was so far away from her parents and family, they were like her 'city parents', and losing Edith had been a big blow to the both of them.

She met John early in her career when they worked for the same company and they'd taken her under their wing as if she were a daughter. They looked out for her as a family would and over the years they became her surrogate family. Dinners, shopping with Edith, even weekend trips to the shore on occasion and holidays spent together when she couldn't get home. Now she felt the roles were reversed and she would keep John under her wing.

They talked for a long time and although Maggie didn't think either of them would be there for that length of time since it was late when she sat down, when she looked at her watch it was long past midnight. It dawned on her by the time she got to bed she would only be able to get a few hours sleep before she had to get up. It wasn't unusual for her lifestyle, and she had the feeling it would be like that all week with the schedule Jackson had created.

"I can't believe we've been sitting here for a few hours now, I either have to go get coffee and pull an all nighter, or get a few hours sleep. I think that photographer probably did this type of schedule just because he knew it would wear me down by the end of the week. I think he subconsciously has it out for me."

"Jackson?" John chuckled.

"Mr. Personality himself. That schedule is for insomniacs. How are we supposed to have a good time and get up way before dawn?"

"You don't have to be there."

"It isn't required but I'll do it because everyone else is. I'm still trying to figure out what the best time is to get anyone to talk to me." Then Maggie huffed. "For that matter, I'm still trying to figure out how to get the photographer to talk to me at all. What's up with him?"

"Jackson is a little reserved."

"A little reserved? That's an understatement if I ever heard one, and you used nice and polite words, more than I would have given him credit for."

"He's really a good guy, he just doesn't open up much to people and keeps himself pretty private, always has."

"Sounds like you two are friends?" She found it odd Jackson would have any.

"I met him a few years ago and we've ended up working together quite a bit. When we're not working, we'll get together on occasion for a beer or two." He didn't go into detail about the photographer's life and wouldn't, only confirmed what he knew. "He's a good guy."

"What's the deal with him? He's awfully unsociable, or maybe he doesn't understand English? I'm beginning to think he speaks a foreign language and that's why he won't talk much. I'm trying to be nice to him, but he doesn't make it easy."

John didn't mention that Jackson casually asked about her also when he found out they were such good friends. He'd merely asked if she was always so persistent, but John got the feeling he'd wanted to know more.

"Don't take it personally, he's pretty much a loner, you just have to get to know him before you can see that."

"Like he let's anyone," Maggie huffed. "No, I think I'll take your word for it but I don't think I'll get to know him. I can probably get through the week, but after that I won't be crying when he leaves. My saving grace is I don't have to be around him all the time."

****

When Nicole was at home, her quiet time in the evenings came when the kids were in bed and it made her into a night owl. She got a cup of coffee in the outdoor café area, knowing it wouldn't help her sleep but it smelled so good and she couldn't resist. Then she sat at one of the many empty tables. There were only a few other people there but when they left she was alone, until a gentlemen sat down at the table next to her.

"Good evening." He smiled and nodded as she did in return. "I've been looking for a perfect spot like this for an hour."

"I was going to take my coffee elsewhere but I couldn't resist just sitting here." Nicole's first instinct was that he had been drinking that evening and needed the coffee to sober up but it didn't appear to be the case.

"Is this your first cruise?" He asked.

"Yes. Yours?"

"No, I've been on a couple. This is my favorite part of the night though, when everything is quiet. I'm used to working late and I'm a creature of habit, I knew I wouldn't be able to sleep yet if I tried." He laughed easily as he picked up his cup. "This isn't going to help."

"No, but there's no alarm clock to wake me up tomorrow and we're at sea all day. I'm giving us an excuse to indulge."

He introduced himself as Derek and it was easy for them to fall into friendly conversation but each remained at their respective tables. It was a comfortable exchange as they laughed and talked together and Nicole found herself just out of curiosity, looking at his ring finger to see if he was married, but saw nothing. It wasn't as if she was interested, it was only habit. And it wasn't as if he were interested, he was merely being friendly.

Nicole hadn't traveled extensively and hadn't been to any of the ports they would visit. Cozumel, Roatan, Belize and Cancun were all a mystery to her, but Derek had been to a few of the islands they were headed to. He told her about Cozumel and Cancun and gave her tips on a few things to see and do. A good restaurant, some of the better beaches to go for sunning, or if she wanted to snorkel he told her the best place.

"I've never been."

"You ought to try it. They rent equipment from the ship, but if you travel to the islands more than once it's worth it to buy your own, really isn't that expensive."

"Oh, this was very spontaneous for me, I wish I could, but unfortunately I don't get away much."

"No?" He questioned with innocence.

Nicole stopped herself from explaining. She didn't know why, but she didn't mention her kids. The mention of them always scared men off, she'd learned that well since her divorce, and even though she'd just met this man and had no intentions towards him, she at least wanted him to sit and converse a while longer.

"Work keeps me busy." She changed the subject back to the islands and listened intently to all the tips and information he offered. Nicole noticed his warm eyes were kind.

The conversation wasn't flirty, and she never felt like he was coming on to her. She thought that was the reason she was so comfortable and stayed until three in the morning, it was simply a nice exchange between two adults, and she thought nothing more of it.

CHAPTER SIX

Their first full day on the ship was a sea day. The ship wouldn't stop anywhere, only sail through clear waters towards the port of Cozumel, which would be their first port of call the following morning.

Jackson composed the schedule and there wasn't a thing she could do about it, only curse him as she rose at 3:30 a.m. because he wanted to shoot during the sunrise. Sunrise, sunset, this time, that time, here, there, Maggie bantered alone in her thoughts as she showered to wake herself up. Did he have to be so particular? And so early?

She dressed as quietly as she could so as not to wake Nicole and Kyla. She knew it wasn't long ago Nicole lay her head down for slumber and she had to stop herself from waking her and asking where she'd been.

Many passengers slept in, perhaps slept off their late night carousing, for them it was a morning to sleep late. They could relax, maybe have breakfast in bed, and Maggie envied them all, especially her two friends in deep slumber when she walked out of the door by 4:00 a.m.

It wasn't a requirement for her to be there and she could have passed on the sunrise shoot, but as acting supervisor she thought it important to make her presence known. Not to boss anyone around, they all knew what they were supposed to do without her, but to show she was willing to work just as hard for this project. Even if she didn't like it, she would give it everything she had.

Her first stop was to one of the rooms that held two of the models and all she heard was their ranting and complaining.

"I told the room man that I needed breakfast early and I didn't have time to eat half of it. How am I supposed to survive under these conditions?" Kelli pulled top after top out of the closet until she found the one she wanted and it didn't surprise Maggie when she left all the unwanted ones where they landed.

Tedi had gone into the bathroom to shower, and when she came out Maggie was surprised a shower could do that to a person. The transformation was obvious and she was one who didn't mind being up so early, but it didn't stop her from complaining about other things.

The other two models were in no better spirits. The room was too small, the coffee hadn't been delivered early enough, and of course both were peeved they had to share the same makeup person, and what a cheap budget it must be to have the makeup person do their hair too.

Simone picked up the phone and dialed room service then loudly demanded more caffeine, also instructed them to take a supply to the top deck where she would be working.

"This is what it's like, this is your true behind the scenes, it's like a war zone." She slammed the phone back down. "There aren't even any assistants. These are impossible working conditions, even when they bring the coffee there isn't any room to drink it. I can't believe they didn't book us suites."

"How much room does one person need?" Maggie shrugged her shoulders. She was as polite as she could be to these women but it was often a struggle not to lose her cool. There was no reason to create ill feelings, they all had to work together and try as best they could to get along for the week.

"Certainly more than this," Simone threw her hands wide. "We even have to share a makeup lady who does our hair too. Talk about low budget." Then she stormed out to the lady she spoke of, forgetting all about the coffee she'd just ordered.

Tiffany would be the last to leave and Maggie spent quite a bit of time with her as she was getting ready. The only one who seemed to be in the mood to talk to her because the others were barely awake, or spending most of their time getting extra work from the makeup artist to hide the telltale signs of all the margarita's they'd enjoyed the evening before.

Her questions seemed trivial, it's why she hated writing articles about it, questions such as... 'Does it make it any better getting up at the crack of dawn being in beautiful surroundings?' or 'Do you try to get to bed early in the evening?', 'When you have such an early shoot, do you go straight back to bed afterwards?'

Trivial, frustrating, but she asked. Then Maggie made her way up to the top deck where Jackson waited as patiently as he could for the first of the girls to arrive. Without looking up from doing camera adjustments, he assumed she was one of the models he waited on.

"You can stand right over there. Simple stuff and the usual poses, little sleepy eyed at the brand new day, you know, that type of thing."

Playfully she did as he asked and when he looked up ready to point his camera and noticed it was Maggie, he sighed and slowly put his hands down.

"Good morning, Mr. Personality." She said snidely. "You said more words in that one sentence than I've ever heard you say."

"It might be your job to talk, but it isn't mine."

"Why is it you seem to get up on the wrong side of the bed every morning? Surely your day hasn't gone wrong yet to piss you off so early, it just started. Actually," she looked out to sea and the sun hadn't really risen so it hadn't even started yet and she pointed that out. "The day hasn't even begun and already you're acting like it's going to be a bad one."

"Is there something you needed?" He asked the question with a bored tone to his voice.

"No, but this is my job and I thought I should be here."

"And this is my photo shoot and I won't need any assistance."

It infuriated her that he knew she posed no threat, Maggie may be the overall supervisor, but Jackson had total control over his photo shoots, and they both knew there wasn't a thing she could do about it. Under her breath she cursed his arrogance, the only reason she didn't openly curse him was because others had shown up.

The morning seemed to start at bad and go to worse. First Kelli wasn't pleased because she said it was too chilly, anything below 75 degrees to her was like being in Antarctica. Maggie wasn't surprised, she couldn't have weighed more than 100 pounds if that, and she wondered what people found so attractive in a body that seemed to be merely skin covering bones.

Tiffany complained standing on the deck in flat shoes made her feet hurt and she'd gotten a splinter on the rail. Which Maggie knew was crap, it was as waxed and polished smooth as the softest silk. There were a multitude of delays and excuses one after the other.

Maggie did get a chance to sit with Tedi after she'd gotten prepared and primped and when she had to leave Maggie sighed with continued frustration. What was she supposed to ask these girls? She could write the fluff article easy. The unglamorous life of the model that had to get up at 4:00 am, go through wardrobe change after wardrobe change, makeup change after makeup change. As hard as she thought about it, Maggie couldn't come up with a different angle. She questioned some of the crew just to get their angle on everything they did, but there was still nothing substantial.

All Wilma wanted were words. She didn't have to find anything worth writing about, but it's what Maggie did. If she was going to do the work, she was going to make it worth reading. Jackson knew them better than she did, certainly spent more time with them than she would ever want to. And she didn't care that he didn't want to talk to her, she talked anyway when she caught him with a moment while changing film.

"You spend more time with these girls than I do, what can you tell me? I need something besides what kind of nail polish they wear. I can't imagine you've struck up many conversations in your day, but ever hear them talk about anything?"

Jackson continued to change his film without missing a beat. "They keep the mouth shut, I get the picture."

"Okay, what about when you're not taking pictures, when you're out with one, or two."

Jackson's hands fell to his sides as he turned to face her. "Do I bother you when you're working?"

"Is this a bad time?" She said sarcastically. "You won't talk to me when you're not working, so when am I supposed to ask you questions?" Maggie huffed in retaliation.

"Are you new at this or something? You're doing a behind the scenes thing, just write a nice little article about what their secrets are to look great in the morning. A makeup trick, a juice they drink. Isn't that what you're supposed to be doing? How difficult can that be?" His voice was harsh and unrelenting.

"It is difficult when I'm used to writing stories of substance, and I can't find any here."

"And you won't. Substance doesn't exist. So can you just make it simple and leave me the hell alone?" He looked back to the subject at hand who posed in a bikini and a sheer white drape of fabric overtop as the sun had risen behind her. "Shit! I've lost the light now."

"There's plenty of light," she argued.

"That's the shoot guys," he turned to the others, then back to Maggie. "Are they paying you to take pictures too? Can you stick to your work and let me stick to mine?"

Maggie's blood boiled. Behind her, John Carob watched the two and laughed on the inside. He felt sorry for Jackson who was about to get some of Maggie's anger, he saw it coming.

"And it's my fault the sun came all the way up? Excuse me, I should have made a few phone calls for you. I suppose you not only expect the world to revolve around you, but at the perfect timing for your needs."

Jackson remained patient and calm, stared at her outburst with no more interest than he had in watching water boil, which this experience was similar. His attitude and silence just made her more frustrated.

"I was hoping to find a few adults in this bunch. Would it absolutely kill you to pretend to be a decent person? Can you at least indulge me so I can get through this week without throwing myself overboard? I don't care if you don't like me or not, I don't need anymore friends, but what I do need is a story and asking for a little cooperation from you shouldn't be too much."

Maggie continued to vent in a relentless rage, as much as she could until he calmly walked away from her without saying another word.

****

When Nicole woke, her eyes opened to see daylight but she hadn't a clue what time of day it could have been. And there was no one else in the room to tell her because both of the other beds were empty. Nicole stretched and wasn't sure if she wanted to get out of bed, hadn't slept later than 6:00 a.m. since she had the flu three years previous. By the sunlight, she had a notion it was past that but she didn't bother to hunt down her watch and check the time, she was on vacation. Maybe she should just throw it out the window and buy a new one at the end of the week. Just as she was about to get into the shower Kyla came in.

"Well, good afternoon," she teased.

"Afternoon? What time is it?"

"Almost. It's 11:30, I was about to check to see if you had a fever and were sick." Kyla placed her hand on her head anyway.

"I guess to say I was making up for lost sleep is an understatement. This boat just rocked me like a baby. Where's Maggie?"

"Jogging."

"Jogging?" Nicole raised her eyebrows in question.

"She thinks its going to help her frazzled nerves that are definitely suffering. There was an early shoot this morning and she said something about the models, her not getting enough money and them not getting enough discipline as a child. Then a little ranting about mean people and arrogant assholes, so we know Jackson was involved in creating her wonderful mood. I met her for breakfast but she talked so fast and talked the entire time and I never did make much sense of any of it."

Outside, Maggie took one more lap and fell exhausted into a chair. How many laps had she done? She'd lost count so long ago, wasn't even sure of how much time had passed. Had she run a half hour? An hour? Two? Three? She'd been so irritated at the morning's activities that she just needed to exert herself in some manner. Jogging was the only thing she could think of that was strenuous enough, odd thing was, she wasn't even sure if it were the models attitudes or the indifference from Jackson that infuriated her enough to push herself to the limits of her physical ability.

She tried to ask him questions about his work but he refused to answer her, ignored her as if she hadn't even spoken. How could someone make it all this way through life without talking? She'd seen he actually had a voice for the crew, it was just her he didn't like or talk to, and she'd done nothing to him. That was fine if it was merely a matter of him not liking her, not everyone needed to like her and she didn't care one way or another. If she thought it would work she'd write questions down and slip it under his door and he could answer them when he pleased, but Maggie knew even that wouldn't help, she'd still be ignored.

Maggie leaned back, closed her eyes, and let the nice breeze off the sea cool her body and her head, which still felt just as hot inside as her skin did on the outside. She could stay right there all day. There was no reason to get up, the ship would sail all day long on her way to Cozumel, so she really didn't have to do anything else, did she?

"Is she alive?" Nicole whispered jokingly to Kyla when they found her a little while later in the same position, lying back with her eyes closed.

Maggie heard them and answered with her eyes still closed. "I think my spirit is, but I can't get my brain to function properly. Spending more than five minutes in the presence of those women seems to make me lose brain cells. Maybe it's contagious. Whatever it is they have that makes them stupid. Could be in the specific pure bottled water they insist on drinking, but they only drink half of it before it gets to 'tepid' and they need a new one. Maybe that's what shrunk their minds, tepid water. Someone please save me before I throw myself overboard because being shark bait seems appealing to me right now."

"Uh oh," Kyla said. "She's still raging."

Maggie opened her eyes then, expecting to see Nicole and Kyla, and she saw them, but she was also surrounded by Alan, Randy and all eight of his friends. All stood silent with smiles on their faces, trying to hold back the laughter.

She continued with a heavy sigh, "Oh good, the cavalry is here. Strong young men who can pick me up and throw me overboard, I won't even have to move a muscle. Please, I beg of you to help me, being fed to the sharks sounds much more promising than having to deal with those insolent children."

Alan laughed as he took her hands and pulled her from the chair, "We won't throw you overboard but we promise to try and make your day better. Come have some fun with us."

"You promise?"

"We'll do our best."

They were all prepared for a day of activities and fun but Maggie needed a shower first and playfully promised she wouldn't do anything drastic and didn't need supervision and would meet up with them afterwards.

The thought of having fun and beginning her day again made her feel a little better as she walked down the hall, but her lift in mood wouldn't last, only worsen. She saw Bo on the outside of a door and heard the demanding voice inside and the boil of the morning reached a peak.

"This is all wrong. I told you I wanted my bed made with all the covers tucked in, including the spread. And I want a full ice bucket at all times. Not just in the morning or the evening, all day long. I never know when I want something cold to drink and it's your job to make sure I have it when I want it."

Maggie recognized Simone's voice, then another's, as Tiffany piped in with her own demands.

"And I have to insist that when you pick up the room service dishes from the hall you be a little quieter. I heard you last night and it woke me up."

Bo began to apologize but Maggie reached the door just in time to stop him, she then banged on the door to the room beside them to summon the other girls. What she had to say would be said to all.

"What is it?" Tedi answered as she rubbed her eyes in sleep. "We were napping and you woke us up."

"I want all of you over here right now," she demanded.

The two had been sleeping and now had no choice but to follow her command so they wandered into the next room but not without a fight.

"You know we were up before dawn, why do we..."

Maggie immediately blasted them all with unexpected fire. "We've all been up before dawn but that doesn't give any of you the right to be rude and I've had about all I can take of it. I don't know where you grew up, but where I come from, we don't treat people the way you've been treating Bo and everyone else around you. He's working hard just to please you and everything he does isn't good enough. Well you know what? Maybe you should make your own bed if it doesn't suit you."

"It's what he gets paid to do." Simone huffed as if it validated the fact he was there to wait on her hand and foot.

"And he did it. He made your bed. His job doesn't revolve around you and your whims because you want your bed made to stupid standards you have no reason for wanting, other than the fact you can tell someone to do it and they will. Like I said, make it yourself. It's a shame you have to be told, but he isn't your personal servant. He wasn't hired specifically for you so I suggest from now on you let him do his job and quit acting like you're the only ones on this ship."

"Who are you to come in here and tell us anything? You're not our boss." Tedi said snidely.

It only made her anger worse and it pushed her directly over the edge as if she'd done so physically with her hands. "Let me tell you something you little snit. Right now I am. My company hired you for a job, which makes you a temporary employee to me. Not only am I the writer of the article, I'm also supervising this stupid little thing and I'm not happy about it. I'd just as soon put your pretty little asses off at the next port, but that shouldn't even be your main concern..."

She continued with a heat of fire. "You ought to be worried about what I'm going to write about all this. Let me put it into terms you'll understand. I write, the world reads. Now I can base my entire article on how you snotty nosed brats complained all week because your pillow wasn't puffy enough or your salad didn't have the right count of bacon bits to suit your taste, or that you sent back three meals because you don't like your meat touching anything else on your plate."

She threw her hands in the air as she looked to the stunned women, all of them silent and motionless. "What kind of crap is that? Where do you come up with this shit? I'd love to tell the world that you had the room steward make your bed five times a day, or come in and fluff your pillows ten times a day just in case you decided to take a nap."

Because of the small size of the room she was already close but moved even closer. As she spoke the words out loud she became even more livid at the absurdity of it all and distaste now took total control.

"I can make all of you look like the biggest spoiled diva's on the planet just by putting pen to paper. Once the industry reads it they'll stay as far away from you as possible, they don't need the headache or hassle of hiring people who are only going to make their job more difficult. So how many assignments do you think you'll get after this? You think you're the only pretty face in town? There are enough models out there that'll replace you faster than you can flash that pretty smile when you want to."

Her last final words were spoken as fact, there was no hesitation to indicate she wouldn't do all she said. "All of you have a choice to make. Start acting like decent human beings or pack your bags and figure out how you're going to get home from Cozumel tomorrow. When this ship docks you can find your own way back to where you came from and if I hear anymore shit I won't even wait until tomorrow. I'll have you in a lifeboat with oars. I don't have the patience to baby sit people who act no older then my youngest niece but it's only in age. At least she has the decency to treat people with respect."

Silence was the only response and when she faced Bo she spoke again, her words a threatening undertone for the ladies to defy her. "I don't think they'll need anything else for the rest of the day, or for the rest of the trip, they may not even be here."

She turned sharply towards the direction of her room and stormed down the hall. Had she looked back, she would have seen Jackson who leaned against the wall just outside the door on the opposite side she faced.

She'd already entered her own room when Bo asked if they would need anything else but was met with mumbles of denial. He left quietly and as he shut the door and turned around, it was then he noticed Jackson standing there.

"Mister Jack, sir," Bo said startled, then wiped his forehead jokingly in the aftermath of Maggie's outburst. It was obvious he'd witnessed it. "Whew."

"Yeah," he laughed. "I guess that should take care of it."

Jackson himself had been witness to their degrading and demanding treatment and would have soon told them off himself had Maggie not taken care of it so well. He didn't feel there would be a need for him to intervene after she'd left them in stoned humble silence. Felt at that point of breaking she would actually put them in the lifeboat as promised, pictured in his mind the women floating in a vast sea with no rescue in sight, and no manicurist to make sure their nails were perfect for any rescuer who might come to save them.

Jackson thought about Maggie and the situation. He'd been treating her with no more respect than they had, and it dawned on him that's all she wanted. She wasn't coming on to him and could care less about him personally.

The shower helped Maggie to put everyone and everything out of her thoughts. She honestly calculated in her mind where she was going to work because she had all intentions of sticking to her word, maybe not so far as to put them in a lifeboat, even though it would have been her first preference, but she would actually put them out in Cozumel if she needed to and they could fend for themselves. Wilma would be furious, she would lose her job, but at that point Maggie didn't care. She went off to enjoy her day.

Alan and the male entourage he traveled with stayed with them for the majority of it and as promised, they all had a grand time. They took Salsa dance lessons, played poolside games which one of Randy's friends won a pretend gold medal in, and overall spent the entire day laughing. She did go to her room several times and found the hall quiet, Bo nowhere to be found. She correctly assumed the spoiled women had gotten her point and all seemed quiet for the rest of the day.

CHAPTER SEVEN

Maggie dressed for formal night before she went to the evening shoot, that way she could linger there while the others got ready and no one would be rushed. She was in a slim fitting red dress that clung to her muscular and fit curves, then fell to her ankles where gold high spike heeled sandals were visible. Dark, thick hair fell loose and free around her face and her only accessory a pair of gold earrings.

A portion of the top deck had been blocked off for their use on an evening that couldn't have been more beautiful. There was a magnificent sun that had begun its descent into the sea and Maggie watched on the outskirts for a moment and it was evident there were no evil spirits among them. There was a definite change in attitudes, she could sense it, and they actually appeared to enjoy their job for once. Maybe all they'd needed all along was the threat of losing it.

Maggie stepped quietly next to John Carob. Although they didn't need any lighting or props that evening he was at the shoot anyway.

She slipped her hand under his arm. "How about you be my date tonight?" She smiled warmly.

He looked to Maggie and whistled low. "And have to fight off all your other admirers who will be forming a line? I'm too old for the competition."

"The only line I see is the one to the buffet." Maggie laughed and almost blushed at his approval and compliment. "How's the shoot going?"

"I don't know what happened between this morning and now but I feel like it's the twilight zone. I haven't heard one complaint, it's the strangest thing."

She raised her brows. "Wow, not even the argument that they have the wrong water?"

"They haven't even asked for it," he shook his head in bewilderment. "I took a nap this afternoon and feel like I may have woken up in some sort of other world, or that I'm still asleep and dreaming this. It's been great."

She didn't say anything about her lecture to them. "Shhhhh... maybe if you say it too loud we'll all wake up."

"I think Jackson's more than pleased. He's accomplished in an hour what normally takes him four with all the interruptions and requests." John could tell just by his relaxed posture that he was content with how things were going.

"Jackson pleased?" She looked over and he looked no different than he always did. "How can you tell?"

"I think you two just got off on the wrong foot somehow, he really isn't that bad."

"Not to you, you're a man. I normally don't judge people, you know that about me, but I'm not thinking the best of him. All I need is a few simple words for a stupid little article, you'd think I was asking for the moon."

"How's the article going?"

She groaned. "All my editor wants is the fluff stuff, the stupid crap that means nothing. But that's not me, John, and I have a feeling I'll keep looking all week for something that isn't there."

"If there's anything there, you'll find it."

Maggie continued to vent her frustration a little, took advantage of his sympathetic listening abilities. "Do you know how hard it is to find something of substance behind a model shoot? Behind girls whose biggest worry of the day seems to be if the makeup girl has the right lipstick color for when she changes clothes every hour? Because the original writer had to have gallstone surgery or some crap, I have to write about the wrong color lipstick. And just think, I've lived my life all along and not realized how important the right color and texture was." She said sarcastically and laughed. "Guess that's why I've never been offered a modeling job, huh?"

"There's not a one here that could hold a candle to you."

He spoke the truth, to him beauty was much more than what one appeared to be. Maggie could have been a model, she was just as beautiful on the outside as any of them, but more important to him was not her obvious physical attributes, but her personality. She may not be sought after for her award winning smile and flawless features, but he would have been proud to have a daughter like her, had he and his late wife ever had children.

Tedi then approached them with her eyes wide, her voice a little timid with a newfound respect and admiration noticeable. "Wow, Miss Maggie, maybe you should be in front of the camera instead of behind it. You look fantastic."

The other women saw her then and Jackson turned to see where their attention was drawn since they'd stopped looking at the camera, had to agree with Tedi's assessment, inwardly. He only took a quick overall glance before he turned away but the impression remained with him as if he'd stared and studied for much longer.

Maggie laughed with the ease she felt. She'd made her argument that day and wouldn't hold it against them for the rest of the trip. As long as they'd gotten her point and took her words to heart, everything from now on should go smoothly.

"Not my area of expertise," she answered. "How embarrassing it would be to make a magazine cover and for the first time in publishing history not one of the thousands printed ever sold. I think I'll stick to what I do best. My editor will certainly bless me for it."

"Just for fun why don't we take a few pictures? You look too nice not to have it etched in film." Simone now stood beside her and the other girls agreed.

They surrounded her and John encouraged it as they drug her to the railing where they'd been posing and wouldn't let her get away. It crossed her mind they were ganging up to throw the tyrant overboard or make her walk the plank. Maggie got the feeling they were buttering her up, their fear of her threats moved them to drastic change and she realized it was their way of apology, one she would accept without question.

She stood motionless until they began posing with highly exaggerated flair and moved her limbs to emulate them. Arms flung straight in the air, spread wide, her head tilted one way or another and they encouraged her to pout or blow a sexy air kiss.

"Jackson, are you getting this?" One shouted with laughter.

He didn't say anything but his camera clicked away as they all laughed. They lined up facing each other's backs and bent one leg in front of them like a line of showgirls in Vegas.

"No, no, no Maggie. You need to pull that dress up a bit. Show some of that leg you're hiding under there." Simone pulled it up for her and put it in Maggie's fingers to hold.

She did as they said then they began dancing like the showgirls they resembled. A few passengers had noticed and began to cheer, clap and whistle as they kicked their legs in unison. Maggie thought she saw the slightest hint of a smile on Jackson's face, the closest thing to him being human she'd witnessed. Then chalked it up to the flicker of sunlight that bounced off the steel of his camera and made her imagine it, for when she spoke to him afterwards there was nothing pleasant there.

"I hope I didn't get in the way too much," Maggie said to Jackson when the episode was over and they all dispersed their separate ways.

"Not too much," he said dryly as he began to pack his equipment, then he looked up from his task and added. "Would it have made a difference if I said you did get in the way?"

"No," she stated firmly with the same stubborn sternness his eyes possessed. For one solitary millisecond she thought she'd seen the hint of something human again but it passed quickly, her mind must be playing tricks on her.

As if there were a silent challenge between them Maggie waited just as he for the first to turn away. Although he didn't turn away, he was the first to speak and she silently claimed herself the winner.

"The way you're dressed, it looks like you have someplace to be." He waited for her to leave, wanted her to leave. She looked too good in that dress.

"Not really. I dress this way every night." She teased and waited for at least a smile but none came. "What are you all about Jackson Turner? What's your deal? Are you a closet extrovert? You go back to your cabin and jump and dance and sing when no one is looking?"

"Is it important for you to know that?"

"I'm writing a story, it's important for me to find out what kind of person you are." Maggie knew it was an excuse. Her curiosity about this silent man was making it impossible not to be drawn to him. The mystery was intriguing, and maybe it was his ploy, like a black widow spider that lured you into the web for the kill.

"I'm not part of this story." He finally turned his attention back to his equipment as he carefully packed it away.

"I have to write about everyone, you're certainly a big part. What am I supposed to write if you don't talk to me?"

"Make something up." He didn't look at her when he zipped his bag and walked away but she followed behind.

"How long have you been a photographer?"

She asked the question casually as if he'd actually respond. When he didn't she continued with a barrage of questions, one after the other, talked the entire way to the elevator, the time they waited and every second on the way down. Maybe she hadn't seen a smile, but she sensed a difference in Jackson. He certainly wasn't chatty, she would never expect that, but it was different. He at least didn't dismiss her.

They reached their floor and Jackson stepped aside then grandly motioned with his hand. "You can get out first, I'm afraid you'll make faces behind my back again."

"Oh." Maggie's face turned instant red at the recollection when she'd done that, obviously he'd seen her, but she didn't care and she recovered quickly. "Had you been nicer, I wouldn't have." Then she scrunched her face up in plain sight.

Per usual, he wasn't going to talk to her at all and left her standing in the hall still trying to ask questions when he unlocked his door, walked inside and shut it behind him. Her first instinct was to bang on it violently. She wasn't a hostile person but he made her feel that way. She saw Kyla and Nicole step from their room, dressed in their finery for the evening ahead.

"What are you doing standing here in the hall?" Kyla asked when they reached her.

"Trying to summon up an evil twin, one who would resort to violence and pound on this door screeching like a banshee."

"What?" Nicole asked with laughter at the words that confused her.

"Never mind," Maggie shook her head as they left Jackson to his solitude.

Formal night on the ship offered passengers the opportunity to get their pictures professionally done and the three of them went to every photo opportunity and got their pictures taken together. There were different backdrops scattered about, then Nicole insisted they needed one with the Captain who was dressed to impress in his best uniform whites. He was quiet until they started cutting up.

"Do you give tours of the bridge? Think I could come up and drive awhile? Do you drive a ship? Navigate, that's what I meant." Maggie said.

"Oh no." Nicole quickly objected. "If Maggie were behind the wheel passengers would always have to wear their lifejackets."

Kyla added her thoughts in. "The way she drives, we could make all of the islands in one day. Now Nicole driving, and it would take us several months."

After a first hesitation, he began to loosen up knowing they were harmless, commented that he'd have to be sure the door to the Bridge area was not only locked, but bolted at all times. Perhaps security guards were also in order.

Alan, Randy and their group of handsome men all dressed in suit jackets, all looked quite dashing, and were just passing through the area when they saw the women and stopped to watch. The three playfully changed positions, posed the Captain with his elbow resting on Nicole's shoulder, or he and Kyla saluting one another. Then he even put his hat on Maggie and told her it would have to suffice, since he wouldn't be letting her take the wheel. There was no one else waiting in line so they played a few moments with girlish fun as the camera clicked away.

The men continued to watch and Randy leaned closer to Alan, his voice low so no one could overhear.

"Have you told Kyla yet?" He didn't need to say the specific words, they both knew what he spoke of, and Randy could see by the look on his face he hadn't, "Weird, huh? Running into her at this time in your life, who would have thought?"

"Yeah," Alan's voice noted surrender to his confusion to the change his life had taken. The day before they boarded the ship, plans for his future were solid and stable, now he felt the college kid he once was, complete with all the mystification and uncertainty he remembered well.

"Are you going to tell her?"

"There's no question I have to, it's just a question of when." Alan looked to his young brother and saw understanding in his eyes along with a hint of sadness for his situation.

"I don't know what happened to you two, you never really explained it to me, all I know was that one day she left and never came back. Eventually I realized she was never going to again. I missed her every time you came home and she wasn't with you, and it hurt a little."

It hurt Randy a little but Alan remembered the intense pain well, it lingered for a long time and seeing her again didn't serve to squelch it. "We had separate priorities."

"Whatever the reason for this second meeting I guess the question is, is it to finally put her behind you? Or finally a chance you thought you'd never have to move forward with her?" Randy shifted his feet and looked away then back again, unsure if he'd said more than he should have.

Alan looked at him with amazement. He knew Randy loved Kyla as a sister, but never realized just how much he was hurt by her departure. He was so young, it never crossed Alan's mind to explain much of the adult world then but he was older now, and understood things.

Randy thought maybe he said too much when Alan was quiet. "I didn't mean to make assumptions, it's just obvious you two either have something to finish or something to start, even if it's something that puts a major kink in your life right now. I just called it as I saw it, I hope you're not mad."

"I'm just wondering where you got all that philosophical stuff?"

"A year of psyche 101 remember?"

"Ah yes," Alan laughed. "The one class you failed."

"So do you think anything can come of it?"

Alan looked to Kyla who caught his eye for a moment and smiled, a guilt coursed through him, one he had to get through but wasn't quite sure how. "I think there are some things we have to get through first before that question can be asked."

"I wish I could give you some advice in that area, but I can't help you out there, as you just pointed out, I failed psyche, remember?"

"Ah, bail on me when it gets tough." Alan put his arm around his little brother. "I'll figure it out."

The three women still cut up with the Captain and a few moments later Randy joined them and egged a few of the guys on and they too jumped in. Nicole, Kyla and Maggie were soon swooped up into strong masculine arms and Randy easily picked up the Captain in the same manner. Alan laughed so hard he had to sit down and the photographer's laughter just as boisterous, he had to put his camera on the tripod so his laughter wouldn't shake it. A distance away, Jackson had been watching the comical fiasco taking place and wasn't immune to the humor.

They all dined together that evening at an extra large table that was put together for their needs, then after dinner went to the Theater for a wonderful production show. Afterwards, they landed at the Disco again where the music filtered into the hall and lured them in. They didn't need much persuasion, they went willingly, everyone in the mood for more fun.

The three women had their choice of dance partners with the young men, only until two of the models, Tedi and Kelli, joined them at Maggie's insistence. After that they became invisible to all but Alan, Randy and two of the others who were attached to women they cared about back home and didn't want casual involvement with other women to be an issue.

Like the two beautiful ladies that now graced the dance floor, who made it a point to assure her they didn't have to be at the 5:00 a.m. camera call, all of the girls bent over backwards to please her. Not only her, but everyone else involved in the shoot. She found she really did like them since they'd shed the ugly facade. Like children, they found their boundaries, actually were pointed rather directly to where their boundaries were, and would carefully stay within its confines.

Several times throughout that evening she'd run into them and took a few moments of quiet time here and there. Small casual bits of time that would eventually add up to the accumulated information she needed. Once the line was drawn that put them all on equal level, Maggie found them more willing to talk to her, confide in her.

Her stories formed on her computer, her paper in longhand, and in her mind as well. Not the specifics, but the basis of what she would fill the pages with anyway. Along with having a wonderful time with her friends, she could see the beginning's of an actual article forming. Probably not the one Wilma originally expected, but Maggie was almost sure her boss knew it would be something more than what name was on the inside of the girls clothes. It was her way.

She didn't know what she would do about the photographer. Do as he said and make something up about him? Maybe for spite she would. Write about a dark sullen man who knew how to use a camera but hadn't a clue how to be kind or interact with humans on any other level. It was a good thing he was sought after for his skills as a professional, it certainly wouldn't be for speaking engagements. Maggie wondered if it was just a simple mean spirit. Then her compassionate side took over and she wondered if something happened to turn him that way.

It crossed her mind what she would write about him. It crossed her mind why he was the way he was, maybe reasons and excuses for it.

But it also crossed her mind that she specifically looked for him when the models entered, then wondered where he was, who he was with.

She would soon find out when Nicole went off for coffee and she left the disco to join Kyla for one last drink at the Wine Bar and found Jackson there with John. Of course John invited them to sit down and when Kyla slipped easily next to him, Maggie was left with the only other option, sitting beside Jackson. They chatted casually and easily, everyone of course except Jackson, man of few words.

"So John," Kyla turned to him, knew she wouldn't get anything out of the handsome silent one. "I'm not around the models much, but I can see a turn around and Maggie didn't threaten to become shark bait after the shoot this evening, said it actually went quite well. Did they just need a day to adjust?"

He shrugged his shoulders with a still confused smile. "A mystery to us all but it's certainly a welcome change."

"Maybe the sea air," Maggie commented lightly.

"Must make it easier on you, Jackson." Kyla was hesitant to even speak to him, his quiet brood was intimidating.

"I've learned how to block most of the disgruntled ones out when I work."

"You seem to block," Maggie was about to comment that he seemed to block everything out, but then she felt like she was attacking him when she wasn't provoked and changed her mind. "You seem to block it out well. I'm not sure I would have as much patience if I were in your position."

"I've seen some lose patience under certain circumstances, and that works too."

Maggie looked at him and wondered if he commented on anyone in particular and wasn't coming out and saying it, wondered if somehow he'd known she had lost patience that morning, but there was no way to tell, his face gave nothing.

After one drink, Kyla made her excuses and left, Maggie knew she was probably off to meet Alan somewhere and didn't accompany her. She should have when John quickly made his exit soon after.

"I think my time is up also, it's been a long day." He rose from his seat and Maggie couldn't see herself staying alone with Jackson so she too moved to rise but John stopped her. Gently but quickly he placed his hand on her shoulder. "Don't let me run you off, Maggie, you're too young to call it a night. I'm the only old one here. I'll see you two tomorrow."

If she were rude, like Jackson, she would have left anyway. But Jackson made no attempt to get up and she wasn't rude. It was quiet between them, then Maggie started talking out loud to herself. She was still sitting next to him, so close she could feel the heat from his body and there was no one on the other side to look at so she looked into her glass.

"How was your day, Maggie? Great, wonderful, how about you? Same here. How's your trip so far? Pretty good, what about yours? It'll be nice to get off the ship tomorrow. Some island sun, a little beach sand. Have any special plans? Not particularly. Okay, it's been great talking to you. You too, have a nice evening." Maggie took the last sip of her drink then set her glass down and moved to leave, but Jackson put his hand on her arm.

"Point made. Can I buy you a drink before you run off with the same notions about me you've had from the beginning?"

She looked him in the eyes and again saw what she thought was the slightest hint of a smile. This time it was real and he looked apologetic, almost sweet, with something of the hard edge gone. And she could see humility, just slightly, but enough that she noticed.

"Wow, that drink must have been strong, I'm actually looking at you and I think you might be human. That could be a bad sign, does it mean you poisoned my drink?"

"I deserve that," he said.

"This is strange, is it the drinks? You need the alcohol to play human? I'm almost afraid to talk to you, in the morning you won't remember."

"I deserve that too, but no, this is my one and only drink of the day. I'll have two if you join me." Jackson finished the liquid and placed his empty glass on the table. "If not, I'll certainly understand. I haven't made the best conversationalist, but you seem to have mastered the skill well. You could take care of that portion for both of us." He referred to her conversation with herself moments ago with humor evident in his voice.

"An invitation and humor too?" Then she thought maybe she'd been the one who'd had too much to drink.

"At least let me buy you one drink, use it as a way to apologize for being a jerk."

"Self admission is good therapy," she stated. "You're the one who said you were a jerk, I didn't. Well... there might have... maybe once when..." She stammered then continued with her own admission of guilt. "I may have used the term loosely in your description. Once."

"And I'm sure it wasn't the only term you've used, and I admit I've deserved everything you possibly said about me."

"I'm still leery, why the turn around? You actually didn't poison my first drink and want me to have another to give you the chance to poison that one. Is that it?" Maggie looked inside her empty glass as if she fully expected to discover something. "Or you did poison it and are just waiting for the pleasure of seeing me go into convulsions any moment now."

"No poison. And the turn around? Truth? When you gave the models hell this morning, I took your words to heart, realized I'd been acting no better."

"Oh, you heard that?"

"I think all of Cozumel heard that, and we were a day away from them at the time." It didn't get past Jackson that Maggie had said nothing to no one, not even her friend knew why the girls had been behaving so well. She was either confident enough to not need the ego boost of her accomplishment, or naïve to think her confrontation with them had nothing to do with it.

Maggie didn't know he'd been anywhere close. It wouldn't have mattered had she known, but she certainly wouldn't have expected him to listen and actually pay attention to what she'd said.

"Well then, I'm glad you got something out of the little talk this morning too, but out of some sense of guilt, you don't have to be friendly if it doesn't suit you."

"I rarely do things that don't suit me, and it isn't out of a sense of guilt." Then he paused and confessed honestly, "Okay, maybe it is, so will you at least let me buy you a drink and then I won't feel guilty anymore?"

The waiter appeared then and Jackson hesitated as he looked to Maggie and waited for her.

She sighed. "Just one, and I'm only doing this out of duty to my job, can't have you feeling guilty all week, Lord knows what kinds of shots I'll get."

They ordered and were left alone again as Maggie spilled out everything she thought about him, she wasn't one to mince words, and wouldn't start now.

"I figured you out, I know all about your kind, Jackson Turner."

"My kind?" He chuckled and raised his eyebrows.

"Arrogant, conceited, you made incorrect assumptions about me without even bothering to get to know me. You thought like every other woman you meet, I would want to go out with you or something, didn't you?"

Jackson was surprised at her directness. He didn't try to explain, nor defend himself from her reasoning. In a sense, she was correct. His defenses had been up for so long it was just the way he was now. "I'm surrounded by models all day, most days. I don't want to sound arrogant, because I'm really not, but I'm approached all the time with offers. From dates, to just simply hopping into bed. I get into this mode when I work, an automatic disinterested attitude I've adopted that seems to keep most at bay."

"You certainly do that, but you didn't have to worry about me, I've decided on a solitary life. Men are bullshit." A man was the last thing on her mind, even if he did make good eye candy as Kyla said.

"Don't hold back on my account," he laughed again at her directness.

Jackson appreciated her honesty, it was refreshing. He also appreciated her natural beauty, that too refreshing and different from the women he saw day in and day out with so much makeup on they probably used paint thinner to get it off. He'd been thinking of her in that red dress all evening, glad she hadn't changed after dinner. Then again, maybe it would have been easier to sit next to her if she had.

"My apologies," Jackson commented with sincerity. "I get so wrapped up in what I'm doing I forget where the line is between work and life."

"The only reason I'm accepting your apology is because John said you were actually a good guy, and he's a good judge of character." Then she paused as the waiter set their drinks down and moved on. "Besides, I'm not ashamed to admit I have ulterior motives. If I don't accept your apology you still won't talk to me and I'll never get my article written."

He wondered if that were the only reason. Stop Jackson, he screamed inside himself. Don't look at her that way, don't think of her that way, and don't think about her at all. "I really can't help you on any story though, I don't know anything about these girls."

He may not know anything about them where their lives were concerned, but she still suspected he knew a few of them very intimately. But that was only her opinion no matter he'd told her he wanted to keep them at bay.

An air of mystery along with his indifference, made him sexy as hell. Maggie of course noticed his physical attraction, it was hard not to, but it still didn't make her interested in him. Maybe that's why she became comfortable with him when he opened up to her just the slightest bit, at least became friendly.

They enjoyed their drink together and casual talk was interspersed with questions that went unanswered, but Maggie tried at every turn.

CHAPTER EIGHT

Deriving its name from the Mayans who believed the island to be a sacred shrine, Cozumel translated to 'land of the swallows'. It was reflection of the birds known in the area that graced the landscape of rocky shore and turquoise sea, one rich in history and natural wonders, rough and rugged in its primal beauty.

The one town on the island, San Miguel, found one wandering the Plaza del Sol and the downtown pier where shops hawked their wares and bars offered refreshing margaritas in a shady spot. While a drive through the interior and to the other side found undeveloped splendor. Rocky shores to explore and ancient Mayan temples on the north side of the island gave one a look back to history, as did El Cedral on the south side, the oldest Maya structure on Cozumel, built in A.D. 800.

One could immerse themselves in shopping. One of many nature reserves such as the Marine Reef National Park, Chankanaab and Punta Sur. Partake in a botanical garden, or laze along the shore of the sea or in it. Underwater life abounded and gave divers and those with a snorkel mask a view into another world as colorful fish seemed used to the intrusion.

A world-renowned ecosystem and natural aquarium, Chankanaab, whose meaning in Mayan language is 'small sea', was where the morning shoot was scheduled. Maggie decided not to go with the crew, instead rented her own open-air jeep and followed along so she would have the freedom to leave when she wanted. Staying for the entire shoot wasn't necessarily mandatory for her, but she found the weather beautiful and the surroundings more than pleasing to the eye.

It was arranged to take pictures with the dolphins and sea lions that were available for tourists to interact with. The models a little skittish but Maggie jumped right in with advance instruction and had the time of her life. With her in the water, they relaxed enough for Jackson to get what he needed. He himself had to smile, even if inwardly, at her boldness and childlike enthusiasm as her laughter resounded in the air and because of her, he got some great shots.

The models couldn't wait to shower and Maggie lagged behind, taking every last second she could to enjoy the dolphins more. When she pulled herself out of the pool Jackson threw her a towel.

"Is there invisible blue dye or something on this? I innocently wipe myself with it and the next thing you know I'm all blotched with blue."

"Not blue. I think red's more your color."

Maggie wasn't sure whether he meant it as a compliment because of her red dress the evening before, then dismissed the thought as being absurd. It was pure coincidence and she felt stupid just thinking it. She wiped her face but still looked at him suspiciously.

"You don't trust me?" Jackson asked.

"I don't fully trust any man that doesn't share my last name."

"You're married?" He asked too quickly, mistook her meaning.

"I'm speaking of seven brothers and a father." She wiped her arms and spoke casually. "What about you? You come from a big family?"

Jackson laughed. "If anyone can't trust anyone, it's me that can't trust you. You have a sneaky way of doing that?"

"What?" She asked innocently.

"Throwing in questions so casually one doesn't see it coming. You're very good at your job." Jackson returned to his equipment and began to pack with a smile as he shook his head.

"There is a difference between Maggie the reporter questions, and Maggie the person questions."

"Which one was that?"

"That was the person, just asking for conversational purposes."

"Had I said I come from a family of a dozen kids it never would have made it into print?"

She took his question seriously and answered truthfully. "I can't say that, but I didn't ask it for those purposes. Do you come from a family of a dozen kids?"

He didn't say another word as he carefully packed his things into foam lined boxes and Maggie left to get dressed, shouting over her shoulder.

"I'm going to make it up, you know. I'm going to write you're one of two dozen kids!"

After she showered to get the salt water off she kept her wet suit on and put on dry clothes overtop. She was only going to another beach so no sense changing again when she got there. The models busied themselves primping as much as they could and she invited them along with her to the beach, but they were going shopping instead.

"There's a store downtown that has the best thongs, why don't you come with us, Maggie, and let us pick one out for you?" Tiffany looked excited at the prospect.

"This behind is way past thong prime, I think I'll stick to being a little more covered."

When she left them to finish she found John and a few of the crew waiting for them and he didn't want to go to the beach either.

"No thanks, a few of us are going around to the other side of the island."

"Are you sure you aren't standing me up for a secret date with a hot mama? If you were its okay, I'll understand."

"You'll be the first to know."

She asked everyone but they all had plans, the only one she hadn't asked was Jackson so she approached him then.

"What about you? I'm going to meet up with some others at a beach, care to join us?" Maggie saw his hesitation. "Don't let your ego get ahead of you, just because I ask doesn't mean you're anything special, I asked everyone here."

"It didn't cross my mind that I was anything special."

"I don't want you getting the wrong idea, you might clam up on me again if you think I might be coming on to you, not that you've opened up about anything, but at least you're not being rude to me."

He chuckled, she certainly laid it all on the line without any second thoughts, and it was tempting to join her, even though she did all she could not to flatter him, but he declined. "I appreciate the invitation, but not today."

"The reply of 'not today' assumes there might be another day. Do you automatically take it for granted I'm going to ask you tomorrow?" She playfully teased with a coy smile.

"Maybe that's some of my arrogance coming out again."

"You have to learn to keep that thing in check, it won't serve you any purpose with me and you're just wasting it when someone else may appreciate it."

"I'll keep that in mind," Jackson flung his camera bag over his shoulder with a smile.

****

The beach she was to meet the others wasn't too far away and Maggie had no trouble finding it with a map she'd been given. Nicole and Kyla were there and after their snorkeling morning at Dzul Ha, known for its bountiful sea life, Alan, Randy and the entire bachelor party joined them for a day of sun. They lounged on the beach with margaritas in hand, the turquoise waters of the Mexican Caribbean surrounded them, pure white sand along its edge a cushion for one to bury their feet and enjoy true bliss of relaxation.

It was an ambience of fun that offered shaded lounge chairs or fun activities to enjoy such as floating on a thin raft, kayaking, there was also a spot to go parasailing. The beachfront restaurant offered delicious Mexican food and of course a full bar of drinks, their specialty the frozen kind with lot's of fruit and umbrella's hanging from the glass. Among the regular bar patrons were two colorful and lively Macaw parrots who entertained children and adults alike, as they too immersed themselves in the tropical atmosphere.

Maggie and Nicole obtained a beach float and lazily spent a good part of the afternoon drifting idly in the ocean. Then Maggie joined some of the guys in kayak races while Nicole opted for a beach massage and Kyla got her hair braided.

Afterwards, they headed back to town, stopped at a popular local restaurant for more margarita's then on to a lively tourist club for even more carousing. Maggie wasn't surprised to see two of the models, but was surprised to see Jackson there among some of the crew. Unlike others though, instead of being loud and boisterous in the party atmosphere, he was quiet and subdued.

The two separate groups merged together when Maggie stopped by where the crew sat and introduced Alan and the party he was with and they all sat together, seemed to take up an entire corner of the establishment. Two of the bachelor party group couldn't have been pulled away from the models by force and everyone else seemed to fall into a comfortable group.

Maggie went around to those she hadn't seen since the shoot that morning and chatted easily. Alan handed her a drink and when she introduced him to John, the two began chatting about the golf club embroidered on John's shirt and then sat down together.

Tedi then pulled her along to the dance floor and there was a group of them, including Kyla and Randy and Nicole when Maggie caught her arm also.

"It's good exercise." Maggie told Nicole loudly above the noise when she wanted to leave the floor.

The song was loud and wild as people moved crazily about and sirens and whistles blew from every corner of the room to add to the noise. Dressed in a white tank top over her bathing suit and a fiery red sarong with fringes wrapped around her waist like a skirt, Maggie looked like a true islander as she moved to the beat of the music.

Afterwards, she saw Jackson across the room who smiled at her, a small turn of his lips, but she was sure it was a genuine smile. Then she was hauled off into the dancing crowd again, became lost amidst the sea of people on the floor. She didn't see him again for the rest of their time there.

Dinner that evening was casual in the outdoor Cafe' instead of one of the main dining rooms, and afterwards the three women found a quiet spot to enjoy while they waited for an evening show to begin. Maggie drank coffee, the early rises and long days were catching up to her already and she needed a caffeine boost.

"Do you know how hard it is to walk out of a room so early and you two so content? I want to accidentally make noise, just so you have to be up also."

"Blame it on him," Nicole nodded across the way to Jackson.

Maggie looked to see him walking with John just before they disappeared around a corner. "He reminds me of one of those 'too good to be true' kinds. I think he's gay, it's what some of the girls say anyway." Maggie said quietly to her two friends, knowing there was no chance to be overheard but she whispered it. She actually couldn't believe it could be true, but what did she actually know about him?

"That's ridiculous. Did you ever think that maybe around women he's a little reserved?" Nicole didn't think he was gay, but he certainly had reservations about people.

Kyla added her opinion. "He could be no different than us. We're always saying we're having nothing to do with men, maybe he's in the mode we get into all the time, and he's fed up with women in general. A few bad relationships, doesn't want to jump in the water right now. Could be he just got over a psycho stalker girlfriend or something. You can tell yourself otherwise, but everything about him is all man." Kyla knew she was right. "Besides, if he was gay, he'd be attracted to Randy's friend Kevin, he's the gay one."

"Kevin?" Maggie whispered in shock.

"That's how you can find out." Kyla said excitedly as if she'd come up with a solution. "If you don't believe me when I say he's all man, ask Kevin, he can pick them out a mile away. He'll tell you for sure."

Nicole smiled. "That doesn't sound half as fun as checking him out yourself. Come on to him, see what he does."

"I can't do that," Maggie almost said it too loudly and changed her voice to a whisper again. "I told him already I wasn't interested, that's the only reason he's at least halfway decent to me now, he knows I'm not after anything."

"So you lied."

"I didn't. I'm not interested." There was a little hesitation in her voice. "I'm not going to say he's not attractive, that's obvious, but I'm not looking for anything."

"So if you come on to him what would happen? You're not interested anyway, so what would you care that he didn't talk to you again?" Nicole almost said it as a dare and Kyla agreed.

"If he's leery of women because of some broken heart, he's not going to come on to you. And if you make the first move, he might just have the unemotional sex because it's there. He is a man, and men do that."

"But I don't!" Maggie pretended to look offended. "Like I'm the kind of girl who sleeps with someone for the sheer sake of sleeping with him."

"With that one, you might want to make an exception to those morals and values," Kyla laughed. "Besides, there's nothing wrong with two consenting adults enjoying a little passionate fling."

Much later that evening she'd left the others to have their fun, Nicole off for coffee, Kyla off with Alan, and she walked along the Promenade deck for one last breath of fresh air before going to bed. She passed few people, but as she got closer to the door to take her inside to her room, she saw Jackson standing alone against the banister that overlooked the sea.

"I should have expected you to find a nice quiet place." She easily stepped next to him and rested her arms on the banister as he had.

"Loud scenes don't interest me much. What did you do? Run out of steam?" She looked good with the contrast of skin that was becoming tan and a simple white dress.

"Working with a photographer who's a slave driver wears me out. Sunrise, sunset, all hours of the day."

"I won't take blame for that, you do a good job on your own wearing yourself out." He'd noticed Maggie definitely knew how to have a good time.

"I blame it on the cruise line. They give you so many options and you don't want to miss a thing."

"How was your day, Maggie?" He asked with a sly smile, it was the start of her conversation she'd had with herself. "Isn't that the proper way to begin a conversation?"

"It was very good, thank you for asking," she said with the same knowing smile.

The more she stood there next to him, the more anxious she became. It was hard for her not to say what she felt, hard not to ask what she wanted to know. She was a reporter, a writer, used to being direct. When she couldn't stand it any longer she gave in.

"Are you gay?"

Jackson wasn't sure if it were some kind of trick question or not. It took him by total surprise but he didn't know why, he'd come to realize Maggie was not shy by any means. He cleared his throat and smiled warily.

"Umm, no. I may not want to know this, but I have to ask, why did you ask me that question?" He chuckled lightly.

"Actually, one of the girls mentioned it. So you have the reputation among some that you're gay."

"That's a good thing." He didn't care what they thought of him, it worked to his advantage.

"I didn't think you'd care."

"It keeps them uninterested, saves me the hassle."

"Are you married?" She bluntly continued then tried to explain her reasons for asking. "I'm just curious, it's general conversation. Just because I'm a woman and ask these questions, don't take it the wrong way. It's not like I'm interested in any way, I guess it's just my reporter mentality, I ask questions."

Jackson wondered if that were the only reason, wondered what Maggie Pace actually thought of him. She didn't appear interested, then again it could be a ploy, and maybe she acted disinterested to pull him in. He wasn't sure, but he felt pulled in anyway, whether she consciously meant to do it or not. He pushed himself off the banister and began to walk inside.

"Goodnight, Maggie."

"Maybe something else, where you grew up?"

He stopped at the door, turned around, and walked back. She now faced him, leaned her back against the banister, and he put his hands on either side and pressed his body to hers. He still couldn't tell what she was thinking, but he liked the fit of their bodies together, Jackson knew he shouldn't.

"What do you want, Maggie?"

She appeared calm and unfazed. "An interview. A few questions answered."

"Is that all?"

At that moment it wasn't. "Of course, I told you, I'm not interested. Just answer a few questions. Maybe where you grew up. How long you've been in photography."

He placed his hand behind her neck and kissed her lightly on the mouth, pulled back slightly then kissed her again, that one a little longer as she opened to him.

"Not that I have anything to prove, but my manhood was questioned. Just something to show in what little way I could that I'm not gay. Don't mistake it to mean I'm interested in any way." He felt a silent draw to her still, just by looking into soft innocent eyes, and he kissed her once more but knew it was a dangerous place to linger. "I don't give interviews, Ms. Pace."

It lasted mere seconds, but remained on her lips a long time after. Maggie didn't put any meaning into it, other than what he said. A man's ego was a precious thing and she couldn't blame him for showing a little of his manhood when she had the nerve to question it. She was glad it was unexpected, if not, she probably would have gone for more proof.

****

Nicole went for her evening coffee to find Derek already there at the same table he was the previous evening.

"Evening," he said, smiled in that warm familiar way. "Did you enjoy any of my recommendations in Cozumel?"

"The beach was the best I've ever been to, thanks for the suggestion, we never would have known about it otherwise. And the place you said to go and buy silver, I'm afraid we found it. My pocketbook is a little lighter and my luggage a little heavier."

"And don't forget that tourist bar I told you about," he laughed knowingly. "I was on my way back to the ship and I saw you and a bunch of people you were with coming out."

"Those people really know how to have a good time," she too laughed. "What about you? Did you have a good day?"

"Great, did two dives."

Derek told her about the dive spots he'd gone to and talked about other places he'd been diving when Nicole was interested to know more. He explained the 'Blue Hole' in Belize he would be going to when they visited that island. Also told her of the few sharks and odd things he'd encountered in his years.

"My only water experience is swimming on top."

"I told you the other night I thought you'd love snorkeling, you really ought to try it. Quite a few of the beaches in the islands have good walk in places you can just go off the beach, you don't have to go to deep water. You want to look for rocky places with coral, that would be the best snorkeling, it's where the fish hang out."

"And the sharks?" She asked a little leery. "Is it where they're lurking around waiting for the humans to hang out?"

"I can't say they'll never be there, but more than likely not."

Nicole found his knowledge of the underwater world fascinating, and the islands he'd visited in order to accommodate his passion for diving sounded like paradise. He tried to make at least two diving trips a year and if he could get a third or fourth in, it was a bonus.

They talked across the tables between them, neither made the move to join the other but there were few people around so it wasn't difficult to carry on their conversation. Each looked at it as physical distance between them, even though emotionally they became closer and closer with every word exchanged.

CHAPTER NINE

Known as Las Islas De La Bahia, are eight islands. Among them was Roatan, the largest and most developed. Located northeast of the mainland Honduras in Central America, pristine beaches, lush rainforests and world-class diving beckoned visitors to its shores. Warm friendly people inhabited the Caribbean's little secret.

With only one major paved road, getting around the 28 mile long island was easy, it was only four miles at its widest point. But just 100 yards offshore lay the world's second largest barrier reef. Formed on the edge of the continental shelf, the reefs were home to an array of brightly colored species and the world's only population of whale sharks that didn't migrate, making it many a diver's quest to find one.

One of the islands most interesting land dwellers was the monkey lala, also called 'Jesus lizards' and they could run like miniature dragons on two legs with their finlike crests expanded. But they could also race across a water surface. They shared the jungle at times with another resident, the red-lored parrot, unique to the Bay Islands. More species could be seen, but these birds were among the few that actually propagated and lived there. They were seen most often when the cashews were in season.

****

Jackson saw Maggie approach from across the deck with a cup of coffee and he was surprised to see her. John's the one that saw her earlier to tell her the shoot had been cancelled, and he figured she'd go back to bed as the others had. She even looked good first thing in the morning, and she had no makeup on, and didn't care that she didn't.

"All the girls are in love with you for calling the shoot this morning." Maggie took a seat across the table from Jackson, next to John.

"They should thank you, I guess you forgot to make the phone call for sunshine today." Jackson reminded her of a comment she'd made previous when she was furious at him. As well she should have been, he'd blamed her for the sun going down.

"I didn't forget. I did it on purpose."

They were probably the only three people awake on the ship. Once the other's found out the shoot was cancelled because of clouds, they'd all gone back to bed. There was a rainy mist now, but they were at a table under the protection of cover, warm coffee in hand.

"Did you at least order it for later?" He asked seriously, as if she actually could.

"I put in a request for mid day, when we get into port."

"That's the worst time of day to shoot."

"I'm not worried about your shoot. I'm worried about having a nice day in Roatan, it's one of my favorite places."

John had been smiling between them, now laughed. "I'm beginning to think you actually did plan this."

"I did," Maggie stated as if it were so. "But to my advantage. The girls won't be tired and I'm taking my now cooperative little brownie troop on an outing. I think it'll be good for them. They need a break anyway." Maggie smiled. "It's worked out perfectly."

"For you," Jackson countered.

"I'll let you come too, and you can bring your camera, I promise a great alternative. It won't be what you're expecting, but I can guarantee you won't be disappointed." Maggie looked to John as if he'd already agreed. "John's coming."

Jackson looked pensive, as if John was right and she'd actually planned the weather. "Where are you going?"

"I have a delivery to make. You can bring your camera along, get some good shots, but I'm not working today. I'll not ask one single question."

"That alone would be worth my time." Jackson drank his coffee. "Or is this a trick? You want to get me lost in the jungle so I can't return to the ship."

"I wouldn't have to get you lost, I told you, Roatan is one of my favorite places and I have many friends here. All I'd have to do is put you in a separate cab, say the word, and you'd never be heard from again."

John got a serious look on his face as he pretended to play along. "Two people have disappeared that way."

"I actually wouldn't doubt it." Jackson looked over to Maggie. "I guess it's a good thing we called a truce before this port of call."

Maggie thought she needed another kiss to seal the agreement. "Who said anything about a truce?"

"An assumption I made."

"I haven't gotten any of my questions answered, I don't think it's actually official, this truce you speak of."

John enjoyed the show between the two as he sat back and drank his coffee in silence. Having known both so well, he inwardly knew from the beginning the sparks would fly.

"Oh?" Jackson raised his eyebrows. "So that's how it's going to be?"

"I have no choice. I can't give you a truce if you can't give me something I want. That wouldn't be fair, it's not an even trade."

He looked with disbelief to John, then back to Maggie. Then decided to challenge her, see what she'd say after being put on the spot. "I gave you exactly what you wanted last night, doesn't that count?"

She noticed the smugness in his eyes, as if he would quiet her, as if she wouldn't say anything in front of John. Jackson didn't know her well. "You gave me a kiss because you wanted, not me. I had no choice in the matter."

John burst into laughter at the look on Jackson's face. "I could have told you she'd call your bluff."

****

The models weren't quite sure they wanted to go with Maggie since she didn't tell them where they were going, but she forced them, in a friendly way. Told them it was part of the assignment. Informed them to wear comfortable clothes, shoes and the like but when they appeared at the dock, Maggie had to shake her head and laugh on the inside. Decked in island resort wear, a few with high heeled sandals, makeup perfectly applied. She had to remember to have Jackson get a picture of them after their day.

Maggie had come to like them, and did think of them as 'girl's', her little brownie troop she led along. Their behavior had been exemplary since her irate discussion, but Maggie also knew once out of her presence they would resort to the type of people they were. She couldn't prevent that, but perhaps maybe she could open their eyes a bit.

Before leaving, she had items shipped to Houston and stored with the crew supplies. There were several boxes she needed to get off the ship and they accommodated her with a rolling cart to do so. It was supplies of school items, pens, pencils, notebooks, backpacks, rulers, but also other more personal supplies for the orphanage. Toothbrushes, toothpaste, toys, clothes, as much as she could possibly bring with her. Most times when she flew to Honduras, she'd have to limit it to the airline standard of two suitcases and a carry on, sometimes she would pay extra to have more bags, so she was excited to have so much this time.

They all gathered by the meeting spot, the models, some of the crew, including John and Jackson, and also Nicole, Kyla, Alan and four of the guys in their party. Randy and a few others had a dive trip planned and couldn't make it. She'd told none of them what they'd be doing, just whoever wanted to go to meet her.

Maggie was surprised so many trusted her. She would have to get more transportation and quickly looked around to find her friend Vinny who would be looking for her. She heard him before she saw him.

"Maggie... Maggie..." Vinny walked down the dock and waved his arms.

They embraced fondly, Maggie excited to see him as always. "It's so good to see you, how's the family?"

"Waiting to see you."

"I've got some others with me, we're going to need your brothers to haul us all. Are they available?"

"They will be... come... come."

Maggie gathered her entire entourage and they piled into several vehicles. She noticed Jackson's playful worried look when he was in a separate one, John teased and said he wouldn't ride with him.

The schoolhouse was a dilapidated house, hard to tell it was a schoolhouse at all unless you knew or a local took you. There was excitement when Maggie entered, even more when they realized she'd brought along friends. Supplies were distributed and a small gift for each child of various age ranges such as new maps, books, pencils, pens, backpacks and more.

The models, quiet and humbled at the poverty, helped in passing out new items to those who appreciated the simplest of things. When they moved on to the orphanage it was more of the same, several of the models near tears as Maggie explained some of the children of Honduras.

Street kids who'd been abandoned, children abused, orphaned. One child abused so badly his beaten and fractured form had been in a body cast, the only thing you could see were his eyes that peeked out. Barely three years old then, now almost ten and thriving. All the kids there also greeted her with warm hugs.

"Mama Maggie." Several cried out and ran to her as others noticed and followed. Soon she was surrounded by dark shining faces.

On the outskirts she saw Katera, a girl of ten who'd come to the orphanage years previous, she had selective mutism, hadn't spoken in many years. Maggie smiled warmly.

"Ladies, can you start opening the boxes and passing out the things?" Maggie left the crowd behind and slowly approached her. When she got within a few feet she knelt down on her knees in the dirt. "Katera, I told you I'd be back."

The girl looked at her with large sad eyes, there used to be more fear there. Maggie told her every time she left that it wouldn't be for long, but she didn't think Katera was ever secure in knowing that. It had taken her years and she'd only come so close, she never interacted with many of the adults, and very few of the children, there were only certain one's she trusted only so much.

Jackson stood quite a distance from the children who now laughed happily as the models pulled the items from the boxes, their faces that of pure joy, their voices uplifted, and much laughter. Like the others at the schoolhouse, the simplest of things brought them pleasure. His attention and camera focused on Maggie and the solitary little girl who moved only a few feet forward, not all the way up to Maggie, and then she turned around and left. Maggie remained there for a long time alone.

They spent the day playing with the kids and Maggie introduced all to the couple who ran the ministry, and she caught up with some volunteers who were still there from her last visit and met new ones. Like the schoolhouse, the models were shown a reality far from their world, the affect seen in their eyes and in their quiet demeanor.

"So this place is real." Kyla and Nicole walked up to her just as Maggie finished helping a few young one's with a block tower. "I used to actually think you just told us that, and maybe you had a boyfriend you hid away down here."

"Lot's of them. There's Ricar, and Emanuel, and..." She pointed to several. "These boys here are the only one's who'll have my heart."

"I'm with Kyla, I didn't really think it was all real, didn't pay much attention, but you didn't talk about it often. You've had a whole other life down here. How did you find this place?"

"And here I thought at least my friends read my stories."

"I try most times." Nicole tried to defend herself. "But I hardly have time to get through the school newsletter."

"I was doing an article about Honduras and discovered an amazing amount of kids abandoned and orphaned. Kids of all ages just left to roam the streets so I made it my mission to tell the world. Well, part of the world, those that read my articles anyway."

When it came time to go, the models were actually reluctant to leave. Maggie didn't think any of them had ever done something so selfless in their lives. They didn't get money for what they'd done, no publicity, and it wouldn't advance their careers, yet all of them thanked her.

As she always did upon leaving, Maggie would have to look for Katera, most times she'd be in the distance somewhere. This time she didn't see her as she scanned the grounds and almost gave up until she came around a corner.

Maggie walked over, and as before, stopped before she reached her then knelt down in the dirt. She never wanted to push the child for affection, didn't want to force anything on her. Story was, her father sold her for prostitution starting at the age of five, and Maggie suspected she had enough scars to last a lifetime.

"I'll be back, Katera, I promise. What do you want me to bring you next time?"

She clung to a stuffed animal Maggie had given her a few years ago, it was dirty and worn now, a constant companion. It was about the only thing she'd ever accepted. She remained for a few moments, hoped the girl would come to her but she didn't, instead she turned to walk away. Maggie rose slowly and turned away herself then heard a noise that made her turn back.

"Ma..."

Maggie turned and knelt again, arms held outward a little to give her the choice to come into them if she wished. It seemed to take hours in her mind but Katera slowly walked towards her. Tears sprang to Maggie's eyes when she moved into her arms and rested her head on Maggie's shoulder.

"You're okay now, Katera," she whispered, clung to her until she pulled away.

The children were gracious, most tried to give what little they had in appreciation. It was a silent message from Katera when she held out the worn stuffed frog.

"No, honey, you keep that. All I wanted was the hug."

Then the girl backed up in silence and disappeared around the corner again. Maggie rose and wiped the tears from her cheeks, her heart filled the child trusted her enough to know she posed no threat, she'd been trying for so long and it was another sign of hope.

****

Their next stop was a Canopy Tour. They were harnessed and Maggie had yet to explain it.

"So you didn't send me off in the cab, is this your chosen way to get rid of me?" Jackson stepped up beside her.

"I don't know. Did you get the pictures I wanted? At the school and the orphanage?"

He wasn't sure how many he'd gotten of the models, most had been of Maggie. "Of course I did."

"Maybe you should tell me where the film is before you go," she laughed.

"Have we called a truce yet? I'm seriously starting to think that if we don't, I'm in grave danger here."

"Not yet, you still haven't told me anything to use in my article, remember?"

"Okay," Jackson finished buckling his harness and stood up tall with a serious expression on his face as if he was about to reveal secrets. "If I tell you something can we call a truce so I can feel safer?"

Maggie looked at him suspiciously, "Tell me what you have to say first, and then I'll decide if it's enough for a truce."

"Oh no, it doesn't work that way, I tell you something and we call a truce or you get nothing."

Maggie sighed, she had no choice and was drawn in. "Okay, but it better be something I can use. So tell me something about yourself."

"I'm not one of a dozen kids."

"That doesn't count."

"It does and you agreed to it."

"You're not out of Roatan yet, and just because you tricked me into a truce doesn't mean you're safe."

All the men in the group were ready for whatever came, the women hesitant and nervous, especially when they were given heavy gloves to put on. They were given instructions on what to do and the most important was how to stop themselves because they would be hanging from a line and swinging through the jungle. Starting at the first platform, from the harness they were hooked to a zip line that hung in mid air and off the base they went to glide through the treetops. From one platform to the next they would swing, and platforms were interspersed throughout unspoiled jungle, and along the way you could view sea and sandy beach in spots if you choose not to look down and out instead.

Screams of fear were the first heard, then the adrenaline rush kicked in. Maggie knew the men would love it, and after initial terror, the ladies couldn't help but enjoy it too. She was impressed when it was over as their hair was a mess, makeup had run and one lost her shoes, but they were laughing and trying to catch their breaths. None of them cared they looked a disaster.

"You know I'm not the adventurous kind, I was expecting something more subdued." Nicole beamed as she removed her harness.

"It's Maggie." Alan thought those words explained everything.

Some of the models got help removing their harnesses from willing young men. Again, it amazed Maggie they didn't care they looked like heck now, actually looked like something that had been run through a ringer, several times, but they smiled anyway. The bonding and camaraderie among the group was apparent after the time spent together and Maggie smiled at the group that had become fast friends.

Their last stop was to Vinny's home where his wife and children welcomed all with open arms. A small hut of a place, but there was more happiness in that one tiny room than if they'd been standing in a castle. Maggie presented them with a new stereo and a box of some of their favorite things. Grape soda and Teriyaki beef sticks.

Afterwards, for being the good sports they were, Maggie arranged to send the models to a beach front spa for the rest of the afternoon but it was a surprise because once again, she didn't tell them where they were going. She just put them in a van with one of Vinny's brothers who would take good care of them and get them back to the ship on time.

Alan and his friends didn't want to go back to the ship, but they had to, they'd prearranged to meet Randy and the others at a specific time. So they all headed back to port where the others had just arrived also.

When Maggie stepped out of the car she saw Mick among the dive group with Randy, one of few men she'd dated and still remained friends with. They gave each other a warm and excited greeting.

"Mick, you're still looking like the sunshine agrees with you."

"What are you doing here? I didn't know you were in town." When they embraced, he didn't let go of her, held her tight. "Did you sneak in? I'm always the second one to know as soon as your plane lands, only because Vinny's brother works at the airport and he's always first."

"I'm only here for the day this time, I'm actually on the cruise with these guys," she indicated to Randy and the group. "And this is a working trip."

"You look like you just came from the Canopies," he laughed. "But you still look great."

"Showing the group a little of Roatan," then she turned her attention to Randy. "I know you must have had a good dive, Mick and his team are the best in the business."

"Awesome. I didn't want to come back, we already have plans to make this our next dive destination, and we're staying a week next time."

"Still reeling in the tourists," She teased him then spoke to Randy again, "Tanner's a character, isn't he?"

Mick answered. "They didn't meet him, he's in the decompression chamber at the medical center right now."

She knew when they came back for a week it would be the time of their lives. Tanner was an old man who Maggie swore had gills under his wetsuit. Full of story's of his years of diving around the world until he settled in Roatan to supposedly retire, but the reefs surrounding the Honduran island of Roatan called to him, it was as if they called his name. Maggie suspected Mick would be the same way, she could probably count on him being there for the rest of his life, it was the only reason their relationship hadn't worked out, because they were always apart too much to have a relationship.

"What are you doing this afternoon? Want to come on our next dive?" He still held her close to him and looked hopeful.

"Not this time. I just have the afternoon left and wanted to do a few more things."

"When are you coming back to stay awhile?"

Maggie felt comfortable in his arms, they were great friends now. "It won't be long."

"Let me know ahead of time, I'll plan on some time off."

"I'll be sure to. But don't be thinking things you shouldn't, since the last time I saw you I've sworn off men forever."

"That's because you can't find anyone like me." He wanted to kiss her but knew he shouldn't. Mick missed her company, they had a blast together and he still held out hope that someday it would possibly work.

"You're probably right, if I'd found you stateside we'd probably be in a different place."

Maggie was honest with him. There was nothing wrong with the relationship except the distance of miles between them, and as much as she loved Roatan, she couldn't see herself a full-time island girl.

Jackson didn't want to think about the thoughts he had going through his head watching Maggie and the intimate conversation she was obviously having. With someone she was obviously close to. He stood a little distance away talking to John, but couldn't help a few nonchalant glances her way. The only one who noticed was John.

"Quite a gal, isn't she?" John asked when he noticed where his eyes wandered to.

"Who? Maggie?" He asked with innocence, looked over again and noticed the way the guy held her tight. He shrugged his shoulders and if he hadn't thought of her every single moment of that day. "Not much you can find fault with."

"That one knows how to live, there's very few who could compare to her."

Jackson didn't know her well, but just from what he saw he had to agree with John. "I'm afraid I didn't give her a fair shot in the beginning, but it doesn't take her long to put someone in their place."

"Maggie's not one to hold grudges, she'll put it all on the line, tell you what she thinks and feels whether you like it or not, but she won't hold something against you."

"You know quite a bit about her." Jackson looked away again as the man in the distance held onto her.

"Like she was my own, she was the daughter my late wife and I never had. Edith loved Maggie, and she was so proud." John paused and shared a memory. "My wife never traveled much, she was always content where her feet were planted, but when she was diagnosed with cancer she went into a deep depression. Maggie brought us here, planned the trip and paid for it. We spent over three weeks and by the time we left Edith was a completely different woman. Of course it didn't stop her death but her attitude changed, and it made what time she had left so much better."

"So that's why you've been a little quiet today. You had to have been thinking about your wife."

"The time that's passed made it easier to be here. Today brought back some memories I hadn't been able to think about before now, and it was nice to remember." John looked around, knew a lot of people that came on cruises never wanted to get off the ship, but they didn't know what they were missing. "Edith didn't dive or snorkel, didn't do tourist things, we simply met some people of the island, made new friends. But most of the time was just spent talking or thinking about life, we stayed in a house on the water and there were no distractions for Edith to clear her mind and come to terms with her fate. It took me much longer after her death to do so, but she was at peace with herself when she passed on."

Jackson couldn't deny that Maggie was the type of person you immediately felt a connection to. He didn't think it was only him that was pulled to her, she had a way about her, a charisma that made you comfortable, made you an instant friend. He couldn't deny it, he could try to suppress it, but it didn't work very well. It surprised him she lived in New York, the city had a way of tainting people, made them sour and immune to things around them, but she'd remained so true at heart, so true to herself, and it was a quality that was admirable. He looked over to her again and didn't want to admit he was relieved she no longer stood in Mick's arms. As he watched her, his heart tugged him back home where someone else waited.

CHAPTER TEN

Nicole had been talking to Kyla who left to buy them another bottle of water when Derek seemed to appear out of nowhere. The last person she expected to see.

"I think this is the first time I've seen you in daylight," he said as he stepped next to her with a broad smile. She looked good, even if a little disheveled.

"Well, hello," she smiled.

"Looks like you had a great afternoon."

"We did. My friend Maggie has some experience in Roatan so we had the best guide," she glanced to all the gear he held and assumed correctly where he was going, "You off to dive?"

"I've been waiting for this all day."

"You must be going with Maggie's friend Mick. He's waiting for his next group."

It turned out he was. As introductions were made all around, Mick assumed Derek and Nicole were together as a couple.

"You don't dive?" Mick asked Nicole.

"Not me. I don't need to be where the big fish are."

"Why don't you ride along with us, there's plenty of room in the boat," Mick asked.

Nicole didn't want to put Derek on the spot, after all, they'd only been coffee partners, but Derek encouraged it.

"That'd be great, why don't you come?" It was something unexpected, but the opportunity of having her along would be fun. It certainly wasn't only over coffee that he found himself thinking about her.

Maggie encouraged it also. She immediately liked Derek, thought he had kind eyes and a warm smile. He looked shyly interested in Nicole and she could tell Nicole felt the same, they were cute together.

"Go ahead, Mick will take good care of you," then she looked to him. "You can trust him as long as he doesn't fill you with margaritas and tell you he wants to show you his whale."

Everyone in the group laughed.

"Every other girl on the planet is easy, you're the only one I've ever had to coax." He put his arm around her again. "And I said my whale pictures. You're the one who wanted to see my whale."

She slapped him playfully. "Don't listen to his lies."

"Come along, you can tell me all Maggie's secrets." Mick urged in the easy friendly way he had with people.

Nicole laughed at what she thought was a joke. "Won't be able to help you there, Maggie has no secrets. She's one of those people that lay it directly on the line and you either accept it or you don't."

Derek's face and words revealed he'd want her to go, even if he hadn't been the one to ask. But of course, it hadn't been his place to ask. He'd purchased a spot on the dive, it was Mick who had the liberty to invite her, so along with the others he waited for her decision. Nicole decided she'd love to spend the rest of the day with Derek, very much so.

When they were alone again, Mick hugged Maggie once more as they were about to leave, again held onto her and didn't pull away.

"You take good care of my friends now," she said.

He still wanted to kiss her, it was hard not to. "Come back soon. Maybe we can give it another try, maybe things could work out."

"They didn't before, what makes you think they would now? You're still going to be here, I'm still going to be stateside." She kissed him on the cheek and pulled away, held onto his hand a moment before she let it fall. "Bring my friends back safe and sound."

"Take care, Maggie."

"You too, Mick," she blew him a kiss.

Kyla decided to go with Alan, some of the crew went back to the ship, some wanted a beach and Maggie sent them off in the safe hands that had driven them all morning, Vinny's brother. She knew he'd take care of them. John decided he wanted to go off by himself awhile and both Jackson and Maggie understood.

"Looks like it's you and me." Maggie thought there would be others left, actually thought Jackson would have taken the chance to wander off without saying anything but he was still there.

"You don't think I'm going anywhere with you, do you? Alone? You haven't gotten rid of me all morning and this would be your chance."

"Come on, you've had fun so far. I'm starving, we'll go get something to eat." She turned to Vinny who'd been talking with a group of men as he waited to see what her plans were. "Hey Vinny, can I borrow the jeep?"

"Sure, you don't need me to drive you?" He asked as he approached her now.

"It's just the two of us left. You can get another passenger for the afternoon and I'll take myself if I can borrow the jeep."

He had several vehicles available to use for his tours and he threw her the keys. "Just leave them with Tico when you get back," he held out his arms. "But I need my goodbye now in case I'm not here later."

They hugged fondly and he turned to Jackson with a serious look. "You ever ride with Maggie? There is a crash helmet in the back seat." Vinny laughed. "I only half joke, she's a crazy one."

Jackson shook his hand, felt he'd found a friend in Vinny, felt everyone who knew him became a friend. "Thanks so much for sharing your island with us. I have a great appreciation for Roatan now."

"Then we will see you again." It was a statement Vinny made. "You come back with Maggie and you see much more. Much beauty here."

He doubted he'd be back with Maggie, and he shouldn't have gone with her then, almost said no, but as he looked at her he realized he wouldn't mind seeing more of this wondrous place. He'd take his camera and get more island shots. It's what he told himself anyway.

There were no threats, she was only being friendly because it was her way, and Jackson was sure she wasn't interested in him in the least, a fact that unfortunately made her even more appealing. Another reason he saw no harm in going, it was probably the dive master who'd gotten her attention that day, certainly not him. Jackson knew it wasn't something he should be thinking about and probably a sign he should have said no, but he didn't.

When they got in the open air jeep he found out quickly Vinny was right and he'd only been half joking. Jackson clenched the bar to hold on, had to in order to keep himself from falling out. "Maybe we should have stuck with Vinny."

"I have my Honduran driver's license."

"That doesn't mean you can drive."

The main roads weren't that bad, it was when she turned down primitive roads and took them with fast ease that he found himself really hanging on. Maggie certainly knew how to handle both the jeep and the rutted roads they encountered. She swerved easily when a weird lizard ran across the road and shot off into the woods.

"Where did you learn how to drive?"

"My brothers. We'd take the four wheeler and dirt bikes every chance we got and took off to the paths in the woods."

"And you carried that over to vehicles and on the road. Not a good thing, Maggie."

"After the four wheeler, when we were old enough, we used a pickup truck. But it was still on the paths in the woods."

Jackson's first instinct was to ask where she grew up but he didn't need to know anything personal about Maggie. He was already more involved than he wanted to be, than he should be. Every thought told him to stay away from her, and every other thought told him the opposite.

"The models actually surprised me when they went through the canopy, I don't think they could have handled this though." He'd taken several pictures afterwards that would never make it to print, they looked like heck but never complained, and that was the surprising part.

"I couldn't believe they actually did it."

"You didn't give them much choice. They didn't know what they were doing, you never told them until they were basically hooked up and pushed off a platform."

Maggie chuckled. "The element of surprise always works best." Maggie thought again, as she had several times that day, about his kiss the evening before. She could still feel it on her lips and decided it best to stick to safe subjects, to ask him questions. "I wanted to ask you, what do you know about Tiffany?"

Jackson shook his head. "I told you, I shoot pictures and do my work, nothing else."

"Something? Anything? Do you know where she grew up?"

"Nothing."

"Have you ever worked with her before?"

"A few times. I don't talk to them, I know nothing."

Maggie sighed. "What about her age? She looks awfully young."

"I don't know anything about any of them, Maggie. Or the tons I've come in contact with over the years. I don't talk to them, I don't date them, and I don't socialize with them."

Maggie had good instincts when it came to people, it's what made her a good writer, and she sensed when there was something else, just as she did now. She felt there was something much more personal there, something he didn't want to talk about, not specifically with Tiffany, just something he didn't want to share.

"Did you ever?" She asked.

"The article is about the models, not me."

"That's not true, you're the one that makes them look good in pictures."

"Half the time it's my computer that does that." He was glad when the road ended and she came to a stop, and it literally ended, the gravel just stopped and she had pulled off to the side in a dirt pullover area. Jackson grabbed his camera bag and got out, even though it looked like they were in the middle of nowhere.

"You still haven't answered my question."

"And I won't." All he saw was a little dirt path through the woods. "Are we lost?"

"I wouldn't steer you wrong. Not unless you don't answer my questions."

"What was your question again?" He stepped close to her. "I can't remember."

"Just curious if you've ever dated models you worked with. I need to know a little about your life. Is it glamorous? Do you have a beauty hanging on your arm? Go to all the right places? Socialize with all the right people? I need to know what kind of person you are."

"And that's why you ask?" He stood much too close to her and liked being alone for the first time that day.

"Of course it's why I ask, what other reason would I have?" He made her nervous and her stomach flipped. If she looked away she could avoid him but he took his finger, placed it on her chin, and gently pulled her attention back.

The tone of his voice was even and serious. "How long are we going to pretend we're not intensely attracted to each other?"

She answered just as seriously. "I don't know. Is there a certain time span that's required? By law or something?"

"What do you think the penalty is if there is a law and we break it?"

"Walk the plank?" The flutter got deeper and more intense when he came so close she could feel his breath on her face, his lips just out of reach of her yearning.

"I can swim," Jackson said, before he finally pressed his lips to hers.

Maggie could swim also, but at that point she felt like she was drowning. Her body seemed to go limp as if in water and the only thing that held her up was his muscular arms that wrapped around her body, held her so close and she could feel his heartbeat against her chest.

His mouth warm and sensual, his hand caught on the bottom of her shirt and as he moved it up he was against her bare skin and the heat coursed through her. "Jackson, I..." She tried to pull away, succeeded for only a second before she placed her lips back onto his where it felt they belonged. She couldn't pull away, her need too great.

Jackson had to finally pull himself away. "That doesn't mean I'm interested. It's the only recourse I have to stop your questions."

"I'm going to have to make a long list." She looked into his eyes as he held her there and Maggie sensed his uncertainty, could almost see regret. "I don't want anything from you, Jackson. I'm not the type of woman who puts any meaning into a..." She was going to say something trivial like a kiss but it hadn't been trivial, it shook her knees.

"I can't give anything, Maggie." Jackson held tight, couldn't let go just yet. There was so much he wanted to know about her, so much he wanted to ask. Yet there was so much he never would know, had no right, for he was not willing to share his life, he couldn't.

"Then we stand on even ground, I don't want anything." The irony of her statement didn't get past her, like her knees that shook, the ground felt less than even.

He looked into her eyes with humor. "Nothing? Not even another kiss?"

"I can barely stand now." Regardless of what she said, she placed her mouth on his once more. Why did he seem so irresistible to her?

When Maggie took his hand and led him through the opening between the brush and along the old dirt path, Jackson had his misgivings.

"I know I joke and I probably shouldn't worry, but we are in a third world country, Maggie. Some people are afraid to leave the ship and I'm being drug through the jungle. You're just right at home here, aren't you?"

"It's my escape from the city."

He thought about the dive master again, wondered what their relationship had been, or possibly was. But he pushed it to the back of his mind, it was something that wasn't his business and something he shouldn't care about, he had no right to.

The path led to a pier then they took a boat through a mangrove and finally came to another pier where they were met by more of her friends at a local restaurant and bar that sat on a deck over the water. Jackson could tell it wasn't a tourist spot. You wouldn't find the Bermuda shorts clad crowd with their flowered shirts and camera's. That crowd wouldn't have been able to find the place with a map, Jackson didn't even think the place would be on any map, the people there probably the only one's in the world who knew about it.

Old worn wood posts held the roof above and three sides had no wall, the only wall was one that faced the jungle, it's where the kitchen was located. A few handmade rickety tables and chairs sat on the wooden boards over the water and a long bar took up one side. Again, there were no formalities as Maggie was greeted by old friends.

"I have too much of the loco drink? Maggie?" An older gentleman at the end of the bar noticed her first, yelled it across the way then yelled louder towards the kitchen. "Gunta! Gunta, our Maggie has come."

They'd gotten through several people and a very, very large woman came barreling through the only door in the open space, the kitchen door. She busted through everyone and seamed to swallow Maggie up in large arms.

"Where you come from? How come I don' know?"

"I'm only here for the day, Gunta, I'm on a cruise for work."

"This no look like work." She indicated to Jackson, also pulled him into her large embrace. "I no work with something like this, I get Miguel." She looked over her shoulder and huffed in her husband's direction.

The afternoon was loud and boisterous. They sat at a table with ten other people, including American friends, while Gunta and Miguel plied them with lots of food and drink. Stanley and Rita had escaped the States for the calmer, subdued island life. Although Jackson conversed with many, some who didn't quite have English down well, it was Stanley and Rita he talked to the most. One, he could understand them well, and two was the proximity, they were directly across him.

Throughout the few hours there, Maggie noticed Jackson was comfortable and enjoyed the company of strangers, some who hardly spoke his language. He laughed and talked with them as if he did understand, perhaps a universal language of friendship. She laughed as one of the women tried to teach him a few words of Spanish which Maggie spoke fluently, but to make him feel more comfortable, she spoke mainly in English.

Given her beginnings with him, when he would barely talk, it surprised her he was so comfortable there. But he'd slowly opened to her and she was seeing a completely different side to him, perhaps a side she wasn't meant to see. It was too late now as she saw he was actually very human, and kind, even warm. He didn't appear to be the same man she met at the airport on the morning of their departure. And she knew he wasn't pretending, she saw a slight disappointment when it was time to leave.

"You take care of our Maggie." Stanley said.

"I'm not sure I can promise anything, I think if I ever tried to do that, I'd hear a thing or two about it."

Stanley laughed. "I guess you're right, she's an independent one. I'll just leave it up to you to get her back here soon. She might live in New York, but she belongs to us too."

"I've certainly seen that today." Jackson had seen more of her life than he wanted to.

Most assumed they were together as a couple even though Maggie tried to dissuade them, but it couldn't be done and she'd given up. Jackson was no help when at times he found himself sitting with his arm around her at times, or took her hand easily in his atop the table without even realizing.

Rita gave him a hug and Stanley shook his hand, held on for a few moments. There was a knowing between them, an exchanged silent look of understanding. Jackson knew who he was and for some reason Stanley trusted him and there wasn't a need to speak the words of silence.

"Is Stanley trying to talk you into a poker game? Don't let him tell you he can't play, he lures all his prey in that way. You haven't made a bet with him, have you?" Maggie said as she approached them.

Stanley put his arm around her. "How come you and Rita won't let an old man have some fun?"

"I saved you, Jackson, you're lucky we don't have time for cards today. There isn't a golf course here yet and poker has become his second passion."

"Maybe next time, you'll bring him back, won't you Maggie?" Stanley asked.

Maggie laughed and teased him. "For you to take all his money?"

"Man's gotta make a living." Stanley hugged her then turned to Jackson and shook his hand again. "Next time we'll play a little cards."

"Yes sir."

Everyone bid them farewell and Gunta cried as she always did.

"I'll be back, Gunta." Maggie stated with a laugh, she was always overly sentimental.

"You always say, and it so long."

"Soon, I'll be back soon."

She pulled Jackson roughly to her again, her smile brightened. "And you brink Señor."

"He'll need some time to save up some money so he can play cards with Stanley." Maggie teased. The statement made no promises and didn't commit her to anything.

The ride back was just as rough as the ride there. Jackson became a little nervous when up ahead he saw some men wielding machetes on the side of the road. All kinds of dangerous situations leaped into his head but Maggie honked the horn and waved as she flew by, Jackson only held on tight.

"What time does the ship leave?" Maggie asked as she slowed a little.

"Eight?"

"Today is your lucky day, Jackson Turner." Just before they reached the paved main road, Maggie took another dirt road, only this one didn't even appear to be a road.

Jackson had to lean in as the brush from the jungle lashed out at him and once he almost fell out when she slowed and drove through a hole in the dirt path that almost sent the jeep on its side.

"I knew you'd be rid of me before the day was out. Where are we going now? To the camp of some of your guerilla war buddies? Is that where you're going to leave me?"

Maggie looked up through the trees to glimpse the sky. "We have to hurry."

"To make the ritual of an American sacrifice?"

"Unfortunately that was yesterday, we missed it," she teased. "I can tell by the light that we have to hurry."

"I don't want to know more."

She slowed almost to a stop and when it looked as if the path ended, Maggie told him to hold on as she sped up a little and went straight through a portion of dense brush. She slammed the brakes on quickly when they came out in the open on the other side and only a few feet from a cliff.

"That's the trickiest part."

Jackson looked around him. They were in the open, but precariously perched on just enough land to hold the jeep, there was cliff on all three sides. He would have been afraid to step out for fear of stepping right off the cliff.

"You've got to be kidding me." He looked down below to the waves that crashed against the rocks.

"I wouldn't get out if I were you."

"Since you brought it up, how do we get out?" Jackson knew that if she attempted to turn the jeep around they'd surely go over.

"The same way we got in, except we have to do it backwards."

He chuckled and shook his head, couldn't believe the gumption this woman had. She didn't look so tough and hard, appeared all woman on the outside, but he knew few men who would have the nerve or courage to go barreling through dense jungle to shoot out onto a cliff.

"Do you always like living on the edge like this? And we're literally on the edge."

"Walking down the middle of the road isn't as much fun."

"It's safer." Words John had said came back to him, Maggie knew how to live.

"You're safe here, I haven't made you disappear yet, have I?"

"And as the day goes on I feel like the sitting duck, just waiting for the exact moment."

"You actually should be afraid here."

"Why is that?"

Maggie reached up to the dash on her side and slid something back, and then she reached across and did the same on the other side as she held the front windshield and let it fall gently onto the hood. Vinny had fixed it up to work that way.

She sat back in her seat again and sighed. "Because being here is like having nothing between you and God, like being fully exposed, and only you two know the truth."

After the initial shock of finding himself in a precarious place, Jackson looked out ahead of him. There was no roof on the jeep, no doors, now no windshield and nothing obstructed the view from all around. He looked out to the immense sea and towards the sun that was beginning to set and end another day. And it was like Maggie said, there was nothing, no barriers to hide behind.

"Did you bring John's wife here?"

Maggie was silent for several moments then she smiled with melancholy. "She actually loved the ride down the path." She paused then turned to him. "How do you seem to know so much about me? Things I don't tell people, or say anything about, and you seem to know them."

He shrugged his shoulders with a coy smile. "People like to talk about you."

"That's comforting to know."

"Truthfully, your outburst with the models I witnessed, I happened to be walking down the hall. And John told me about you bringing him and his wife to Roatan when she was sick."

Maggie looked back out to sea and into the setting sun as the sky filled with color. Her voice was soft as she remembered. "Edith loved it here."

They became quiet again and Maggie started giggling. "You thought I was bad, you should have been with us the day I let her drive."

"You let her drive down that path and shoot out onto this cliff?"

"I've never told John, he wasn't with us that day, it's why she wanted to drive because she knew he would probably object to it. We probably have at least a couple feet in front of us, that day I think it was mere inches if that. It crossed my mind that she was feeling like she was going to die anyway and decided to do so in a blaze and just keep going."

"Were you prepared to bail out?"

"Never, I told you, walking down the middle of the road isn't nearly as fun." Maggie leaned her head back and sighed. She'd seen many a sunset in this exact spot, but it looked different that evening, all sunsets were different but this one seemed especially so and she wondered if everyone else saw the same thing she did. "This is the best spot on the island to see the sunset."

"And it's never crowded, you have to have it all to yourself, no one else fits. What on earth would you have done if there was another car here and you barreled through and pushed it right off the cliff."

She casually waved her hand through the air as she joked but said it as if she were serious. "That's only happened once."

It was quiet between them and Jackson began to think of his extraordinary day. A day with Maggie was definitely one to experience, and he wouldn't even begin to be able to explain it to anyone, it was truly one someone had to experience for themselves to get the full effect of.

As the sun descended before him he thought about the people he'd met, especially Stanley and Rita. They appeared to be the nice older retired couple who'd taken the simple life, when in actuality Jackson knew exactly who they were. It took him awhile, but after a sense of seeming that he knew Stanley somehow, he'd finally figured it out.

Ivan Straner. He'd been one of the biggest investment bankers implicated in a scandal a few years back. It involved billions of dollars, the biggest financial scandal ever, and he'd been acquitted while four others went to jail. Rumors abounded still about his involvement and whereabouts. Often people speculated he was the one who set the others up then took off with the money and disappeared. Others said different things, everything from he'd been used as a scapegoat and it hadn't worked, to he had actually worked with prosecutors all along, was placed there. No one had ever solved the mystery.

"I liked your friends." Jackson commented.

"They're good people."

"Stanley and Rita are interesting."

Maggie looked to him and saw recognition. She would never have taken anyone there who would have posed a risk to Ivan, and went with her gut instinct to know it was safe to take Jackson. She was confident the world would continue to presume they knew the story and continue to make guesses. Even now, when she knew, that he knew... she still believed her gut instinct to be right and he would remain a mystery to the outside world.

She didn't say anything as she turned away from him again, kept her eyes on the sunset ahead.

"An old fisherman, huh?" Jackson asked with a sly smile.

Maggie smiled softly, her voice a low whisper. "Yeah, just an old fisherman."

And that was all that was said on the subject. Many a journalists would sell their children for a scoop like that, a story on his whereabouts, an exclusive interview. As much as Maggie had surprised him, at the same time she didn't. No matter how much money or fame a story like that would bring her, there were things more important that would prevent her.

He never wanted to know about Maggie's life. He didn't ask any questions or didn't try to guess, but he'd been in her world for one day and what he'd witnessed spoke volumes. It would be easier if he had continued to ignore her as he'd done from the beginning, if he had turned the other way and simply gotten through the week. But he hadn't, and now Jackson felt as if he were somewhere he shouldn't be, it certainly wasn't a place he belonged, and he could have gotten by if all he knew was her name. But it was too late now.

CHAPTER ELEVEN

"So you have no secrets about Maggie?" Mick asked as he sat down beside Nicole, someone else out with the divers.

"If you know Maggie well, you know she makes no excuses for who she is. It's all out there and she has no secrets."

He laughed. "Only one of many things that make her so attractive. Should I hold out hope she'd ever move here?"

"Don't ask me, I'll leave that between you and Maggie." He was open, and Nicole could tell he sincerely cared for Maggie. She liked Mick, he made it hard for one not to, but what Maggie would ever do was anyone's guess.

"I think if I could get her to dive once, she'd be hooked and move here. She saw a whale shark once and that was enough to keep her out of the water."

"I'm just as chicken."

"As much as Derek dives and you've never gone with him?"

He still assumed the two were heavily involved. "I just met Derek the first night of this cruise."

"You're kidding? I thought you two... you just looked... well." Mick laughed.

"Strange to me too, this was the last place I thought I'd be today, I just happened to run into him on the dock."

"Shows how much I know, I certainly thought you two were definitely together."

That morning, Nicole wouldn't have guessed she'd be on a boat with Derek in late afternoon, but she was. And even though she didn't go in the water, just to see his smile when he climbed onboard again was enough to make her day. She got those feelings in her stomach that told her something special was going on.

Odd to think such a thought with a perfect stranger, someone she knew so little about, but more and more they got to know one another and she had never been so comfortable with someone so soon after meeting them.

"I'm glad you came today." Derek enjoyed her company and decided he wanted more of it. "Maybe we could have dinner this evening?"

"Maybe we could. This isn't a trade, is it? Do I still get our coffee date?"

Derek leaned in and kissed her, her lips tender and gentle then he pulled away, feeling guilty for his impulse. "I'm sorry, I..."

"It's okay, Derek, you don't have to apologize."

"I'm not normally this forward."

He looked shyly embarrassed and Nicole felt the same as she took the opportunity and leaned into him then, indulged herself in a kiss and lingered a little longer than he had.

She'd never done something so brash, to meet a man who she would probably never see again and be so forward. They were on a week long cruise, it felt like the beginning of a one night stand, which she'd never had, yet it felt more than that. Hard to explain to herself or anyone else, but why couldn't she enjoy a man's company for however many days they had?

There could have been many assumptions each made about the other but neither did, it felt right. Nicole discovered he was divorced also, his wife the one to have broken the marriage vow and he'd held his reservations on meeting anyone else. She revealed her husbands infidelities and feeling the same way he did.

She kept her children silent. From experience as soon as she mentioned them, men ran as far away as they could get. Nicole felt he was different but felt she didn't need to risk that chance just yet. What would, or could, ever become of them she was unsure of, but she wasn't prepared to give up his company just yet.

Nicole had no explanation, didn't know what it was. Only knew that she liked the feel of her hand in his and the touch of his lips as she turned up to him and kissed him again. Then settled comfortably in his arms for what little time they had left alone.

When the boat docked Derek gathered his gear and Nicole waited for him on the dock as Mick approached her with a wink.

"Only known him a few days, huh?"

"Strange," she laughed.

"Sometimes those things can be." He thought of Maggie. "Maybe I just had a premonition about you two."

"Could be."

"I think I had a premonition about Maggie too. I don't think I can count on her and I again, can I?"

"I never know what Maggie's thinking."

"You're kind not to burst my hopeful bubble immediately." Mick picked up his own bag and looked around the port but didn't see her. Not that he expected to, but it would have been nice if she'd been there to see him once more. He remembered a time well she'd be waiting for his boat to come in, he missed that. "You two come back and see me, you and Derek. I've got plenty of room to stay and any friend of Maggie's is welcome," he paused and glanced around quickly once more. "And you tell Maggie I wish her the best, will ya?"

"Sure Mick. Thanks."

****

She dressed that evening with particular care. Neither Maggie nor Kyla were there when she showered and began to dress, but Maggie had come in just as she finished up and Kyla followed.

"Wow. You didn't have to dress for me." Maggie teased. "I take it you had a good day, and it looks like you plan on a great evening."

Nicole wore a brightly colored print skirt with a straight and slim fitting that came just above her knees, with a bright yellow sleeveless light sweater. She'd gotten some sun the last few days and it went well with her newly tanned skin.

"I can't even believe I'm going."

"Why not? He seems like a great guy, and you obviously had a good day with him today."

Kyla entered then, smiled broadly at Nicole. "Look at you, a hot date?"

"A dinner. I'm not interested in men," she told herself. "Besides, it's a cruise, I'll never see him again after this."

"Could be a great arrangement." Kyla shrugged her shoulders.

Maggie knew the smile on her face. "Kyla Reeves, you didn't! You slept with him."

"It isn't like we'd never done it before." Then a huge smile covered her face, she couldn't hide the truth of what had happened between her and Alan. "But he did surprise me, sweet Georgia, it was better than I remember. I guess maybe age has its benefits after all."

"I knew that glow," Maggie laughed.

"Can we cover it up with makeup?" Nicole commented with laughter too. "I haven't had any in months, probably closer to a year, do I have to see that glow all week now to remind me of that?"

"I'm in the same boat you are, Nicole, even though it hasn't been a year it's been a few months and even then it wasn't very satisfying. I say we hang her overboard to get rid of that after sex glow." Maggie began to look through the closet to get her things together to change for dinner.

"There's something wrong here." Nicole said. "Here Maggie and I have been the single one's for years, you get separated not even a month ago, find an old boyfriend, jump into bed and discover each other again."

"Discover we did." Kyla said coyly and they all laughed.

"I am jealous. A relationship I could do without, but great sex is hard to come by." Maggie's mind went to Jackson and she quickly pulled it back again.

"Like you couldn't have Jackson as quick as you could have Mick, who by the way, is quite the cutie," Nicole turned from the mirror and looked at her. "And he still has it bad for you. Why didn't we know anything about Mick?"

"Yeah," Kyla added with the same questionable tone. "There was an island boyfriend after all."

"The only ex I've remained friends with."

"I can see why," Nicole commented. "He's a great guy."

"And Jackson?" Kyla raised her eyebrows in question.

"What about Jackson?" Maggie busied herself.

"Instead of threatening to hang me overboard, there's no reason you couldn't indulge yourself in uncomplicated satisfaction."

Maggie questioned the uncomplicated part as a few simple kisses had sent her almost over the edge. "We might have to work together again, that makes it complicated." Then she turned back to Kyla. "Is that what yours is? A simple matter of uncomplicated satisfaction?"

"Right now it is, why complicate it with thinking about anything else?" Kyla answered. What did she plan on doing? What was she thinking about? They split up years previous because they couldn't withstand the long distance relationship and it wasn't any different now. He was in Texas and she was in California. Nothing had changed, not even their feelings for one another. The same scenario that was years ago would play itself out again. Why did she think it was possible for a different outcome?

Kyla couldn't think about that now, it wasn't the time. They were rediscovering one another, enjoying the time together and she wasn't going to ruin it by bringing up talk of the unknown. She didn't know what he wanted anymore than she knew what she herself wanted out of all this.

Kyla didn't question Alan's avoidance of any affection towards her during the day while they were in public. She too liked the distance, the secret only known to them that they rekindled a passion long ago lost to separation. Other than her telling Nicole and Maggie, no one else suspected. To others, they were two old friends. But as she lay in his arms after making love that afternoon she certainly knew it was much more.

"I think this is good exercise for my leg, it's been feeling better." Kyla stretched her bare leg over his as she lay across his chest.

"I'm glad I could assist as your personal trainer." Alan became a little quiet when he spoke again. "We have to talk, Kyla."

"No we don't," she whispered in the dark of his room. "Not now."

****

With Nicole off to dinner, Kyla and Maggie decided on a pre dinner drink where they ran into Alan. Randy and his friends elsewhere, Maggie opted out and left them to enjoy an evening together and she decided to check on the models and talk awhile. She found most getting ready for their evening and after the others went on their way, Tiffany was the only one left alone in her room, as she'd waited for the others to leave before she attempted to get ready.

"Do you have a little time?" Maggie asked as she made herself comfortable across the bed.

"Sure."

"All the others had a good time today, what about you?" Maggie had seen the rest earlier, had checked to make sure they all got back safe and sound but Tiffany had been sleeping after a long day.

"It was heaven," she sighed. "This morning and this afternoon, the spa was what I needed to rejuvenate myself. We got massages, laid in the sun. What about your day? I saw you coming back with Jackson. Just a heads up, he's a waste of time."

"Oh?" Maggie said casually.

"I didn't have the benefit of knowing, came on to him for months before someone finally told me he was gay," she huffed. "It was a stupid phase, I should have known the first time he said no to me."

"Thanks for the heads up, but it's nothing more than work. I do appreciate it though." Maggie was laughing on the inside.

"He's a mystery man. I think he's gay, some say he's married."

"Married? I hadn't heard that one yet." She'd asked him about marriage and remembered he hadn't answered her.

"Like I said, I'm one of the one's who thinks he's gay. All the good one's are gay."

Maggie had to laugh. "Your world is so much different than mine, my friends and I say all the good ones are married."

"I think if he were married, he'd still go for it, most of them do. And I prefer married one's to single men because it gives me all kinds of freedom in the relationship with no commitment and hassle. They're more secure too, love to spend money on me, pay for things and buy me things."

"Is that all you want out of life?"

"What else is there? The best clothes and jewels, furs in my closet I haven't worn yet. And I have a great apartment, compliments of a businessman who only gets to the city a few times a year. One man even bought me a car once but I sold it when I moved to New York though."

Maggie stared at her in disbelief over her confession of her lifestyle she commented on so casually, Tiffany was immune to how it sounded to others. "I know I'm going to sound harsh, and don't take offense because it's just the way I am, I speak my mind. But don't you feel a little like a prostitute?"

Anger crossed over her face but it wouldn't stop Maggie from pursuing the topic. Then Tiffany's face softened, even saddened a little. "Hey, I use what I have."

"You're worth more than that." Maggie's direct statement was candid and heartfelt. "How can someone so beautiful have such a low self-esteem? You must if you let men treat you that way."

"It's what I have, a beautiful face, and a beautiful body. So I put it to good use to get somewhere in life." She shrugged her shoulders. "And I don't take advantage of men, they don't want anymore from me than what I want to give in return."

Tiffany looked away from her but not before Maggie noticed a dark look, a foreboding that came from somewhere deep inside. "It's nothing but an exchange of something for something else in return, there aren't any real feelings involved, there can't be."

"Why would I want to complicate things?"

Maggie left the direct subject alone for the time being. "Where do you want to get in life? What are your aspirations for the future?"

"I plan on marrying rich someday and getting as much plastic surgery as I can."

"Certainly that isn't what you dreamed about as a little girl. I know when I was little I dreamed of being a librarian," Maggie laughed. "I know, pathetic, but I loved to read. What did you love as a little girl, Tiffany?"

"I was never a little girl, Maggie. The way I grew up was entirely different from the norm. I thought it was normal, I thought everybody's mother was a prostitute."

Maggie talked for quite a while to Tiffany after her revelation, but Kelli had forgotten something and interrupted. If not, she would have talked longer but Tiffany quickly transformed back into the persona she wanted everyone else to see. The carefree beautiful model who had the world in her hands, when Maggie had caught a glimpse underneath to the sordid world she hid.

Kelli stayed and chatted for awhile also, she too mentioned Jackson.

"I noticed you and Jackson are at least a little cordial to one another now. Quite a fine piece isn't he? Wish I'd caught him and made him a family man."

"I've heard everything from being gay to being married. Now you tell me he has a family too?"

"I hear he does. Course we hear lot's of things, who's to say what's true. I can't say for certain, but it makes sense to me. He seems very committed, photographs beautiful women all the time and won't give any of us the time of day." Then Kelli remembered something she'd been told six months previous. "There was one girl I worked with who bragged about sleeping with him, so maybe he isn't so committed, maybe just picky in choosing girlfriends."

Tiffany laughed. "See? I told you that you would get all kinds of stories about him. He's a mystery to us all and we all have our own opinions about him. I still think he's gay. He's been hanging around that older man quite a bit, the head crew guy? Maybe that's actually his boyfriend."

"John?" Maggie questioned, tried not to let her amusement by the statement show too much.

"Yeah, nice old man, but I think maybe the two of them are more than friends."

"No," Kelli disagreed. "I think Tiffany is just disappointed because she wants him. I'm telling you he's married and has a family he hides away somewhere." Then she looked to Maggie. "What do you think? You've probably found out a thing or two about him."

Maggie sighed, still trying to suppress her amusement. "He doesn't come from a family of a dozen kids, that's really the only thing I know about him. He hasn't said much and I don't know what I'm going to write about him in this article."

Kelli rose then, had found the earrings she wanted to borrow from Tiffany and was ready to go, invited Maggie along. "Tiffany is going to go hang out at the bars, why don't you come with me? They're having something in the lounge tonight, I think a comedian."

"Not tonight." Her concentration wasn't on entertainment that evening.

Several of them had begun to open up to her much more than she would have expected. They'd been very good at accommodating her when she asked for a little time for questions and some of them commented they looked forward to it. It became like therapy, or talking to their mother.

"Thanks," Maggie sighed playfully when Simone said it and joked with her. "As if my ego wasn't put in its place enough having to hang around you beautiful women all day you say I'm like your mother."

"Not that you're old enough to be my mother," Simone tried to explain. "In the sense you're someone I feel comfortable with. I have friends, but they don't offer advice, they're all as confused as I am about things. You're a great listener, most of my friends can't have a conversation for fifteen minutes if they're not talking about themselves, and I don't want to hear about them."

"There's your problem right there, in order to get someone to listen to you, you have to be a listener yourself." Maggie had the benefit of knowing a little about Simone, she was often very open when talking about her wealthy family, and she suspected some of her problems came from that.

When they truly began to open up about things she knew a therapist should have handled, Maggie promised she would print nothing they didn't approve of, and Simone was less hesitant to reveal things when she realized that. Maggie had picked up things and suspected her eating disorder came from inner problems more so than trying to keep her figure for her career. It wasn't something she had control over. When she directly asked about it, the models first words gave her clue to what those problems were.

"Simone, I don't see you eating much, you pretend to, you push the things around on your plate but they never really make it to your mouth." Maggie suspected she was anorexic, the thinnest of them all, and just enough on her bones to still be a model but if she was any smaller her bones would poke through her skin.

"My mother has always been a certain size and since I've been a little girl it was never acceptable to be pudgy. We had to present ourselves in a certain way, and our appearance was important she always told me. Being even a little overweight showed that a person had no control, it wasn't a quality that was acceptable to her."

"Do you have a good relationship with your mother?"

"Sure, we talk." She shrugged her shoulders but didn't elaborate on more.

"Talking and having a relationship are different."

"When we have time, my mother is a busy woman. She likes to travel and isn't around much."

During that conversation, as with the other models, Simone had her opinion about Jackson and offered it to her without Maggie asking. She thought he was just an egotistical jerk, someone said he came from money and she'd seen his kind and thought he was just a snob. Things were shared, none of which she put any credibility into. Maggie never took someone else's word about anything, she judged someone herself and formed her own opinions, and she had to admit that when it came to Jackson there were many opinions. Everyone seemed just as mystified by him as Maggie herself did.

Maggie thought about what she was getting herself into with Jackson. Was he married? Did he have a family? Did he fool around on his wife? Rumors, she told herself, just like the one he was gay, no different. There was no wife or family and it wouldn't matter anyway, she wasn't getting into anything. Nothing had happened, a few kisses that meant nothing, a few feelings that meant nothing, there was nothing.

Why was she thinking about it so much? Left on her own that evening, Maggie didn't seek out company, subconsciously didn't want to run into Jackson and wanted to distance herself so she meandered around alone, and it was easy to distance herself physically but emotionally she was in a different place. All she could think about, all her thoughts centered on the day together, and the passionate kisses that left her reeling still.

Maggie stood on the Promenade deck and took in the night filled with the sea before her and many stars above. She tried to let the soft breeze take her thoughts with it, pass over her and possibly carry anything she was feeling out to sea with it. Just as she was about to turn to go inside, Jackson came up from behind her, put his arms on either side as he placed his hands on the railing.

He pressed against her and she closed her eyes as he kissed her neck with several slow, sensual, light kisses, barely a touch that she felt straight to her toes. It certainly wasn't something she needed as she tried not to think about him but the feeling it gave her washed everything else away. All the things she'd been fighting rushed back and she didn't try to stop it.

"How was your day, Maggie?"

"It was wonderful. Yours?"

"I survived it, much to your chagrin I'm sure." He teased then whispered close to her ear, it had driven him crazy not to see her for hours and Jackson let his feelings overtake him, lost all self control when he shouldn't have. "Where have you been all evening?"

Maggie found herself being totally honest, "Trying to stay away from you."

He thought of her words, knew she too struggled with what was happening between them. "Should I take offense in that statement?"

"You should take yourself somewhere, I'm not sure I can be trusted right now, this Caribbean air is interfering with my rational thinking. And you being so close to me doesn't help."

"Maybe we should stay away from each other."

"Maybe we should." She agreed with him but neither made any attempt to move.

He turned her around to face him but still held her there with his hands on the rail. She placed her hands on the tops of his arms and could feel the muscle underneath his long sleeved white shirt that showed off his now tan skin. Maggie felt relief at seeing him, the turning of her stomach she experienced before now, turned to the flutter of excitement.

"You seem to be taking liberties, Jackson. A few kisses and you feel entitled?"

"A few kisses and I can't stop thinking about you."

"I'm not interested in you." Maggie seemed to hold her breath, didn't know if she were breathing as the hunger for his lips on hers consumed her. The smell of his skin so close sent thoughts of anything else into oblivion.

"And you mean nothing to me."

"This could complicate things." She argued in her mind why she should leave but the smell and feel of him as he pressed closer prevented her from moving. "We have a working relationship."

"I think we both want to stick to simple basics." Like her, Jackson battled in his mind of how far they should go. She was a stranger in passing that would do nothing but complicate his life, but she was like no one else he'd ever known and he was drawn to her as if by magnetic force. It was something powerful he couldn't explain, but his need for her overtook all of his normally reserved senses.

Maggie felt lost, he stimulated fears and doubts and she didn't feel in control as she normally did. Jackson stirred things in her, things long buried and hidden deep, things she didn't have much experience in such as something possibly real. In that moment, it didn't feel casual though she knew it was, and she pushed aside sentimentality and tried to bring herself back into control. She was over-romanticizing it, the night sea air and light breeze as the ship sailed through water made it impossible not to let go of a little reserves, but she didn't have to let them get out of control.

The instant Jackson pulled her to him and kissed her hard, the fire traveled and exploded in their bodies. Maggie hadn't been drinking, but she couldn't recall getting to his room where the passion overcame any sense she had, any notion of remaining in neutral territory, and she let everything else dissipate and had no second thoughts.

When she woke against his chest before dawn there was no guilt or regret, only a satisfaction of being in Jackson's arms and in his bed. She hadn't known she wanted him so much, nor had that much desire that needed to be released. Hidden desire for him and the intensity they experienced together was different than anything she'd ever experienced before, and Maggie chalked it up to the fact she hadn't been sexually satisfied in a long time. She thought he was still asleep when she went to move away but his arm tightened and held her there.

"Where do you think you're going?"

"It's your room, I've never had one but from what others have told me I think a woman normally leaves quietly after a one night stand. Aren't I supposed to sneak out now?"

He chuckled at her directness again, Maggie was certainly not shy in being blunt and honest, and he suspected it was what made her good at her career. She wasn't one to dance around issues. "You're not going anywhere."

She snuggled back against him. "You're more experienced at this than I am, I'll take your word for it."

His voice revealed the hurt he felt. "I know you don't know much about me, but if you know one thing make it the fact that I'm not experienced in this. Women do come on to me, it's the position I'm in, I'm surrounded by them, but that doesn't mean I partake in every offering. At least give me credit for a little decency."

She leaned up and looked at his face, she hadn't meant anything by it and didn't mean for him to take her so seriously and now she regretted her flippant remark. "Credit granted. Is that something else I can add to what I know about you? That you don't come from a family of a dozen kids and you deserve credit for some decency?"

"You probably came to bed with me just to see what you could get out of me, didn't you?" He playfully accused her. "What lengths you go to for an article."

"I might even do it again if you tell me something else."

"I don't have to, we've already made a truce so I don't feel obligated anymore, you know all there is to know about me."

"You tricked me into that and it didn't really count."

"This makes the truce official."

"We could have just shook hands on it," Maggie said.

"That wouldn't have been nearly as much fun."

The curtain was open and Jackson looked to her face swathed in moonlight and gently pushed her hair aside as he placed his hand on her cheek. He had betrayed himself but he wasn't able to fight the intensity that had consumed him. He felt he needed to be completely honest and she needed to know upfront where he stood.

"This isn't a one night stand, but I don't date, Maggie."

"I don't want a date." Was it because he was married? She forced the question from her mind as it was total nonsense to even think about it at a time like that.

"I don't want you to think..."

"Jackson, I told you where I stood, I'm through with relationships because they're all bullshit, and I'm not the type of woman to read anything into two people sharing sex. If you think my heart's going to be broken when you don't call me after we get home, it's not what I want. It's not what I expect."

She kissed his neck, the stubble of his face scratched gently as she nuzzled deeper. She didn't want a date, she wanted nothing from him but to feel his skin so close to hers again, wanted him to take her to the heights of exhilaration he was so good at.

"I just want to make sure we were both understood upfront. This can't go anywhere but here." He voiced his thoughts out loud as he tried to convince not only her but himself as well.

"This is all I want."

Jackson rolled her on her back, leaned over her, tasted the sweetness of her skin, felt the softness of her neck in his hand. "The rest of this week is all I can give."

"I don't want anymore than that." Maggie arched her back. It was easy to give in to the powerful feeling of pleasure, the craving to have him close again.

"When this trip is over, that's it, it ends." Jackson needed to explain there would be no expectations, no false promises. At the same time he was trying to convince her, he was trying to convince himself also. As he said the words he already suspected how difficult it would be to follow through with them.

His body touched hers, they lay against each other and she gave freely of herself but he had the sensation it wasn't enough. He couldn't get close enough to her even though they were as physically close as two people could possibly be. But he wanted deeper inside her skin, his hunger so extreme it made him ache.

"I don't want to lose my reputation, we can't let anyone know. The models knowing would only give them incentive. It would be like sending me to the wolves."

As he talked, his mouth moved to the tiny places on her neck, her shoulder, then to just out of reach of her lips. The space between them so close the tiniest movement would cause them to connect.

"Jackson," she said with frustration, almost screamed with the urgency he made her feel. "This is it. Sex. It's what we both want and nothing more. I understand that, you understand that, so could you please stop talking?"

He laughed. "A little impatient, aren't we? The one full of questions, the one who can hardly keep her mouth closed. Since when do you not want to talk?"

"It's a rare occurrence so the least you could do is indulge me, and you're normally a very quiet man, do you have to pick now to ramble on?" She pressed her lips hard to his, the craze she felt enormous.

CHAPTER TWELVE

Previously known as British Honduras, in the heart of the Caribbean Basin on the East coast of Central America, lie the natural paradise now known as Belize. 8,860 square miles of total land area included over 1,000 offshore islands. It bordered Mexico to the North and Guatemala to the West and South and it was flanked by the Caribbean Sea to the East that served as a playground of Cayes, pronounced keys. Offshore atolls and the barrier reef, which was 185 miles long were among its wonders. The barrier reefs the largest in the Western Hemisphere and second largest in the world.

Blessed with the best of both worlds, in Belize one could visit the mainland cities, towns and interior. Or discover the underwater world that revealed another life. Historic sights offered ancient Maya culture to be discovered. Maya temples and palaces, and archaeological sites abounded. It was believed Belize was the heart of the Maya civilization at one time. The most extensively excavated ruin in Belize was Altun Ha, Water of the Rock. A major ceremonial center, as well as an important trade center, that linked the Caribbean shores with other Maya centers in the island interior. Its ruins consisted of two main plazas with surrounding temple's and residential structures.

Located in the Vaca Plateau of the Cayo District awaited Caracol, one of the most inaccessible ruins in Belize, but offered one of the most scenic drives to get to its destination. Permission had to be obtained by the Department of Archaeology and the Forestry Department in order to visit. Its largest pyramid rose 140 feet high and stood as the tallest man-made structure in all of Belize.

Other Mayan centers included Cerros, Lamanai, Lubaantun, and Xunantunich that overlooked the Mopan River. All offered a look into history and the beauty of Belize as getting to most presented a tour itself, from driving interior mountains with lush tropical jungle to a boat ride over the sea to a place that overlooked a beautiful bay atop ancient temples.

At the other end of the spectrum, Belize's marine environment was well known around the world. Outlying Cayes, atolls and numerous mangrove systems both offshore and along the coast created an incredible wetlands environment. It was home to many species of birds, fish, mammals and reptiles that propagated in natural splendor. The marine environment was a favorite destination among divers, biologists, fishermen and people wanting a true escape from reality.

Protected areas and reserves established by the Natural Parks System Act created environments for an ecosystem to thrive. Half Moon Caye Natural Monument at the southeast corner of Lighthouse Reef Atoll was the first reserve established to protect the Red-footed Booby bird. Some ninety-eight species of birds have been recorded on the Caye, with winter migrants such as Osprey, Mangrove Warblers and White-crowned Pigeons.

Permanent residents included the Iguana, the Wish Willy and the Lizard. Loggerhead and Hawksbill turtles came ashore annually to lay their eggs, and the waters surrounding the island were home to many species of marine life.

Another popular spot, southeast of San Pedro town, was Hol Chan Marine Reserve. The first of its kind in Central America, it included three zones to create a five square mile area. All interdependent on one another, the first included the reef both inside and outside. The second the sea grass beds inside the reef. And the third included the mangroves of southern Ambergris Caye. Making it illegal to fish or collect coral in these areas gave the marine life room to flourish and grow. Divers and those who chose to snorkel were rewarded with sightings of large fish and healthy coral.

One of the newest National Parks was Laughing Bird Caye, named for the original large number of laughing gulls that once graced its boundaries, but due to excessive human encroachment they migrated elsewhere. Outstanding scuba diving and snorkeling opportunities drew people to the shelf atoll with deep channels.

Outlying Cayes and Mangroves gave the sea, beaches and massive coral reefs to explore. Making it easy to escape the human world easily and immerse oneself in underwater adventure.

****

The ship docked at 7 a.m. that morning. An early shoot required everyone meet and board a boat that would take them to an outlying Caye. Nicole, Kyla and Alan accompanied them that day.

It was a large boat and everyone scattered about, some in the shade on bottom, others up top in early rising sun as it was forming into a beautiful day. Maggie sat with Nicole in the aft of the boat, stretched out in the early sun on the molded plastic seating as they watched the land pass by.

"It's hard to believe these are the same people you started with." Nicole motioned discreetly towards the models.

Maggie smiled. "Isn't it? And I'm actually getting a story, a real story, something I didn't expect."

"I think quite a few things have happened none of us expected." Her thoughts were on her dinner with Derek the evening before.

Maggie looked towards the sea, the line of the horizon spanned wide, and she remembered what they'd said leaving Houston, how empty it looked. She didn't know all this was on the other side. She didn't even know what 'all this' was. It was as if the three women who left the Houston port, also left behind their inhibitions and their senses. Maggie hoped hers were waiting for her when she got back.

She glanced quickly to Jackson but couldn't look long, noticed he too had avoided any eye contact. She turned her attention back to Nicole. "How was your date with Derek last night?"

"I wish I could say I found out he was a jerk like the rest of them," she laughed. "I don't know, Maggie, I got up this morning and wondered what I was doing. I've been thinking about a man I'll probably never see again four days from now."

"Didn't you say he only lives five hours away? What's wrong with seeing him again?"

Nicole looked at her with light amusement. "Like yours and Kyla's long distance relationships have ever worked out?"

"I guess you have a point there." Maggie shrugged her shoulders. "But that... well Mick..." Then she gave up, had no explanation.

"I have a feeling I'll be chalking it up to a memory when this is over."

"It isn't to say none of them work out. Situations are different, people are different."

"What about Kyla this time? Think her and Alan are going anywhere after this?"

"I can't imagine they won't." Maggie looked over to the two of them sitting towards the front of the boat talking with a few crew members. "See, there's perfect example. Situations are different. When their long distance relationship didn't work out, they were young and just starting their careers. Now they're more settled, they've done things they wanted in their youth, made their careers. With you and Derek you're starting out settled, you're both at the same place in your lives."

"What about you, Maggie? You and Jackson live in the same city."

Maggie laughed. "But our difference is, neither one of us is looking for the relationship. We might have something here, but once we hit home land we'll want nothing more out of it."

"No?" Nicole questioned.

Maggie looked indifferent, shrugged her shoulders. "I look at it for sex, both of us do. You're not like that, Nicole, you're a mother and you think you'd be irresponsible no matter that you're single, if you don't have a relationship with the man."

"We're not talking about me anymore. I asked if you didn't want any more out of it than sex."

"It's not an option. Not for me, or him. Even if I had the notion, he's made it perfectly clear, just as I have, that it won't go any further."

"And that's what you want?"

"At this time in my life? Yes." Maggie's statement was strong as she said it with no question in her voice, it was easier not to concentrate on anything else, they understood each other and made it clear, and she wouldn't break her end of the agreement.

Hundreds of coral and mangrove isles, known as cayes, lie off the Belize coastline. Isolated stretches of sand compared to bigger islands that offered more than sand and palm trees. Off the magnificent Barrier Reef, was a wonder of many small worlds to explore, their boat headed to Caye Caulker.

Only five miles long by one half mile wide, it was one of the larger cayes, but large, by small standards. Most times if you lie on the beach in glorious sun, the shimmering clear turquoise and emerald green waters of the Caribbean at your feet, the only sound you'd probably hear is that of motor boats pulling in and out of their docks.

A tranquil place to while away a day or a life, as in other Caribbean islands, there were some Americans and others who moved to its calm shores to retire and make their homes. Swimming, diving, fishing, snorkeling, there was much within reach. They were met at the dock by an older gentleman and his son who welcomed them and gave them an overview of the island, a small hand drawn map, and provided them with golf carts to get around the sand roads.

Maggie was standing with John when Jackson approached but didn't notice her there right away, his concentration on his camera as he prepared some adjustments.

"John, I'll go to the first spot and I won't need anything so you can take the crew to the second spot. I'll just be there for a few quick shots and we won't be far behind you." He looked up then and averted his eyes from Maggie as if John would see the connection somehow if he didn't.

"Want me to drive you?" Maggie asked with playful innocence.

"I had enough of your driving yesterday."

John laughed and knew what he spoke of. "Don't ask me how she got that Honduran driver's license, I think she bribed someone."

"I've discovered Maggie has a way of getting what she wants." Then he quickly went back to the subject at hand before she spilled out with what they shared the evening before, as she'd done on the first kiss they shared. "I'll be working with some light by then, so it will have to be artificially adjusted, but you know where to set up."

John looked to his clipboard, "I've got the location right here."

"I'm going with the crew, unless you're sure you don't want me to drive you." Maggie called to his back when he walked away from them.

"That's a good idea, you go with the crew."

Her friends didn't need to work so they took off on their own cart to explore the tiny island and would meet up with her later and Maggie helped John load the equipment from the boat. There were three other men who tried to stop her, said they could handle it but she didn't listen.

"I'm not going to stand around and watch." She said as she picked up and easily carried an extra large tripod.

"No sense arguing with her," John said. "She's going to do it anyway."

She spoke with the crew as they set up, she couldn't help in that because there were particular ways things had to be placed and adjusted so she used the time to get information. Maggie knew these men, liked them, but found it sad that one had lost his wife because he preferred the traveling jobs and she tried to force him into something more stable where he could be home more.

He shrugged his shoulders as he made sure a light tripod was firmly implanted into the sand. "Hard to be married and on the road, I always asked her to come with me but she never wanted. It was difficult to find the compromise line so the line just broke."

"What about you, Maggie," he asked her. "I know you have the office job, but you travel too, how do you keep a balance?"

"I don't have to balance my schedule with anyone, it's just me."

"Doesn't make for a very fun life."

"I have my fun, I'm just not obligated to any one thing but my job, makes for an easier life."

When they finished setting up, the men took a spot underneath a shade tree to wait and Maggie took off her sandals and walked with John along the shore.

"So how was your day yesterday?" She'd worried a little about him being in Roatan again but saw yesterday there was no need to, and he confirmed that when she asked.

"Made the entire trip worth it. It's the main reason I took this assignment, other than I like working with Jackson. And you were a surprise bonus since I didn't even know you were going to be here."

"I think about her all the time, but especially yesterday." Maggie looked down to the water that washed over her feet. "She'd be proud of you, she would want you to get past it and live and I know it was hard for you to let go and do that."

"Hardest thing I've ever done, and I can't explain it or find reason for her death, I just have to be grateful and feel lucky I had her all the years I did."

"You and Edith shared what my parents share, and you are lucky, it's rare in this society to have anything so lasting. So easy to give up and get divorced, people don't want to fight for marriage anymore."

"Is that what you're so afraid of?"

She looked at him and laughed a little. "What makes you say that? I'm not afraid of anything."

"Aren't you? I've never known you to be afraid of a fight, but maybe you are. I've met a few of your potentials and you've always remained on the outskirts of relationships. You might be in one, but you're never really fully in, there's always a reserve."

"Maybe I'm just looking for that lasting one, why waste the time with others in between?"

"This may be off subject, but I see you and Jackson are getting along much better."

"Way off subject, but yes, we're getting along a little better." She hoped her face didn't give anything away when she felt flushed. "Only because I trust you and you said he was a good man so I gave him all the benefit of the doubt I could, but he didn't make it easy."

"And the article? How's that coming?"

"When it comes to Jackson I may not have much to say, he still hasn't given me anything to use, but I'm getting somewhere with the models, farther than I expected."

"You've gotten underneath the gloss and the lipstick, haven't you?" He never had a doubt she would.

"You could say I've found some substance."

John looked across the sand and noticed Jackson and the others had arrived, also noticed Jackson looked towards the men in the shade then looked around further, as if he searched for something, or someone. When he saw John he looked content but the man knew it wasn't him he'd searched for. He waved as if it was and went about his business.

Maggie hadn't noticed and his voice was soft as he spoke again. "I for one want to thank you, Maggie, you have a way of changing peoples lives."

"Changing lives? What do you mean?"

"You changed Edith's life, gave her a whole new perspective on her last days, and you can say you've changed my life, you've been a daughter to this old man, one I thought I'd never have. It's a comfort to an old man like me to know there's one person who's going to worry about me a little."

"Sometimes a lot when I don't hear from you." She put her hand through his arm and held it there as they walked.

"And these models haven't been the same. Jackson confessed to me that the credit belongs to you on that one, told me about your little talk you had with them."

"It may have been what they needed for now, but I'm sure as soon as they're out of my sight and off this project they'll resort to normal. Just a temporary fix, I wouldn't say I changed their lives. I don't hold that much power."

"I don't know about that."

"You give me more credit than I deserve, people have decency in them, sometimes it just takes a reminder."

"Life changing and humble about it. There's a lucky man somewhere in this world, I just hope your eyes aren't closed when you find him."

The shoot began and Maggie stood out of the way and let them all work, rested with the models under the shade, those that weren't required for the moment. She and Tedi were alone when Maggie broached the subject of drug addiction.

"How long have you been addicted?"

Tedi looked at her quickly, and then when Maggie didn't turn away, she did. "Addicted to what?"

"I'm not exactly sure but something. What is it? Meth? Crack? Cocaine?"

"Maggie," she tried to laugh it off. "I might be a little insane at times, but I'm not that insane."

"And I'm not naïve. I've been around it all, Tedi, the line of work I'm in gives me the benefit of meeting all different kinds of people from all different walks of life. The homeless crack head in the street to the wealthy rock star who goes bankrupt over an addiction he can't control."

"I've got control." She didn't admit nor deny she was involved in drugs.

"Most think they do, I wouldn't expect you to be any different."

"It's a requirement in this business, like a part of my makeup bag, you don't know what its like trying to be everything to everyone, trying to take on as many jobs as you can because the next big face is breathing down your neck."

"No, I don't know what that's like." Maggie empathized with her and sat casually as she sifted the sand through her fingers. "But after your career is over, you may have lost the jobs but you won't be able to lose your addiction so easily. Where are you going to be then?"

She shrugged her shoulders. "I won't need it then so it won't be a big deal."

"I don't know if anyone has ever lectured you on denial or not, and I'm certainly not going to start. But I've seen people like you, Tedi,

I've seen firsthand what happens to the beautiful people who once shone in the spotlight and then lost everything."

"I won't be like them." Her words sounded confident but Maggie openly disagreed.

"Yes you will, and it scares you to know that."

It was a beginning. They would have talked longer but Tedi was called towards the shore and Maggie watched after her with great sadness. There was a good heart in Tedi, a child inside who was lost and scared, but she used the drugs to suppress it. More than one article could be done on models, an entire book could be written about the sad women who were so picture perfect on the outside, but on the inside there was so much pain.

She was reminded of a long ago song about tears of a clown, it fit these girls, all of them. Maggie could talk to people, she did have that way about her, but John gave her more credit than she deserved and she couldn't change some lives as much as she wanted to. She'd learned long ago from people she interviewed that she couldn't change the world, she could just report about it, write about it, and hope that people would share her compassion for humankind.

****

The morning seemed long as the sun rose higher and Maggie could tell Jackson was trying to hurry, full sun shots didn't do well for him.

"Want me to call and slow it down a bit?" She asked as she stepped beside him, it was the first time she'd been close to him all day.

He didn't look up at her but she could see the smile he was trying to suppress. "Go away, Maggie."

"What do you mean go away?"

"How am I supposed to keep my mind on work with you right next to me? Go away."

"Isn't work almost over? The little ones are getting restless." She indicated the models who she could tell needed a break, even if they were afraid to voice it.

"Them or you?"

"You have a million shots. I think you have the perfect one in there."

"I actually do. I have one of you practically falling out of the golf cart when you reached over to the ground for something and John took off," he steady clicked his camera, tried to ignore her presence.

"Sounds perfect for the magazine's cover material."

"Are you going to let me work?"

"I'm going to be selfish, you've worked long enough. Besides," Maggie picked up his bag next to him, the one that contained the film, and began to walk away. "You're out of film."

Jackson finished the roll in his camera and called it quits. Everyone wandered down the beach either on foot, or in the golf carts where they would meet up at a restaurant on the water. He found Maggie leaning against the cart with the equipment.

"I asked John to drive Simone and Tiffany, they had to go to the bathroom quick. I told him we'd bring the equipment."

Jackson never stopped walking until he reached her then kissed her immediately. He couldn't stop thinking she should have stayed out of the shoot that day because she was more than distracting to him. When someone close by cleared their throats in an obvious attempt to interrupt, they both jumped and turned quickly to see Alan.

Maggie looked as if she'd been caught with her hands in the cookie jar. "We were... discussing the film supply."

"And did you come up empty? Did you find out Jackson doesn't keep it in his mouth."

The two men laughed and Maggie blushed. "Did you come to tell me you've lost my best friends?"

"I came to tell you where we'd be. Found a nice little place over by the split."

Maggie rode with Alan to the restaurant the crew and models had gone to because it looked better than showing up with Jackson alone. The shoot over for the day, most decided to eat and go about enjoying the rest of their day. Maggie invited John to come with them, but he was going Cave tubing with some others that were headed back to the mainland.

It surprised Maggie when Alan asked Jackson if he wanted to stay and fish. When he agreed, Alan told Maggie to take his cart and go meet Kyla and Nicole if she wanted.

Alan obviously saw their situation and among a group, it was difficult to get away alone without someone having suspicions. It was his solution, which worked without anyone thinking otherwise other than he and Jackson were going fishing.

Maggie knew he'd only done it for that reason, he hated to fish, there were no questions asked though and she took the cart and left. As she passed a pier, a dive boat had just come in from their morning dive and she stopped and waited at the end of the pier, watched as Derek finally looked up and took notice. She got the feeling there was something that was meant to be somewhere.

"How was your dive?" She asked with a smile.

"It was great. I didn't expect to see you here."

"We did some shots around the island this morning. I'm on my way to meet up with Nicole now, if you're not going back out, you're welcome to come with me. I'm sure it will be a nice surprise for her." Maggie saw his face change at the mention of her name.

They found Kyla and Nicole where Alan said they would be. Sitting in a chair, lounging in the sun and both their eyes were closed as the two snuck up.

"Excuse me, ma'am, can I get you something to drink?"

Nicole had been half asleep, she didn't open her eyes and Derek's voice hadn't registered. "I don't think so, but thank you."

He knelt down closer to her chair. "We have many specials today."

It halfway registered then, but she wasn't sure if it was coming from her dreams or if it was real until she opened her eyes and screamed, then laughed. "Where did you come from?"

"The sea actually. I just came back from a dive and Maggie happened to be passing by."

Maggie watched the two, knew from somewhere deep inside that something was meant to be, she was sure of it. Fate had thrown them all together, Nicole and Derek, Kyla and Alan, and even herself and Jackson. Who would survive the ending was anyone's guess, and Maggie wouldn't have bet on herself, but the odds were good for the others.

Hers may not have the potential as theirs, but on this side of the horizon she'd found the unexpected. As she watched him walk across the sand towards her, she had nothing to complain about.

On the beach that day, on the little caye in Belize, there was hardly anyone around but them and no one had to be discreet. Randy and his friends weren't around and neither were the models or any of their working crew and the three couples gathered as normal couples would.

The six easily relaxed in an atmosphere of island ambiance. All three men got along tremendously well, they could have been old school chums themselves by the time the day was over, and Kyla and Nicole saw a different side of Jackson than they'd seen previous.

They were all easy and comfortable around each other. A few had gone in the water, now Maggie sat in the sand just on the edge of the surf with her back against Jackson's chest, her arm around his bended knee beside her. It was one day, but she felt like he was in her life. How did he get in her life? It wasn't how she planned it, didn't think he'd be socializing with her friends, infiltrating a space he wouldn't be in after the trip was over, but he was there in the middle of it.

"Maggie Pace has no words?"

"Hmm?" She didn't hear him, lost in thought as the sun beat down on her.

"You're quiet, a very unusual practice for you."

"You made me get up at the crack of dawn."

"I didn't. You didn't have to come," he said.

She now wished she hadn't. Maggie liked this place, in his arms, him in her life. She got up and walked into the water to wash the sand off and then turned and smiled.

"Of course I had to come. I had to make sure you didn't overwork the little ones, don't want them to get obstinate again." Maggie turned again and walked straight ahead, looked to the horizon now, wanted to be back on the other side. She could get hurt on this one.

****

The men gathered and Kyla and Nicole were in the water when Maggie saw a few island children up the beach and put her shorts and shirt on and approached them. They were playing soccer and she joined in to their surprise. Even showed them a trick or two with the ball and they wanted her to play then fought for her to be on their team, so she played a little while with one team then a little while with another.

She'd never played soccer in the sand before but it sure strengthened one's legs as at times she struggled, but kept up with them all. When she heard her name being called, Alan stood on the sideline and waited for her. They had to go, their boat was leaving and they had to catch it.

All of the children gave her high fives and Maggie used her shirt to wipe the sweat off her forehead as she joined Alan.

"Whew, I haven't had a workout like that in ages."

"I got tired just watching." He laughed and put his arm around her. "You're still a kid at heart, haven't changed a bit."

She and Alan had been friends for as long as Kyla and he dated, and she'd missed him when they split. It saddened her as well, knowing two people who she felt were meant to be together, weren't going to be. She told him she'd missed him as they walked down the beach together.

"I've missed you. I think it's great, you and Kyla again. Talk about destiny."

"Is that what it is?" He looked unsure.

"What would you call it?"

"I'm not sure. I still love her, Maggie, I've never stopped. As much as I still feel she loves me, is it enough for her to change her life?"

"She loves what she does, and she does it well, but I would think she knows now that there's more to life than that."

"That's a question only she can answer." There were many things he'd yet to talk to her about, one thing in particular he struggled with daily, knew when that time came there would be a price to pay, he had to wonder how high that price would be.

"I think faced with you again she'll have to ask herself some serious questions. Have you asked her about anything yet? Like your futures? If there is one?"

"And risk her shutting me out so early? I don't want to create tension so soon, I'm just enjoying it again."

"Life certainly isn't simple is it? Remember when we were younger and we talked about our futures? Not one of us was true to it. Nothing we ever said happened."

"You mean like when we were going to buy a van and drive across country? I was going to play in a band, you were going to write a great novel about the experience and Kyla said her contribution would be to drive, she didn't trust either of us."

"And Nicole was going to keep us all out of trouble. Our ideologies were a little immature at the time but is your life really the way you thought it would be?"

Alan had his arm around her as they walked. "I always feel like I'm waiting for the fun to begin. Day after day I wake up and think this is the day. But at the end of it, it was no different than the day before. This week has been different though, I don't have that feeling."

Maggie felt for him, she wished there was something she could say to give him hope but she remained in the dark just as much as he, didn't know what would happen between them. If there were a future, and what that future would be, neither one of them knew. She could feel it there, but that wouldn't make it so.

"What about you, Maggie? Is it the life you wanted?"

"Actually someone else has my life and I want it back. I think its Jennifer Lopez but she won't return my calls."

His voice exploded in laughter. "I really have missed you, it's good to see you haven't lost your edge."

"Nah, I keep it pretty sharp, keeps most at bay."

"Must not work on Jackson. I like him, seems to be a guy I could see your brothers approving of."

"Where did that come from?" She pulled back a little and laughed.

"He's a nice guy. Lives in New York also, doesn't he?"

"I don't choose my companions based on locality. We work together, rather, we're working together this week and I will probably never see him again after this."

"Why?" Alan asked with all seriousness.

"Because I've sworn off men, I don't need the hassle. I'll be an old maid but I'll look damn good, no telltale signs of stress lines on my face. Besides that, what do my brothers have to do with it?"

"I know how they are, I've met them and had to go through the third degree because I was seeing one of your best friends, I know what you go through when you take someone home to meet them. I can't imagine that's changed."

Maggie thought about the last time she'd done just that and confessed it. "The last guy I took home was two years ago and he left with a broken leg. It was an accident of course, happened while they were playing football, but Grant is proud to take credit for it."

"A tough crowd to face and I still remember how scared I was the first time I met them."

"They loved you, used to ask me about you all the time." Maggie thought back and remembered all of them having a great time when they went home to visit.

"They'd love Jackson too."

"It won't happen, Alan."

"There's no reason for it not to. Not as far as I can see. You're not old maid material, that's someone like my Aunt Dee, who after six marriages gave up. Course it didn't help that she has ten cats and every husband she picked is allergic to cats."

"A woman who makes the right choices, I like that." They reached the others and Maggie looked up to see Jackson deep in conversation with Derek.

He hardly stopped talking when she walked up, looked at her just quick enough to see who it was then casually put his arm around her and pulled her close as he continued the conversation.

Maggie stood quietly and listened as they talked of photography. She liked being in his arms, liked that he'd pulled her there as if it was natural for her to be there, and she realized Alan was right. Her brothers would like Jackson, but it wouldn't matter, they would probably never meet him.

CHAPTER THIRTEEN

The men went back to the ship while the women took the very little time they had left to meander through the shops at the Tourist Village, and then took the next ferry. It was quiet among them until Maggie spoke up with what she thought they'd all been thinking.

"Insane isn't it? Nothing about this week has been normal. It's some other universe we've stepped into."

"And you think you can step right out of this little universe or whatever world it is?" Nicole added. "I saw you and Jackson today, both of you can tell yourselves what you want, but I don't see anything ending at the port."

"I'm not a relationship person. Yeah, he's attractive, he's a great guy, and I'm going to take advantage of it while I can. But that's it."

"I'm with Nicole. There's more there than a one night stand, rather a one week stand."

"You two are romanticizing it. Its vacation, we're in glorious surroundings without a care in the world and nothing to do but lie around on the beach and have fun. We get home? He'd turn into Godzilla man. Expect dinner on the table by five, his laundry perfect, his shirts starched, isn't me men want, it's a maid."

"I think we can tell he's not that type, you wouldn't be attracted to him if he were. Your instincts wouldn't let you."

"They change on you. Half the guys I've dated I didn't know were that type."

"Come on, Maggie," Kyla began to think she was seriously going to ban men from her life all together and if Jackson didn't have a chance, she wasn't sure who would. Like Nicole, she thought there was something much more between the two.

"You two know my track record, I can pick the losers out, like I'm constantly being tested to see just how much crap I can put up with."

"You haven't had many losers, you just haven't had any that you've stayed interested in. You label them losers instead of telling yourself you're bored."

"Maybe I am too hard to please. Who's to say I wouldn't be bored with Jackson? But the main thing, what do I know about him? It might all be some act he puts on that he doesn't date models, separates his work and his life. Maybe he picks up a woman in every town he's in."

Nicole looked at her. "Why are you trying to talk yourself out of it?"

"There's nothing there to talk myself out of. It's a non emotional, purely physical thing. Lust, passion, infatuation, all of those describe it, surely nothing stable and lasting. And that's fine with me, that's all I want, not everyone needs more than that." Maggie didn't need any more than that. Did she? She didn't answer the question, it wasn't an option, she wouldn't have a choice and didn't want one.

When they reached their deck Maggie walked behind them down the hall. Kyla was first and had her key out, then Nicole was in the middle of a conversation in front of her, then without being seen, Jackson grabbed her from behind and pulled her into his room.

He shut the door, pressed her up hard against it and entwined his fingers with hers, raised her hands high above her head. "How was your day, Maggie?"

"You're getting good at this conversation thing now, aren't you?"

"It wasn't really conversation I had on my mind. What took you so long?"

"I didn't know you were waiting." She squeezed his hands tight, pleased she wouldn't have to wait until much later to see him. Maggie lifted her chin as he kissed her neck.

"I can't sit by tonight and watch you with all your male friends. An entire entourage at your beck and call, I can't compete."

"All my male friends?" She raised her eyebrows, he sounded a little jealous and she liked it. What was it about the slightest hint of possessiveness that made a woman feel something? Maybe because it was another emotion shared, a display of protective instinct, and she didn't want to like it but she did.

"An entire entourage of admirers," Jackson continued as he let her arms come down slightly.

"They're much too interested in the models to ever take a second glance at me, I'm old enough maybe not to be their mother, but their babysitter at one time."

"I never had a babysitter that looked like you, all mine were old." He kissed her lips several times, light pecks that teased her desire for him. "Let's eat in. Room service. Any objections?"

"Just one... do we have to eat?"

****

"I guess we're on our own this evening, Maggie ditched us." Nicole took one last look in the mirror, liked her newly tanned skin as it made the blond highlights of her hair appeared brighter.

"We're liable not to see her till tomorrow. Think they'll come up for air tonight?"

"Why? Like she said, guess she's going to take advantage of every minute. I can't blame her. But I still don't understand why there couldn't be anything afterwards."

Kyla slipped her high heeled sandal on. "You know how Maggie is, she gets something in her mind and it sticks sometimes. She's hell bent on living the rest of her life alone, she won't even open her eyes."

"Both of them are hesitant. Wonder what his reasons are?"

"I sensed that too, just a few things he said."

Nicole leaned against the wall as she waited for Kyla to finish and thought about it, but it was a mystery to her. "You don't think Maggie could be right about him, do you?"

"Right about him?"

"When she was talking about him picking up a different woman on every trip, maybe he could be that type. After all, what do we know about him?"

"Knowing him at least a little now, I don't see him as that way. I can't picture it, it doesn't fit."

"I can't either, really."

Kyla slipped her other shoe on and stood up, finally ready. "She can say what she wants, but I can almost bet after they get off that plane in New York after this trip is over, they'll be in the same cab."

"What about you, Kyla? You haven't said much about you and Alan."

"Denial and avoidance are a great defense. Let's go, I'm starving."

They left Maggie a note just in case, and decided on the Italian restaurant that evening, then a show. Much later they sat at a table on the top deck for an outdoor party when Derek happened by and joined them. Then Randy and a few of his friends showed up and eventually Alan and Maggie. Two of the models followed, some of the crew, and the last to show was John and Jackson.

The group of them, who'd all come together in an odd way, enjoyed the night air and lively conversation. It was a jovial crowd and it was quite some time before they began to break up and disperse their separate ways.

Afterwards, Maggie discreetly tapped on Jackson's door when she knew the hallway would be safe.

"I knew you'd come knocking on my door." He teased and pulled her in.

"Get over yourself, Jackson. I'm only here for my pleasure not yours."

He laughed and pressed to her. "If I did have a big ego, it certainly wouldn't survive around you."

Maggie looked around the empty room, asked what she'd been thinking. "How did you get a room by yourself anyway?"

"A good contract."

"Remind me to talk to my boss." She kissed him lightly. "I'll have to remember to thank her."

****

Later that evening, Kyla and Alan sat alone in the Piano Bar and enjoyed a glass of wine.

"We've got to talk, Kyla." Alan leaned to her and kissed her.

Kyla moaned. "Not now. Let's not think about anything serious, I'm having too much fun."

It was romantic between them. The place was quiet with only four other people that evening and they knew Randy and his crowd were somewhere much more energetic and they wouldn't be seen. Both of them still hesitant to have Randy think things that might be premature.

"Have you thought about us? What we're doing? Where we're going?"

"We're going to Cancan," she said.

He looked at her for a long time. Was it avoidance because she wasn't feeling what he was? Denial she was feeling what he was? Like her, he wanted to put it off, but he knew he was only making it worse on himself. When he told her what she needed to know, he didn't suspect she'd take it lightly. But again, at her insistence they didn't talk about it seriously, he pushed it away for another time.

Kyla enjoyed her drink and enjoyed his company, how strange life was to throw him at her at that time in her life. It was all so unexpected and she didn't want to talk of serious things, not when she was so unsure of everything. She wanted to take advantage completely of what they had left in a carefree 'in love' state. She knew she loved him desperately still, but was it enough for her?

"I like Derek and Jackson." Alan held onto her hand tightly, needed that connection to her when he could get it. "This has been one strange trip, hasn't it?"

She laughed. "That's an understatement. All three of us vowed to stay away from all men, now look at us. All three wrapped up in one way or another. It was the least thing I would ever have expected from this trip."

"I always pictured the three of you settled into a marriage by now, all kinds of children between you."

"Maggie's the only one who hasn't taken the plunge, I'm not sure she ever will. I don't even know if she and Jackson would date after this and they live in the same city. And Nicole surprises me, it's been a few years since her divorce, but she's stayed away from men because she was so hurt. I certainly wouldn't have expected her to so easily fall for someone."

Kyla knew there was an obvious connection between the two and was disappointed Nicole couldn't have found someone so similar in her own hometown, someone her friend could possibly have a decent long lasting relationship with. She knew Nicole better than she knew herself sometimes and one thing Kyla was sure of, she wasn't one to have a sexual fling and forget about it.

Nicole would take the time to get to know someone but she wouldn't be able to in a short week's time. And a simple tryst in bed was out of the question, unlike herself who was caught up in Alan, but it wasn't a simple tryst. Or was it?

****

Even though they'd been together earlier that evening, and left with others, it didn't stop Nicole nor Derek to show back up alone for their late night coffee rendezvous.

"It was getting late, I was about to give up on you." Derek smiled as Nicole sat down with her cup of coffee at the next table and he laughed. "Nicole, I think you might be safe in sitting at the same table with me now." He moved to her table and gave her a quick kiss before he sat down.

"I didn't want to seem pushy."

They shared so many of the same feelings it scared her. Each of them had experienced similar situations, now harbored the same fears and emotions because of being hurt by people they once loved, a common bond that made it easy to share with one another. They talked and laughed, never ran short of things to say, even more now as conversation flowed easily. Before they parted they agreed to spend the day in Cancun and set to meet early on the port.

"Anything special you want to do?" Derek was mindful to ask.

"You pick something, I've never been anywhere, remember? I'm the new traveler who needs guidance."

He bent down and kissed her tenderly. "Until tomorrow."

****

Maggie didn't stay long in Jackson's room, she'd gone briefly then left for her own even though he tried to persuade her to stay.

"It's early, why aren't you staying?" He protested.

She had to be away from him for awhile, he was invading too many of her thoughts but she didn't say so when she left. The next morning, she stood on the top deck and watched as the ship made its way into its berth at their last stop, the Cancun port. It was their last destination before the vessel would turn around and head for home. The last thought on her mind that evening was Jackson, the first thought that morning was Jackson.

She was glad she hadn't stayed, the night away from him gave her the space she thought she needed, though she hadn't gotten much sleep just thinking about him right down the hall. Now she was anxious to see him and thought he'd be up and about by now but she'd seen neither him nor any of the crew. After awhile she decided to go to his room with the pretense of asking who was to meet them at the port.

He set up the shoots so he was also responsible for any extra contacts they needed in order to be able to take photos in any special areas. She was just checking to make sure everything was taken care of. That was her job, wasn't it? Okay, so she also wanted a friendly face to have coffee with and both Kyla and Nicole were still getting ready for their day and she saw no one else she knew.

Maggie knocked lightly on the door. Like her, he was normally always up early and she didn't think he'd be sleeping, but she had to knock twice and just as she was about to give up the door opened.

"Hey, Maggie," Tiffany said with heavy sleep that still lingered. Her naked body was loosely covered with a sheet pulled from the bed. "I'm not late, am I? Is it afternoon? I have the afternoon shoot."

"Its morning, I was..." Words didn't seem to be able to come to her. She couldn't think of what to say then her brain began working again. "I just needed to know something from Jackson."

"Jackson?" The girl said and turned around to the dark room but there was no one there. "He's not here."

"Thanks," Was all she said before leaving. What did she thank her for? The knot in the pit of her stomach? The icy coldness that made her skin clammy?

Her mind actually tried to justify it. It was Jackson's room and there was a naked Tiffany in it that obviously had spent the night. No, Maggie told herself easily, there was no justification, don't even try.

Maggie walked quickly to her own room to see if she'd missed Kyla and Nicole as they didn't expect her to go with them that day since she was going to the shoot, but she'd missed them, they were gone. She searched the dining rooms and their usual haunts they enjoyed but found them nowhere. She was on her way to get off the ship to catch up with them when she heard Jackson call from behind.

She didn't want to stop, didn't want to see his face or hear his voice, but he quickly caught up to her and gently grabbed her arm.

"What's the rush? Hold up a minute."

She stopped and turned and as much as she tried to hide her anger she couldn't, it was all over her face. "Actually I'm glad I ran into you, I won't be making the shoot this morning like I thought, so don't wait for me. And I won't make this afternoon either."

His face held disappointment and confusion. "I thought..."

"I changed my mind, your environment is a little too crowded for me today." She tried to pull away but he stopped her.

"Am I supposed to know what that means? What's this all about?"

"Don't flatter yourself and think it has anything to do with you, Jackson, I can't make the shoot. I have my reasons and I don't have to explain them to anyone."

"Hey!" He screamed as she jerked away from him.

Maggie actually ran in the opposite direction, had to get away from him, and couldn't look at his face. Her turmoil inside consumed her and she realized she was actually shaking. She found Derek and Nicole waiting along the port for the others who would join their excursion and stopped quickly, chatted for just a moment.

As hard as she tried to force Jackson from her mind, he wouldn't go away. But she did smile, brightly and earnestly, no one would ever guess a handsome stranger bewildered her, and she didn't even know why. He was nothing to her, absolutely nothing.

If they hadn't any set plans, Maggie was going to go with someone but everyone seemed set. Derek and Nicole were going on an excursion and Kyla and Alan had signed up for a tour, so Maggie decided she would spend the day alone rather than impose.

How odd life was to test them. As if it meant to dangle the hope of true happiness with someone in front of you only to take it away. Was it meant to strengthen one's character? Instill faith that it was out there somewhere? Maggie thought about it philosophically and then just said to hell with it, it was all bullshit and nothing more. She was about to get into a cab alone when Jackson grabbed her arm.

"I want to talk to you," he said.

"I want you to quit grabbing me like you have a right to." Her eyes were hard, her voice a quiet hiss.

"Where do you think you're going?"

"It isn't any of your business."

"You're not going anywhere until you explain this to me." Maybe he should have let her go, maybe it was time he started to let her go in preparation for their return home, but he pressed. "I don't know what this is about, but I'm not leaving you alone until you tell me."

"Don't you have a job to do?"

"I canceled the shoot."

"What do you mean you canceled the shoot?"

"I canceled it, told them I was having equipment problems and everyone was happy about it."

"Well I'm the supervisor of this job and..."

"Don't pull that shit with me, Maggie, it won't work. I work on my own and do as I please." He pulled her from the cab door and told the driver she wouldn't need him.

"What do you think you're doing?" Maggie wanted to pull rank. Tell him she wanted pictures taken until the sun set and then they had to work the whole evening on the ship, and tomorrow from sun up until sun down. She didn't make a very nice woman scorned with the thoughts she was thinking.

"We need to talk, and I'll talk right here, and I'll talk very loudly." Jackson threatened and Maggie knew he wasn't bluffing.

"Someone who a few days ago wouldn't open his mouth, now he's demanding to talk," she huffed and walked with him when he pulled her out of the way of the crowd of tourists vying for a cab.

He remained silent for a long time as Maggie stared at him in fury. "What is it you need to talk about? I don't have all day to stand here and wait for you to speak. Is something wrong with the shoot? You're the one that picked the spots, I didn't have any control over that. The models? They've been fine, or are they acting up again? Are you running out of film? Sorry, can't find any to purchase so I guess your job is over. I can use the expense account to get you a flight out today. All of our problems are solved now, aren't they? There's nothing more to talk about."

"Maggie..." He tried, but she wouldn't let him get a word in as she went on and exposed her reasons.

"I guess when I didn't stay in your room last night, you found easy replacement. Be my guest Jackson, help yourself to anyone you want, who am I to question it?"

He sighed and realized what she was so angry about, he'd forgotten all about Tiffany. Would she believe the true story of the events that landed a beautiful model naked in his room? And if she didn't, why did he care so much? Both emotions of relief and concern mixed into his mind.

"Damn you spit fire when you're mad!" He actually liked the way she was mad, the reason she was mad.

"And I'm only getting madder. If we have nothing to talk about this is a waste of my time when I could be planning your flight out."

Though she squirmed to move past him she couldn't get away, he moved in front of her and she was against a pole as he held her tight.

After she'd had her tirade, Jackson began his explanation. "As supervisor of this assignment, you might want to talk to the models a little about safety. You see, last night I found Tiffany so drunk at one of the bars she could barely hold her head up. She was alone, meaning there was no one there she knew, but there were at least five men probably waiting for her to pass out just so they could take her back to their rooms and take advantage of her. She could barely talk but they kept buying her drinks. I didn't even know what room she was in, and she was passed out, couldn't even tell me. So I took her back to my room, had to carry her when she passed out in the elevator, and left her there to sleep. I slept in John's cabin last night."

Maggie stared at him. It was all a lie. He'd found out she stopped by and to cover his ass thought of a story that sounded plausible, wanted to continue with her and keep her on the sideline just in case Tiffany backed out on him one night, and he'd use her as a back up.

What did it matter whether it was the truth or a lie? She asked herself. Let it be, leave him alone. So he slept with models, preferred long and lean beauty over anything she could possibly offer. It didn't matter. You didn't want him anyway, Maggie, you don't want or need anyone, remember?

Maggie knew it was the anger that lingered that made her think the worst of him, the anger and her weariness of men who disappointed her time after time. She could easily check his story, John was a man of integrity, if she casually asked about Jackson sleeping in his cabin he wouldn't lie to her. The story was plausible, it sounded like the truth. Why did she believe him? Maybe because she wanted to so badly.

He pressed closer to her, could see her anger dissolving. "Ask John, you trust him, even if you don't trust me."

"I hope you're only telling me this so I can tell the women to be more careful and not because you think I care if you slept with Tiffany or not."

"Oh, no, I knew you wouldn't care if that were the case. It wasn't that I had to explain myself, just the situation. And you should tell them if they're going to get that drunk they should at least have someone with them, it isn't safe."

"I'll talk to them. Is that all?" Maggie still needed to get away from him. Her roller coaster of emotions had taken its toll from one extreme to another and she didn't want to be so close to him. But Jackson just pulled her closer and held tight so she couldn't get away, literally wrapped his arms around her. She didn't want to be there, yet didn't want to be anywhere else. She wished she could keep the coldness that now edged away.

Jackson felt her tension ease from her body. "We have the whole day. What do you think we should do with it?"

"Who says I'm going to spend the day with you?"

"You want to."

She did. As she looked into his eyes, felt his arms around her, she didn't want to be anywhere else and the thought scared her. Both being with him, and being without him.

"I still can't believe you canceled the shoot. You, Mr. Workaholic."

"Some things are more important." He wished it weren't so, wished she didn't tear his insides apart when he thought about her but she did, and there was nothing he could do about it now.

CHAPTER FOURTEEN

Located on a tiny elbow shaped sandbar on the very eastern tip of Mexico's coast, Cancun lie in the state of Quintana Roo. Once a sleepy fishing village with a population of 120, it was now a bustling activity center for tourists with a population of half a million. Glittering resorts perched along the shore, golf courses inland, shopping, drinking, sun, sand and sea gave one many pleasures to partake in.

Maggie and Jackson chose a relaxing day far from the crowd. Between Cancun and Playa del Carmen on the Riviera Maya, Tres Rios was an ecological park of low subtropical jungle and mangrove along the coast. A natural reserve with minimal intrusions from man left one with a feeling of serene paradise along Mexico's Caribbean coast, and one could explore in many ways. By foot, kayak, canoe, bicycle or fins.

On the large white-sand beach you could walk along and seek shell offerings of the ocean or take a trek on horseback. They were on their own to discover the beauty within the park, and the beauty of each other as it wasn't crowded that day and they seemed to be on their own.

On horseback they trotted along playfully with a guide in unspoiled beauty, then swam and frolicked in crystalline waters. Afterwards, they relaxed in a hammock along the shore where Maggie fell asleep in the comfort of his arms as gentle ocean breezes caressed her skin. When she woke she couldn't imagine anywhere else on earth she'd rather be.

The hammock hung beneath a large straw roofed covering that not only would provide shade if it were sunny, but served to keep the rain off them when it came.

She reached across Jackson, held his wrist and pulled the knob up on his watch.

"What are you doing?" He asked confused.

"I'm stopping time."

He laughed. "Unfortunately, the only thing that's going to do is cause us to miss the ship."

"I don't care," she snuggled closer into him, crossed her leg over his.

"You're not making this easy to lie in this hammock with you. While you've been lying there sound asleep I've been trying to stop thinking about you."

Maggie kissed his chest and rubbed her soft hand across his stomach, let it rest precariously just below the elastic of his swim shorts.

"Whoa. I think we'd better get up, I for one need a dip in the water."

Maggie held tight when he tried to move. "This is all this relationship is going to be, pure unadulterated sex, so the least you could do is oblige me."

"I'm not sure the other guests in this park would understand if we were caught and I told them I was merely trying to fulfill my duties."

"There are hardly any other guests here to worry about. We're back here in seclusion, who's going to see?"

The instability of the hammock prevented them from remaining there but the soft sand beneath, surrounded by underbrush and trees gave them a perfect spot to explore one another again. A constant need for him was something she'd never known. He fulfilled her lust with a fiery passion she was sure no other two people had ever experienced before, was sure it was only them with a connection of skin that made her feel like she'd never felt before. Maggie had never acted that way with any other man that had been in her life. Maybe the difference with the others was that she looked for a relationship, sought something that could be her future and she never found it. With Jackson she looked for nothing. This was what it was, each fulfilled a sexual need for the other and it was enough for the moment.

Situated under a beautiful palapa, they dined on excellent cuisine and enjoyed a few frozen drinks. It only enhanced her sexually driven mood around him and another secluded spot along the shore became a safe haven for them as he satisfied her once again.

"I may not make it home alive if you keep going at this rate." Jackson sat in the sand with one leg bent, rested his arm atop it as Maggie sat in front of him, her back leaned against his chest.

"Me? You make it sound like I'm alone in this. I didn't hear you object."

"And you won't. I'll deal with being dead next week. Think of the days we missed, all you had to do was tell me you were interested in sex alone," he kissed her neck softly.

"I couldn't tell you anything, you wouldn't talk to me." Maggie held his hand in hers.

Jackson could smell her hair, her skin. Even so soon after making love he wanted her again although he'd been completely fulfilled just moments ago. For the second time in less than a few hours, and yet he already wanted more. Maggie brought to life something beneath his skin that made him feel alive. Something about her heightened every sensation as if electricity coursed through his veins and all he needed was for her to turn the switch. Just to sit next to her was enough to feel it. Again, as he'd done several times, he wondered when or if he had ever felt this way.

He already knew it would be difficult to have Maggie, to be so intimate with someone so genuine and then have to walk away. Often reminded himself over and over that it was the way it had to be. It was what they both wanted, what they both silently agreed upon and nothing more.

Jackson thought about other alternatives, it crossed his mind there could possibly be a way to continue when they got home. They lived in the same city, it would be easy to continue a sexual relationship that was satisfying to both of them. But he was bound by other things, knew it would have to come to an end.

"I might have to start rethinking my assignments, I normally don't get to come to places like this. You've probably been all over these islands several times, haven't you?" Maggie asked as she looked out to serene beauty.

"I have, but I've only seen it through my camera lens. I've never really taken the time to enjoy it much, looked at it as just another assignment." For Jackson, there was never anyone to enjoy it with, that was in the day he was a very solitary man and that man seemed a distant memory now.

"Is that my hint that you're all work and no play? Sitting here like this I find that hard to believe."

"Guess I've never had the chance to sit here like this."

Maggie thought about the chances he could have had, the models that threw themselves at him only to be ignored, women more than willing to sit in his arms on an isolated beach. Was there someone at home he was committed and devoted to? A girlfriend he was so totally in love with he saw nothing else? The wife that was rumored?

He said he didn't want to be bothered by the models he worked with. That was why he didn't mind the rumors that floated around about him, kept them all at bay, kept him out of their claws. But why? Maggie had to wonder now. Wasn't it every man's dream to be surrounded by models that thought nothing of jumping in bed with this handsome, young, virile man? He could have his pick yet he distanced himself. Wasn't he interested in beautiful women? Her mind asked the questions, her writing reporter's brain went around in circles.

"What are you thinking about?" Jackson asked quietly, his mouth whispered close to her ear.

Maggie didn't answer with what was on her mind at that particular moment, but she answered honestly with what she'd been thinking previously as they made love. "How free this feels. How I can give myself so completely to you and I know how it ends, there's no question. It's like true freedom."

"Maybe we can at least send Christmas cards every year. Just as friends, since we're not interested in each other."

"I can't promise you that," Maggie pulled his hand to her face and kissed it as she entwined her fingers in his.

"That's right," he laughed. "We promised no promises."

"Can I make an exception to that?"

"No exceptions," he teased.

"I have to make one. I just wanted to say that I promise I'll never forget this."

"That I agree to and can promise the same, Maggie," he whispered against her as they looked out to turquoise Caribbean Sea. Over the horizon they'd come, neither had been prepared for what they'd found on this side.

****

Derek made her feel bolder than she was. He insisted she drive the 4x4 jeep to experience it and once she came to the conclusion the rutted dirt roads weren't going to get any better, she drove as the rest of them did. Fast and carefree as she dodged iguanas, screamed, then laughed. When they reached their destination of a secluded beach she was happy to hand the keys back over to Derek.

"I'm through, it was fun and I can say I did it."

"And did it well, I'm impressed." Derek smiled and took the keys.

"Maybe I picked up some things from Maggie, she drives like a maniac."

The dust and dirt from the road made the water feel that much more refreshing when they took a swim immediately, then an overhead downpour of rain drove them under the protection of a covered cabana.

"We're already soaked." Derek laughed.

"But that rain is cold." Nicole had probably gotten too much sun over the last few days and a slight burn still lingered, gave her the chills at times. Goosebumps appeared on her arms and she tried to hold them close to her.

"We don't even have a dry towel."

Without waiting for her to stop him he took off for the large covering where dry towels could be found, grabbed several, then ran back again and wrapped her inside their warmth. She took one and began to dry his hair and face.

"You're really soaked now." The closeness of him made her shiver, it wasn't her sunburn skin now.

"Are you still cold?"

"Not really."

Derek slowly put his hand behind her neck and pulled her to him. Placed his lips upon hers and it was barely a whisper of a kiss before he pulled away.

"I'm sorry," he apologized, always so respectful.

"Don't be, I wish you'd quit apologizing." Nicole touched his face but he made no move to kiss her again, so she pulled him to her this time.

This time it was more than the slightest of touches. This time Nicole gave him the kind of kiss she'd been longing to give, the kind she'd dreamed about. As the rain poured outside, they made out like two teenagers inside until Derek finally had to put a stop to it.

"I think I might have to stand outside in the cold rain." They found themselves lying down on the towels placed on the sand and he stood up quickly, forced himself to pull away from her and step outside.

Nicole laughed. "You're getting soaked again."

"But you don't understand, I need to, this feels much better. Well not much better, but comfortable. I was getting uncomfortable." He stammered the words, decided he needed to move further away from her so went and got them a drink.

"Is this my consolation prize since you don't want to kiss me anymore?" She playfully teased.

"That certainly isn't the case. I'm afraid I was getting greedy and wanted more than a kiss."

"And there's something wrong with that?" Nicole said brazenly, she too wanted more.

"I respect you Nicole, I'd never want you to think otherwise."

"I never would," she pulled a rope that untied the front curtain and let the flap give them more privacy, they would need it.

Then she willingly seduced him, made him throw his true gentleman values aside, as she assured him it was something she wanted. Nicole didn't know how much she actually did until she was naked in his arms and he gently made love to her in such a slow sensual way it drove her mad.

****

Not having any intimacy during the day only made their sexual tension greater in the evenings, but that day, Kyla and Alan didn't need to feel secretive as it was only the two of them. In an air conditioned bus they toured Cancun, relaxed on a beach, then enjoyed a late afternoon lunch in a local restaurant that offered native cuisine.

"As much as I love Maggie and Nicole, and my brother and his friend's, I'm glad to have you all to myself today." Alan took her hand in his, glad they had the freedom to act the way two people in love acted.

"It's been great, hasn't it? I keep wondering if the boy's are staying out of trouble though." She referred to Randy and his friends and they laughed.

"Hard to say, I guess we can only hope. Like having kids to watch over."

"Randy has a head on his shoulders. And he's so completely in love he won't do anything to jeopardize that."

"And you, Kyla?" The words came before Alan could stop them. It had been on his mind as the week was winding to a close and his impatience was beginning to crowd him.

She was quiet for a few moments before she answered. "I can say now, I never stopped loving you."

"And I never stopped loving you, I love you more today than I ever have. But not loving each other was never something we had to deal with."

Kyla looked away from him, she didn't want to discuss things she wasn't ready to discuss. Wouldn't it all just flow together somehow? Miraculously they found each other again, wasn't there something miraculous that could happen to make it work out this time?

"We have to talk, Kyla." Alan said it with urgency, his guilt had grown and he couldn't keep it to himself any longer.

"Not now. We've had such a lovely day and..."

"If not now when? We've got one day left and then we'll be home."

"Then I'll stay in Texas a few days." Kyla tried to postpone it as best she could.

"A few days? Is that what you think I want? Is that what you want? A few more days of being in love and you'll go on with your life again?"

"I don't know what I want," she sighed. "But I can't figure it out now on the spot like this."

"You're avoiding it."

"I'm prolonging it."

Alan took both of her hands in his. Maybe it was the wrong place, maybe it was the wrong way to tell her, but he could hold back no longer and blurted it out quickly.

"Kyla, I'm engaged to be married," he held tight to her hands when she immediately tried to pull away, saw silent shock then instant anger as it flashed across her face. "I've been wanting to…"

"You took me to bed and you were engaged?"

"When I saw you and felt everything I've always felt, maybe it's a poor excuse, but I couldn't help myself."

Kyla jerked her hands away from him and got up from the table, as she did she knocked a plate onto the floor but didn't pay the slightest bit of attention as she rushed away. "You son of a bitch."

Alan threw down enough money to pay for several meals and a new set of china and chased after her.

"Kyla, wait!"

"For what?" Her head spun around and there was fierceness in her eyes, she was poised for battle. "An invitation to the wedding? I'll be busy that day, or did you think I could go on the honeymoon and stay in the next room to be your mistress."

"Kyla, I saw you and I saw our second chance for a future."

"You saw me and you saw an easy bed partner for a week away from your girlfriend."

"It isn't like that." Alan tried to grab her arm to stop her and she roughly pulled it away from him.

"Don't touch me."

"Will you listen to me for a minute?" He tried to plead with her.

"Listen to what? More lies? You're an engaged man who took a lover, that's explanation enough, I don't need to hear more." Kyla didn't let him stop her, or join her in the cab she jumped into and instructed the driver to speed off as fast as he could.

CHAPTER FIFTEEN

Kyla couldn't remember the cab ride that took her back to the ship. Cancun whizzed by her in a blur as her torn emotions now split in two and cracked completely, left her with a single emotion of pain. How could Alan have done this to her? Engaged, and he'd carried on as if they had the possibility of a future again. All when he knew after the ship docked he would go home to a future wife and wedding plans. She would go back to her empty house.

As much as she blamed him for her pain, she had to blame herself also. How stupid she was to assume he was the same loving man she'd known him to be, when obviously he merely took the opportunity for an easy shipboard romance. It wasn't like she made it hard for him.

Without question, without an indication he was committed to anyone else she went head first into something familiar. Only to discover he was so completely unfamiliar after all. He wasn't the same loving man she assumed, only a stranger who took advantage of what she offered. Only herself to blame for a stupid mistake she'd have never made with a stranger, her trust had betrayed her, Alan had betrayed her.

As the rain pelted down, everyone around her ran for cover or towards the ship. She seemed not to notice as she stepped from the cab and walked slowly in her dazed state, didn't notice or hear Randy who called to her from a covered bar.

"Kyla!" When she didn't hear, several of them repeated her name in playful unison and everyone within twenty feet heard except their target.

Randy watched as she continued by and a feeling in the pit of his stomach told him she now knew of Alan's unforeseen dilemma. Randy was close to his brother, knew the complicated agony he suffered throughout the week of when to tell her and what to say to make it understandable for him to delay the news. Her reaction wasn't a surprise.

"Want me to run out there?" His friend asked from beside him.

"No," Randy answered, thought about it himself, thought maybe if he talked to her he could make it understandable somehow, defend his brother and his reasons. But Randy ultimately knew it was something they would have to deal with themselves and nothing he said or did would make a difference to the choices they had to make.

When she reached the room, Kyla closed the door and leaned her back against it then closed her eyes as if she could shut it all out that way. Her clothes and hair were soaked, rainwater dripped from every inch of skin but on her face it was mixed with the tears that escaped her eyes. Kyla tried to remember the last time she cried about anything and couldn't place when. She hadn't cried over her first divorce or her second. There had never been a man who moved her to tears, except Alan, and she couldn't stop them now as they streamed down her face. The pains in her heart a physical jab as if it had been punctured with a knife.

Only Alan had ever made her cry. So long ago when their life together ended, and now as her second chance turned out to be a farce, a lie. The unexpected surprise of finding him again now revealed as nothing but the anguish of knowing he moved on with someone else. On the verge of starting a life with a woman he obviously loved enough to ask to be his wife, obviously not enough to be faithful to, but committed nonetheless.

Married twice herself, Kyla couldn't fault him that. But he hadn't been in her life then, she certainly never led him on to believe there was hope and possibility when all the while she'd been devoted to another. It tortured her to know that he never loved her enough to be upfront and honest, now turned their relationship into a deceitful lie. Nothing but a seedy affair he would have ended in a few days.

****

Nicole liked the feel of Derek's arm around her, then the feel of his hand in hers as they walked under the cover of a few stores before going back to the ship. It had been a long time since she felt like she'd been in an actual relationship, and that's what it felt like to her.

As odd as it was, she didn't have any indication to believe she would ever see him again after the ship docked, and she felt okay with that for now. Nicole wouldn't rush into asking about any possible future between them, didn't want to appear clingy and needy, but it crossed her mind what would become of them, if anything.

That she wasn't sure of, what she did know was the feeling of being naked in his arms. The whispers of softness against her ear as they made love with a quiet passion. She'd never done something like that before so soon after meeting someone, she'd never been that kind of woman who would, but it felt natural and easy to do so. She would recall it with vivid detail over and over again.

They were rushed getting back to the ship, had taken every moment they could together and though Derek didn't have to take the elevator, he walked Nicole there and waited with her, pulled her into his arms quickly as no one else was there.

"Would your friends understand if I stole you for dinner again this evening?"

"They would," she answered, so they set it up to meet at eight.

"I don't want to wait until our coffee date, I can't."

Nicole had begun to feel a little edgy after they'd been so intimate, felt as if she wasn't being honest with him, and feeling guilty that she hadn't told him about her children. Perhaps it was the wrong time or the wrong way, but she felt urgency, as if she had to get it off her mind quickly.

"I have children," she blurted out just before the elevator reached them.

He looked at her in silence, unsure for a moment of her words. "You," he paused for a moment. "How many?"

"Two wonderful children, Anthony and Elizabeth, I should have told you earlier, but…" The elevator doors opened and Nicole slipped in. "We'll talk about it at dinner?"

She was a coward. She'd told him quickly then ran off so she didn't have to face his reaction. What was his reaction? Nichole thought to herself now. His face was blank, she hadn't seen a reaction, not an obvious one anyway and she couldn't really recall one. She'd shocked him by blurting it out so quickly but it had to be revealed.

Nicole went to the room but found it empty and noticed Kyla's bag there so knew she was back from the day, and she decided to seek her out before she showered. They would often linger on the deck chairs by the pool, or somewhere on the top deck, but she looked everywhere and didn't see her. She and Alan must be in hiding somewhere, she hoped they had a good a day as she herself had.

As she lingered in the open air and enjoyed the last of the day, she noticed Derek on the deck below talking to an attractive woman by the pool bar and wondered who she was. Her dress would indicate she was a member of the staff, but it didn't really tell her exactly in what capacity, or maybe she could have guessed. She would have waved but he didn't see her, his concentration on nothing but the woman and Nicole didn't think about the tinge of jealousy she felt. Absurd, she told herself. You made love to him, you've no right to feel possessive and jealous, and who she was isn't any of your business. The thought of their quiet dinner together bought a smile but she still wondered about the woman as they walked through the doors to the inside together, still in deep conversation.

****

Jackson's arm was around her and Maggie leaned into him and closed her eyes. She felt comfortable, content, even with the sense of urgency they endured. "Are we going to make it?"

"We're almost there, don't fall asleep now. We'll have to run to catch the ship."

"The entire fault lies with you that we're late. It's your watch."

"You're the one who stopped it," he defended himself and laughed as he thought back to the moment they realized he hadn't started it again, and they now had less than five minutes left to make the ship before it sailed without them.

"We could stay in Cancun. I have an expense account remember? We can call Wilma and tell her we've been delayed for a week, missed the boat and can't get a flight out." It sounded a good plan to her, delay the inevitable of parting in a few days and extend it.

Even to Jackson it sounded good, but they couldn't avoid the unavoidable. "Sure, my other scheduled clients, who booked months in advance I might add, would understand when I tell them I wouldn't be there next week."

"Who do you do most of your work for? Any one client, or are they mostly varied."

"Are you ever out of interview mode?"

Maggie raised her head and looked at him. "It's conversation."

"Conversation that would make it to print?"

"Possibly, but in all likelihood the probability is very low, you still haven't told me anything about you to print."

"I keep telling you this article isn't about me."

"You're an important aspect, without a photographer there would be no shoot, without a shoot there would be no behind the scenes. It really all revolves around you."

He shook his head. "You make me sound much more important than I am."

She looked to him and decided to ask something she'd been curious about. Knew she should throw it off as the other rumors that surrounded this mysterious man but it came out anyway. "I heard you were married before," then she laughed lightly as if she thought it was a joke. "Even heard you were married now."

Did she notice a sudden change in his expression? Or was it her imagination? Maggie couldn't be sure because it was so quick, but his voice was not as soft as it had been moments ago. When he answered she thought she heard a slight edge, or was it her imagination?

"I don't want to be with Maggie the journalist, I want to be with Maggie the person."

"Is it true?" She persisted and felt his arm tighten.

Jackson was not prepared to discuss his life with her at that moment, not in a quick cab ride with the pressure of missing the ship ahead of them. He would be saved from answering as the cab pulled up as close to the dock as possible and they had to run through the rain, made it to the open entrance just in time as they were about to close up the doors. They were laughing as they entered.

"You two almost had to take boat to meet us." The door attendant said as he too laughed.

"No," Maggie teased. "We should have missed the ship and stayed here, but he wouldn't let me."

"You enjoy your day in Cancun then?" The man asked with a smile on his face.

"It was bearable," Maggie sighed and joked with her comment.

"Yeah, I managed to struggle through it." Jackson playfully pinched her behind out of view of others.

The attendant looked a little confused as they got into the elevator and the doors shut. Jackson pushed the button for their floor then leaned into her and pressed her against the wall.

"One more kiss before I'll have to stay away from you."

"Not for long."

"Long enough to drive me crazy," he pressed his lips to hers, felt the tenderness of her lips he'd come to need like water. When he pulled away he knew they had to take their chances, it could always be played off, and he didn't want to wait until much later to see her so he took advantage of the empty hall and pulled her into his room.

Maggie didn't think about the odd moment in the cab when she asked about marriage, it still haunted her, but it wasn't what she thought about when she fell into his arms and his bed once more. Jackson had a way of consuming her. Every thought, every emotion went into him, and everything else was pushed to the back of her mind.

CHAPTER SIXTEEN

Nicole couldn't contain herself at the thought of having dinner with Derek and more alone time to enjoy. An evening with a man she actually knew she enjoyed. They wouldn't sit in silence and wonder what to say to each other, they wouldn't wonder what would happen at the end. Would he try to kiss her? Would he not? She thought about the afternoon and a comforting warm feeling ran through her. Even though it wasn't like her to have such intimate contact with someone she basically just met, she enjoyed it beyond belief. It seemed so natural for them to be so intimate and she felt no guilt in doing so.

She thought about him the entire time she showered, changed clothes, applied make up and did her hair to absolute perfection. With the approval of both Maggie who couldn't say enough, and Kyla who assured her with a smile she looked fantastic, Nicole went on her way with the uneasy feeling that Kyla only seemed to pretend to be happy for her. There was something that lay beneath the surface she couldn't quite figure out.

When asked, Kyla laughed it off, said she was fine. And as Nicole looked to Maggie, she knew Maggie had the same feeling she did. There was something amiss that Kyla didn't want to discuss, but each of them let her have the space she needed. Both thought to themselves it was Kyla contemplating her feelings, her future, as the trip wound down. Neither had any suspicion of the blow Alan had dropped that afternoon.

Nicole arrived at the French restaurant to find Derek hadn't called ahead for a reservation, but they had a table available due to a cancellation and she was escorted to it, but decided to wait for him before ordering anything. She'd been a bit early and didn't think anything until she looked at her watch and realized she'd waited ten minutes, then twenty, then thirty. After an hour, she decided sitting alone in a romantic restaurant waiting for someone who obviously wasn't showing up looked pathetic. Nicole paid her tab for the few drinks and left.

All kinds of things went through her mind. Maybe he was ill, maybe he'd forgotten, she thought of everything to give him the benefit of the doubt but the main thing that kept returning was the fact she'd revealed her children. It sent men running, surely Derek wasn't like that, surely it hadn't been that, but Nicole had to admit she could think of nothing else.

And the woman she'd seen him with kept invading her thoughts also. Who was she? Someone he found himself attracted to after he had what he wanted from her? Although deep down she knew he wasn't that type of man, it crossed her mind. Then again, she didn't really know what type of man he actually was, she didn't know him at all.

Yet she'd thrown herself at him, he'd gotten what he wanted and now was off to greener pastures. What had she expected? He was basically a stranger she knew nothing about. As much as Nicole tried to talk herself out of it, the back of her mind convinced her she'd been taken advantage of, more so when she met at their usual late night time for coffee and Derek never showed up.

She tried to make excuses to herself why she had to wander the ship before she went back to her room. Of course she happened to pass through all the public places and a few lounges. She knew it was ridiculous, what would she do if she saw him with someone else anyway? She never saw him, but walked into the Wine Bar to find Kyla sitting alone and it was obvious she'd been there quite awhile.

When Nicole asked the reason, all she got was a sad smile and words she didn't understand.

"Stupid me, same broken heart, and stupider still, over the same stupid man. I feel brainless. Isn't age supposed to make one wiser? How come I feel so stupid?"

Nicole tried to talk to her, asked for specifics, but got no more than confusion. She didn't reveal any details to her dilemma, only rambled on with words that were senseless to her. Then Maggie entered and revealed to Nicole in private she'd run into Alan who explained things.

"We had a disagreement this afternoon," Alan said when Maggie questioned the mood Kyla had been in.

"About?" She raised her eyebrows with concern.

"I told her I was engaged to be married."

Maggie stood stone silent at the revelation and then found her voice again. "I'd say that caused a little more than a disagreement."

"I'm in love with her, Maggie, when I saw her I looked at it as our second chance when I knew she still felt the same about me. Had I told her upfront she would have avoided me all week as if she hadn't even seen me. I know it was stupid but I didn't feel like I had another choice."

After that, Jackson understood when she reneged on any plans he may have had for them and went in search of her friend.

"Bartender? Can we have what she's having?" Maggie asked politely.

Nicole cringed when she saw the bottle of Scotch. Couldn't she have been drowning her sorrows in something easy and frozen? She moaned, "Oh my."

"You can't drink that, Nicole you hate scotch." Kyla said.

"But I like you more than I hate it, and I won't stop until you do. Besides," she accepted the glass and took a long sip through a scrunched face. "Scotch might be just what I need tonight."

Kyla looked to her then looked to Maggie. "Ladies, prepare yourself, this could be a long night. I've been here awhile and I'm not feeling better. We might be here for days."

Not one of them mentioned the problem. It remained silent between them, nothing they could do or say would solve it that evening, would make Kyla feel any better or come to any conclusions or make any sense. So nothing was said as the three of them sat in the fairly quiet atmosphere for some time then slowly emerged from a subtle calm to boisterous rowdiness as they joked and laughed. Scotch made them lose all control as the hours passed and when the bar closed, the bartender offered them help to their cabin, which they politely refused. The three held onto each other to stay upright as they made their way alone.

"I don't think it's us. It's the ship, there's a storm." Nicole said as she tried to point towards the sea on the open deck they walked for fresh air.

"If it were a storm, wouldn't it be raining on us?" Kyla looked up to the clear sky so full of twinkling stars it brightened the dark night.

"We're special, it doesn't rain on us, we're special... special... dry people." Maggie could think of nothing more to say than nonsense and they all laughed again.

As they made their way down the hall to their room all of them were at least cognizant of the fact people were sleeping and tried to be as quiet as they could.

"Shhhh..."

"That wasn't me," Nicole said. "It was Kyla."

"I didn't say anything." Then she stopped in the middle of the hall. "I don't think so anyway. It was Maggie."

"What did I do? I didn't do it." Maggie defended herself against something she didn't know anything about.

When they finally made it to their cabin no one could get the card in properly and they began laughing, making it even more difficult. They jumped in surprise when a hand came between two of them, took one of the cards and easily slipped it in to unlock the door.

"Jackson." Maggie beamed as her heart took a jolt at the sight of him, she had missed him terribly in the short time apart, probably even more so than normal due to the large consumption of alcohol.

"A knight in shining armor." Nicole commented. "Ladies in distress and here you are."

"Where did you park your horse? Aren't you supposed to have a white horse? Do they allow animals on the ship?" Kyla squinted her eyes to see him better.

He'd heard them as they passed his door, had been awake wondering where Maggie was since she cut their evening short. Now he laughed at their lack of sobriety.

"Are you ladies in for the evening?" He asked with a smile. "Or should I expect to have to come back out and open your door again?"

"We're in, and out." Kyla answered as she hit the bed immediately, her head rested atop the chocolate mint placed on her pillow.

Nicole began to undress without thinking of Jackson standing in the open doorway and he turned to hastily make his escape.

"Good night," he said quickly and was out in the hall in a flash.

"No, wait." Maggie protested and went with him.

When they reached his room he was holding her up. Tried to talk her into letting him tuck her into her own bed, back in her own room, but she refused.

"I missed you," she admitted. "I thought about you all night."

"I missed you too." He held her face in his hands and chuckled. "Let's get you into bed."

When Maggie rolled over the next morning she moaned. The ship seemed to be rocking but when she remembered the night before, she knew it wasn't the ship but her head that seemed to shift back and forth.

"Morning sunshine, how are we feeling?"

"We? Do you feel like this too?"

"That privilege solely belongs to you." Jackson laughed at her which only made her moan louder. "I guess that's not true, it's something you share with Nicole and Kyla I'm sure."

"Kyla," Maggie said softly, remembered why they'd gotten drunk.

Jackson sat down beside her on the bed, he'd been up and dressed for hours. "I'm sure she's feeling the pain. I hope there's enough aspirin on this ship for you three to share."

"She was drunk last night, but I'm sure in the light of day she's going to see a different picture. I've got to go make sure..." Maggie rose quickly then groaned and held her head.

"Hold on, what's the rush?"

"Hers isn't just sex, Jackson, hers is love."

"What are you talking about?" He was baffled by her words.

"You and I have this perfect thing, just sex with no feelings involved and no emotion. When this ship docks tomorrow morning we say goodbye, its ideal, isn't it?"

All night he'd thought of nothing but Maggie and the possibilities of changing the rules. Maybe pursue something further with the incredible woman he never thought he'd meet, never thought existed, but her words shut all those feelings down again.

"Isn't it?" She repeated and waited for his answer.

He glanced casually at her as if he hadn't been paying attention. "Sure, yeah."

"It's different with Kyla. She finds Alan again, realizes they're still in love with each other after all these years apart, and then yesterday he tells her he's engaged to another woman. And he's been sleeping with Kyla all week."

"You know Alan, is he the type of guy to casually sleep with someone for a week and go back to his fiancé as if nothing happened?"

"Of course not. He said he was afraid if he told her upfront she would have avoided him, and he would have missed any second chance they might have had."

"Sounds plausible, but that's a judgment call she'll have to make. I don't think it was his intention to deceive her by omitting the fact he was committed to another woman. And I don't know Kyla that well, but she doesn't strike me as the kind to hear a man was taken and go for it anyway."

"I hate to take the men's side on this, but I think Alan's right with his explanation, and so are you to agree. She would have said 'Great, nice to see you again' and that would have been the extent of it."

"Can't really fault him, he felt like he didn't have another choice."

Maggie looked at him with an odd expression. "A man with some actual sense, wherever did I find you?"

After Maggie showered she went back to her cabin to find Kyla still sleeping where she'd fallen the night before. She was fully clothed and her head still lay atop the chocolate mint, which had melted onto her face and pillow and chocolate goo smeared everywhere. Then she found Nicole sitting at a table on the outside deck having coffee.

"And how are you feeling this morning?" Maggie laughed, knew she felt as bad as she did and Nicole agreed.

"As bad as you." She wore her sunglasses even though the sky was cloudy.

"It's a good thing we're at sea all day. I just checked on Kyla, she's still sound asleep, will be for the rest of the day. She started way earlier than us. I feel guilty for not pressing when I saw her mood, I just thought she was beginning to think about what she was going to do about finding Alan again."

"Yeah," Nicole agreed. "I feel guilty now too. I was caught up in my own thoughts about dinner with Derek."

"How did that go by the way?"

"It didn't." Nicole said with a huff.

"What happened?"

"Guess he got what he wanted from me and moved on." She explained the intimacy they shared, then her revelation, and then seeing him with someone else, assumed his interest was now drawn elsewhere and she was stood up.

"I can't believe that, that's so odd. He didn't seem like that type of guy at all."

"I for one will be the first to admit I relapsed and thought I'd actually found a decent one out of the bunch, even if I hadn't a clue what was to become of us. Guess now I know any sort of a future wasn't an option anyway, and to think I wasted precious time thinking about it."

Her friend looked so disenchanted, Maggie saw it there in her face, the sadness of her expression even if she couldn't see her eyes through the dark glasses. Casual, uncomplicated sex had taken its toll on both Nicole and Kyla and Maggie had to wonder about herself. She had no right to expect anything else from Jackson but the more they went along, the more she began to think about other possibilities and now tried to shut them out even more. It would only set her up for the disappointment that was sure to come.

They sat for a while and talked about the situation with Kyla, knew it was something Kyla would have to work out on her own as there was nothing they could do. Maggie suspected that if she didn't forgive Alan, she would use that as reason she wouldn't give up her fast paced job and career. Use it as the excuse she wouldn't have to. Maggie had to wonder if she had been considering it, the small town in Texas Alan came from wouldn't be fast enough for her and perhaps now she felt like she wouldn't have to make that choice. It would be easiest to blame Alan for their demise and Maggie suspected she'd already set in her mind a closure to it, no matter Maggie would try to make her see Alan's point.

When Jackson joined them, the three sat for close to an hour until Nicole left to check on Kyla again and take a nap herself. She rose slowly because if she rose too fast she got dizzy. "I certainly am thankful for this lazy day at sea, I feel like it's going to be a totally wasted day."

When they were alone, Maggie took Jackson's hand in hers underneath the table, entwined her fingers with his as she looked at him with longing in her eyes. "It doesn't have to be a totally wasted day. I think I need to go back to bed too, but sleep wasn't what I was thinking of."

If it was all she would have with Jackson, Maggie wanted to take advantage of every moment before she'd have to let it go. With the passion she now craved from him as if it was the only thing to quench a long dry thirst, they made love several times.

She'd fallen asleep and when she woke he was showered and dressed again.

"Where are you going?"

"We have one more shoot, Maggie, and I know you don't have to be there, but it would be impossible to accomplish without me and my camera."

"See? I told you you're imperative to this article, the most important thing." She stretched and grabbed the belt loop of his pants to pull him closer.

"I'm just the guy with the camera." He sighed and sat down on the edge of the bed even though he knew it would be difficult to get back up and leave her there.

"Are you ever going to give me something to use in the article? Or is it wasted breath to keep asking you anything at all."

"People don't need to know anything about me."

"They may not need to, but what if they want to. Say people like me? Say I promise it won't make it to print, tell me something I might want to know about you. And not the technicalities of shutter speed on a dawn shoot." She waited for him to say something but he just stared at her for a few seconds, in his eyes she saw so much he wouldn't, or couldn't say. A look that told her he was much deeper and more mysterious now than he had been when they first met.

She shared his bed, intimate moments being as close as two people could physically be. She craved him, yearned for him, and knew nothing about him, not much more than his name.

"You want to complicate things? I thought you wanted to keep it as simple as possible, this and nothing more."

"Maybe I've changed my mind. Knowing something personal about you doesn't commit us to anything, does it?"

So maybe he should have told her of his life then. It was a thought but he was pressed for time, had less than thirty minutes to set up equipment and prepare for the shoot. It wasn't the right moment, there never seemed to be a right moment to tell her he was committed to something, to someone. There were things she should know about him but it would take much longer to explain than the few moments he had. Then again, if this was all they would have, was there a need for explanations?

"You've changed your mind about keeping it simple?" He asked.

"I don't know," she spoke the truth. Her emotions when she thought of it went in all kinds of directions and she truly didn't know an answer to the question. Did she want anything more? Just when she simplified her life and vowed to keep men from it, he'd come barreling in to shake and stir her solid ground. Was it only a sexual desire? The intimacy they shared so well together? Was there anything else under the surface of that?

Jackson spoke softly. "Maybe it's something we'll talk about when we both know."

He kissed her lightly. He did feel the need to talk, wanted to tell her everything, but again, other responsibilities waited and he pulled away from her though she tried to hold on, and he jumped out of the way when she tried to stop him. He was weak, wouldn't be able to leave at all if he sat one second longer knowing her soft skin was just under the light cover of the sheet.

"That wasn't even a real kiss." She beckoned him to return but he stood at the door and refused.

"So I owe you one."

"Come back soon?"

He stood for a long time, the temptation was great and she smiled, knew he hesitated, but he didn't give in. "As soon as I can."

"Hey," she stopped him just as he was about to walk out the door. "I'm still not interested in you, ya know."

CHAPTER SEVENTEEN

When Kyla did wake, her hangover was not the first thing on her mind, it was Alan who centered her thoughts. Engaged to be married, the thought of it repeated itself over and over again, and she tried to tell herself it wasn't real but there was no ignoring the facts. He deceived her, lied to her. Somewhere inside she felt herself close off, felt everything she'd been feeling the past week recoil and go away to hide somewhere. She would get past this, she kept repeating to herself. It wasn't the end of her world and she wouldn't let Alan destroy her because she was stronger than that. Kyla was anxious now to get home and immerse herself in her work.

She and Nicole wandered the ship that afternoon. They grabbed a casual lunch at the buffet, relaxed in the cloudy warm breeze and read a book, and napped in lounge chairs until Maggie joined them and insisted they do something constructive. She forced them to partake in some of the ships sea day activities. Nothing too strenuous, as no one had the energy for it, but they played the jackpot bingo game and watched a few shows, as it was about all they could handle.

Tiffany and Simone caught up with them and those two joined them for the art auction. She knew with the two being there the photo shoot was obviously over and she wondered where Jackson was and found herself anxious to see him again, then she had to force her mind to not think about him. How foolish, how ridiculous she couldn't sit here like a grown adult woman and think of the art, think of the nice afternoon she was having with her friends.

So Maggie partook in a few glasses of the champagne that flowed and concentrated on the art instead of where her thoughts wanted to take her. Both Tiffany and Simone seemed truly interested in learning about the paintings from the auctioneer who was very knowledgeable about the work he presented, and Maggie shared what little she knew. Both of them bought a few small pieces and Maggie bid on a few small ones also while she waited for the one she really wanted to come up, but when it did she found it quickly got way over the limit she'd placed on herself and she was disappointed.

It was a beautiful work of an artist she wasn't familiar with but she loved his use of bright colors. She found herself one day standing before it when it was on display in the atrium as if she was mesmerized by it, it caught her and she stared as if she were in a trance. Bright tropical colors dominated the bold painting of abstract. Although it seemed a haphazard placement of the brush, at the same time, it made sense. She saw many pictures in it. It seemed you looked at it one way and saw a landscape of an empty beach, yet in another way it looked as if there were a city next to the beach. Yet another gave her a glimpse of Spanish style houses hanging over the edge of a marina filled with boats, rather than the white in the water looking like whitecaps on a vast sea.

"Aren't you bidding anymore?" Simone asked when she noticed Maggie wasn't.

"Going above and beyond my means, I foolishly thought I might have stood a chance."

Nicole was astounded. "I liked it too, but I never would have guessed how much it would go for and it's still climbing, shows how much I know about art."

"It's already up to four thousand dollars." Tiffany looked around to the bidders, there were only two now, one man and a woman. "It looks like they might be slowing down."

Kyla watched the action too, tried to pay attention and concentrate only on the art auction but it was difficult. "I don't know about slowing down, they're just going in increments of five hundred dollars now."

The auctioneer skillfully continued the bidding war going on and there was hesitation on both parts of the two bidders he had left when it reached above eight thousand dollars. He was about to award the winner at eighty five hundred dollars when a new bidder piped in.

"Ten thousand."

The auctioneer looked to the two previous bidders he had who both shook their heads in a negative motion and he announced the winner. "Going once, going twice," he paused and waited once more but it was obvious the other two were completely out. "Sold to the gentlemen, number three sixty eight for ten thousand dollars."

"No wonder you liked it, Miss Maggie," Simone commented. "That was Jackson that won that, and he must know his art, it was obviously something worth having."

"So it was." She looked over to see his handsome form leaning casually against the wall.

Maggie wasn't aware of when he'd entered the room, but she was aware of the flip of her stomach at the sight of him, but she nonchalantly only took a quick glance before her attention was back to the auctioneer who was about to start the next auction. How childish to act like strangers, but they barely glanced at each other, acted as if they didn't notice the other was there. He was gone soon after his purchase and they remained for the rest of the event, then the two models went one way and Maggie, Kyla and Nicole another.

It was the last she'd seen of him for the rest of the day, and not once did they run into Derek or Alan. Both Kyla and Nicole encouraged her to go off and leave them, but Maggie didn't.

"Who says I want to be with Jackson?"

"Why not? You're the smartest of the bunch, have a physical relationship and leave the emotions out of it, the safest kind of fling to have." Kyla's voice held the bitter hurt she felt at being blindsided. "I was encouraging you to put some emotion into it before, but now I've changed my mind. Emotion has no place in a relationship."

"Won't find me arguing with that," Nicole commented, she too feeling bitter.

They were feeling pain, and Maggie wasn't sure what she was feeling. Confusion, infatuation, whatever it was it engulfed her when she thought about it, though she tried not to. For dinner, Nicole decided to order room service and finish reading her book in the comfort of their room and when Maggie and Kyla were on their way to the dining room, Alan appeared and talked Kyla into joining him alone.

"You've been avoiding me all day," Alan said after they were seated. "We can't leave it like this."

"What is there to leave? You've had your way with me all week, now you'll go back to your fiancé, get married and live your happy little life." Kyla's voice was cold and unforgiving.

"You know the kind of person I am, Kyla, you have to know it wasn't my intention to lie to you."

Kyla was quiet as she looked about the dining room. Happy people with happy lives, and she wondered why she could never be one of them, it didn't seem to be in her cards. "Do you love her?"

"I thought I did."

"You wouldn't have asked her to marry you if you didn't."

He took her hand. "It isn't what I feel for you."

"Marry her, Alan, be happy. Nothing's changed with us."

"How can you say that?"

"What's changed?" Kyla asked sadly.

"That's the point, nothing about our feelings have changed. We still love each other just as much as we always did."

"And we still live hundreds of miles apart, loving each other isn't enough to make our lives work."

Alan heard her words as they seeped through his brain, he understood them well because she'd said the same thing so many years ago, and he knew he would be faced with the same thing he was faced with before. Whether she forgave him for not telling her of his impending marriage or not, Kyla was right, things hadn't changed. She was still unwilling to sacrifice her fast paced life for the slower atmosphere of his small hometown, and it hurt just as much now as it had then.

"As much as I'd love to wait forever, Kyla, I can't. When are you going to place more importance on us and a lifetime together?"

"I have a career, one that I'm proud of, one I've worked hard for."

"That wasn't the question I asked. I know you have a career, an important one, but is it going to be everything to you for the rest of your life? Is it going to be enough for the rest of your life?" Alan hesitated before he spoke again. "Not everyone ends up like the women you represent. You're so immersed in the bitterness of divorce you're scared of anything that could possibly end up that way."

"That isn't true." Kyla said in her defense.

"Isn't it? Think about it Kyla."

Maybe he had something. Kyla wasn't ready to fully agree, but in her subconscious she couldn't deny that what she dealt with day in and day out did have an effect on her outlook. She'd seen so many couples that once promised to love forever end up in her office in a bitter, hateful battle to the end. A fairytale world turned sour and angry.

Even though she'd been married twice, she hadn't devoted much emotion into it. Both of her husband's understood where her loyalties lie, and that was with her career and nothing else. They'd accepted it with ideas of changing her and left when reality proved otherwise. A relationship with Alan meant total commitment, and maybe it did frighten her a little, giving fully of her emotions and experiencing the devastation if it didn't work out.

He spoke as if he read her mind. "Kyla, I can't see into the future, I don't know how things would work out but I'm willing to take that chance for us to have a lifetime together. All I'm asking is the same from you. If you give it a try, at least we can spend the rest of our lives knowing we gave it a shot. If not, we spend the rest of our lives wondering what might have been."

"You can't leave the family business, especially not now since your father is gone. So you're not willing to move to me, you're asking me to sacrifice everything I've ever worked for and move to you."

"I am," he said honestly, knowing it was a lot to ask of her.

"So you want me to give up everything."

"I want you to give us a chance to have everything." Her 'everything' was so different than his.

****

Maggie was going to grab a quick bite at the buffet when she ran into Jackson who whisked her away to the ship's smaller, more intimate restaurant. The atmosphere was quiet and romantic and they didn't have to worry about being seen as it was late and both were sure they wouldn't run into anyone they knew. She looked across the candlelit table to Jackson who studied the menu.

Maggie felt as if she knew him, and at the same time felt as if she didn't know him at all. "I didn't know you had such good taste in art."

"Oh, the painting I bought?" He didn't look up from the menu as he said it casually. "I almost missed it, I got there halfway through the bidding. I happen to know that the artist, Joshua Canner, is only doing a certain number of abstracts. I bought it as an investment." Jackson paused and his voice became softer. "I probably went a little overboard, but some things only come along once in a lifetime."

It was quiet between them again but it was a comfortable quiet as he studied the menu and she studied his face. Chiseled, strong features that seemed carved of stone, yet she'd seen the softness. The way he looked at her from across a room, that small turn of his mouth that wasn't a full smile, but she knew it was meant just for her and it held secrets, the secret they shared between only them.

He looked up at her then and gifted her with one of those smiles. A slow draw of his lip, higher on one side than the other, and the intense gaze of his eyes pulled her to him.

"Maybe we should have gotten room service like Nicole," she said.

It had been tempting to him also but he laughed. "We had to come up for air, Maggie."

"If I didn't know any better, I would think you were tiring of me."

"Never." It wasn't an option for him now, wasn't a thought that crossed his mind. If anything it was opposite, he couldn't get enough.

"This is a little different for us, a quiet evening alone."

"You mean a quiet evening *out* alone."

Jackson ordered a bottle of their best champagne and Maggie got quiet. The ambiance, the mood of the restaurant as soft music surrounded them, and the moonlight as it crossed the open sea, it all came together and made her sentimental. It wasn't an emotion she was ready to deal with yet, had set in her mind she would deal with the aftermath when the time came, not beforehand.

"You don't like the champagne? Would you have preferred scotch?" He playfully referred to her drink of choice from the evening before when she didn't lift her glass.

"All of a sudden I feel like it's a celebration to our demise," she said then added. "And I'm not sure I'm ready to celebrate that."

"We're not celebrating our demise." Jackson took her hand in his, he knew it was something they had to discuss, and he wouldn't be able to walk away from her and suspected she felt the same. "We're just celebrating this night."

"See? It's our last night and you're celebrating, you can't wait to be rid of me," Maggie teased and playfully pulled her hand away.

"No, we're celebrating this night and we'll talk about things later."

"Talk about things? Are you finally going to give me something to use in this article other than the fact that you don't come from a family of twelve children, you deserve a little credit for being a decent man, and you're knowledgeable about art? I'm going to use that by the way."

"I've no doubt you will."

"So let's talk about more. Have you always collected art?" Maggie encouraged him but he went back to the menu.

She knew he meant they would talk about where they were headed, maybe talk about a relationship, so why was she trying to avoid it by directing the conversation to the article? Why didn't she just head full throttle into a discussion about them and what would happen to them? Because Maggie was actually afraid to discuss what she was feeling, afraid to admit there was anything real to the emotions that seemed out of control now.

Maggie admitted only to herself she was afraid of what was to come. Both Kyla and Nicole had suffered heartbreak, who was she to think she would be the lucky one to escape it? Why wouldn't she be like them and walk away with a scar? If she avoided it, maybe it wouldn't happen. If she pretended her feelings were merely on the surface and no deeper, maybe she wouldn't get hurt. But she also only admitted to herself, that she was in much too deep to ignore it.

With the immense passion between them, one would think it was their only connection level, but there was so much more that didn't revolve around the bedroom, their level of attachment exceeded way beyond that. There was a bond of friendship, a loyalty to one another as they felt like one union, one soul, in a few short days. They had the freedom to enjoy a tryst with no commitment, and in doing so they unintentionally let the openness with one another reign, and each found they'd invested so much of themselves in the other.

It was their last night on the ship, and that evening their lovemaking wasn't as wild and frenzied as they'd experienced, it was slow and sensual as each took their time, seemed to study every inch of exposed skin. She couldn't remember falling asleep but when Maggie rolled over and opened her eyes to see the light color of the room, it meant early morning and she didn't want it to be. Maybe if she closed her eyes again she could get the night back but as she placed her head on Jackson's chest, felt his heartbeat and the evenness of his breathing indicating sleep, she knew the night was gone. It wasn't possible to get it back, no matter how badly she wished.

Jackson sighed and smiled before he opened his eyes, felt her soft hands caress him, her mouth placing heat against the skin of his chest. "You are insatiable."

"You've made me that way." There was no one else who ever made her feel the way he did.

Afterwards, while he went to get coffee and rolls, she jumped into the shower but found him still gone when she was through. She dressed and while she waited for him to return found paper and pen and decided to write a little note and place it somewhere to be found much later when he least expected it. It brought a smile to her face thinking of him opening his bag, possibly not until his next shoot, and seeing her little surprise greeting. Simple words, she wrote... 'As promised, I won't forget the time we spent together. I'm probably thinking of you right now with your kiss that still lingers. Thanks for the sweet memory. Maggie'

Since the luggage was placed outside the evening before and already gone, she would put it in his camera case, perhaps on the bottom. As she opened it she carefully pulled one of his cameras out of the way then saw a framed picture and pulled it out so that she could get to the bottom.

Staring her in the face was a beautiful picture of Jackson and two other people, and Maggie could almost hear her heart break in the silent room, the sound of the crack resounded in her brain. Jackson and a woman stood with their arms around each other and he held a child, a beautiful little girl smiled up at her. My God, she thought, this was his wife and child. Jackson was a married man and the rumors were true after all, who else could it possibly be? What single attractive man carried around a picture of a woman and a child if it weren't his family? And the child was his spitting image with dark hair and dark brown eyes that peered beneath curls.

Maggie was frozen as hints came back to her. She remembered well the edge she saw on his face when she asked about marriage, a reaction she shunned away as imagined at the time, now she held the truth in her hands and couldn't deny its existence. Her mind reeled and her stomach churned as blood boiled to the surface. Heat of anger made her skin burn then was replaced with cold blood as if ice coursed through her, turned her to stone once more. The coldness that once helped her keep her distance from men now returned with full force.

How stupid she was to have let the magic of the Caribbean erase all logical sense, make her vulnerable and weak to passion. She'd slept with a married man. Made it so easy for him to have an affair on this beautiful family she held in her hands. Maggie quickly crumbled her note in her fist, placed the picture back just as it had been, and then bolted from the room. In the hall she almost literally ran into Bo as she was blinded by the pain that struck her.

"Whoa, pretty lady," Bo held onto her arm as he looked into her eyes then sighed knowingly. "Ah, my pretty one, you suffer as I said."

"Guess you hit all three on the mark." Maggie almost choked on the tears that threatened to sting her eyes as his premonition of cleaning up the pieces of her broken heart hung silently in the air.

"My mama had a gift and she give to me. I no use to cause you pain, I use only to tell you your heart will break, but more important, that it will be whole again. No worry, pretty one, no worry."

He said it as smooth as silk. It was meant to soothe her for the moment but she couldn't believe his words, wouldn't believe she would ever be in a position to have her heart whole again, would never expose it to anyone for the rest of her life. The only thing she knew for sure in that moment was the intense sting that shot through every nerve ending and a hate that boiled deep inside.

Maggie stormed into her own cabin and threw the rest of her few things into her carryon bag. "Can we get the hell out of here?"

"This isn't a pleasant morning for anyone, is it?" Kyla put her makeup into her own bag and looked to Maggie with concern and couldn't get the words out to speak before she stopped her.

"I don't want to talk about it right now." The look on her face was deadly and neither Kyla nor Nicole questioned anything further.

Nicole barely had enough time to grab her bag before Maggie was out the door and at the airport she changed her ticket to another flight, another airline than one the others used. She couldn't possibly sit on a plane with Jackson so close by because she never wanted to see his face again, the thought of it made her feel nauseas, and the anger of it made her break out in a sweat. Her flight would land an hour after theirs and she could avoid any confrontation.

Maggie wasn't running from him, she never ran from a fight, especially one where morals were involved. She thought of confronting him immediately, wanted to scream and vent at the wrong he'd done, wanted to face him and expose him. But that would give him the satisfaction of knowing she'd come to care about him, and she didn't want to do that. She'd made a mistake in letting the carefree environment relax her guard but it was something he wouldn't know, let him think the sex was all she wanted and she was through with him now. Let his arrogant ego suffer a blow at the thought that a woman wouldn't want more from him.

She waited with Kyla and Nicole at their gate until their flight left. They bid their farewells for the time being and it was difficult. When the three parted, each was lost in their regrets.

"Maybe next time we'll just spend a weekend closed up in a hotel room together."

"That way we won't get ourselves in trouble?" Nicole asked with a half hearted smile. "This trip certainly didn't turn out the way I expected."

"No," Maggie commented. "Life just keeps throwing us curves, I'm wondering when the man in charge is going to figure out we can't play baseball well, isn't our best sport."

Kyla looked outside the door to Texas as they stood in the airport concourse. "I knew I couldn't play years ago, I don't even know why I bothered to try again."

"I wouldn't have expected a strike out, but it seems all three of us missed." Nicole looked to Maggie, they still didn't know what had happened between her and Jackson but she could see a deep pain on her friend's face, one she'd never witnessed before. She knew Maggie had suffered her first and very last fatal blow. "Why don't you two plan to come see the kids in a few weeks, they'd love to see you."

Maggie smiled, the only thought to brighten her day. "I'll call you when I can manage to get away."

"That's a great idea, we'll spend the weekend with children and do nothing but play, it's what we all need right now."

Maggie's flight was smooth and she was satisfied to know she didn't have to face anyone. But what she hadn't known was that Jackson's flight had been delayed and they'd actually arrived around the same time. When she stepped outside of the terminal and hailed a cab, she heard the excitement of a child's voice that caught her attention.

"Daddy! Daddy!"

Maggie turned to see Jackson standing on the sidewalk with his bag as a little girl ran to greet him, then a woman stepped out of the car and gave him a warm hug. How cruel was God to have timed it so perfectly? She suspected what he'd done, he'd chosen another airline to be picked up at, one other than the airline he'd flown in on, for fear of his personal life being discovered by others. It was verification if she needed it, and she felt like she was again caught up in the sick deceitful game he played. Maggie quickly stepped into the cab and couldn't watch any more as it pulled away.

Of all the things about their departure that went through her mind, it was not the ending she dreamed. She felt just as both Kyla and Nicole explained their feelings, as if the beautiful days together had been negated by the fact he was a deceitful liar. Jackson was nothing but an adulterous husband who used his quiet charm to seduce her. If it hadn't been her, it would have been someone else, and when she thought about it, it could have been someone else also, along with her. Maybe he'd lied about Tiffany also, had actually slept with her that night instead of the false pretense of letting her sleep there when she'd passed out. Maggie had never questioned John, she trusted him after he explained.

He'd pulled her in, lured her with his pretend innocence in affairs, she remembered him seeming hurt when she referred to their first night together as a one night stand. Jackson was a professional, one that knew all the right buttons to push, all the right strings to pull, and Maggie never thought she would be a woman to so easily be taken advantage of. Always gave herself more credit than she'd obviously earned, had listened to others talk about being taken advantage of and never put herself in that sort of situation, always thought she wouldn't be so stupid. She'd obviously proved herself wrong and learned a lesson she wouldn't soon forget.

After all her heart had put her through before, she sincerely thought Jackson could possibly be the one to wrap her world around, but she was wrong, so completely wrong again. How could she have been so taken? Guarded Maggie, careful Maggie, who knew how to avoid situations like that. Where had she been? Who was the vulnerable woman who'd taken over and let her be burned? And so badly burned she'd been.

****

Wilma smiled broadly from down the hall. "Well, don't you look tan and refreshed?"

"I'm tan. It was the only thing I got out of that stupid trip and I'll never do anything like it again. Here's your article." Maggie practically threw it at her, she wanted to blame someone and it was part Wilma's fault for sending her, wasn't it?

"Want to talk about it?"

"Nothing to talk about."

A little while later Wilma called her to her office.

"What is this? I wanted stuff, meaningless things such as how long it took them to get ready for a shoot, what they thought of traveling to different locations, that sort of stuff. This isn't what I asked for, this is an expose' on child abuse and eating disorders."

"It's not all peaches and cream behind those cameras. You wanted behind the scenes and this is truly behind the scenes."

"But, Maggie..." Wilma couldn't get her protest out.

"People look at these models with envy. They have this glamorous persona of beautiful faces and exotic places, this is true behind the scenes that shows what it's really like. Simone doesn't eat for days because she's anorexic. On the opposite end you have Kelli who eats everything and throws it up. Tedi is so high on cocaine half the time, every day it's a battle whether she'll wake up the next morning alive or dead. Tiffany was sexually molested as a child and seeks approval from married men willing to pay her way through life with material things. She's a glorified prostitute, just as her mother was a real prostitute but she was dirt poor, she prostituted herself for drugs." Maggie stood stone faced in front of her, never wavered from her stance and she would stand strong, she refused to back down.

"I wanted the four a.m. wakeup calls. The tricks on how to keep hair in great shape when you're working in salt water and hot sun." Wilma flipped through the pages as if she'd find something there when she knew she wouldn't.

"Well this is what you have and I'm not redoing it. To come forward is their cry for help, they're tired of pretending life is wonderful. These girls know what's going to be written, they were willing enough to talk about it, the least you could do is respect that and run it."

"This isn't what our readers want." As much as Wilma loved it, as the head of the magazine she knew what her readers wanted, and this wasn't it.

"Your readers want to pretend there's a beautiful world out there somewhere, they want to bury their nose in the sand and not think life sucks. Well that's reality, life sucks, and no sense sugar coating it. And not only does is suck for the readers, it sucks for the people they envy." Maggie walked to the door then turned around with a strong voice that never wavered. "I won't redo it. If you want something else, have Marsha write the bullshit she's used to. Make up the words for the behind the scene's you want if you don't like the truth, Wilma, but the truth is all I can write and I refuse to write less. And if you think I went through all that bullshit for nothing, think again. You don't run this story and I'll take it elsewhere and you can print my resignation in your next issue." Then Maggie walked out, not only out of Wilma's office but out of the building and into a taxi for home.

A few days after their trip home, Nicole called her with excitement. "You'll never believe this. Derek called and he's coming to see me this weekend."

"What happened to him? Coming to see you? I thought when you told him about the kids..."

"It was all a mistake, I misconstrued everything. He has kids too, two of them. He never told me for the same reason I never told him, every time he ever told a woman he'd never hear from them again. Especially not when he told them he had shared custody and had them quite a bit."

"But what happened to him?"

"Remember the day in Cancun we spent together? Well, after he got back to the ship he found out his son had become ill, they were actually thinking meningitis, so he flew home right away. When I saw him talking to that woman, she was a person from the ship and helped him get the next flight out. He didn't even have time to leave me a message, didn't even get his things out of his cabin, they had to be shipped home to him."

Maggie could hear the excited relief in her voice, the happy heart again. "That's great, Nicole." Maggie said it with all the enthusiasm she could muster and it was enough that Nicole didn't question it. In the back of her mind she wanted to tell her friend to run in the opposite direction.

"Neither of us has the kids this weekend. We've already talked about getting the kids together, but we'll wait for awhile."

Maggie thought it sounded as if she were moving too fast but who was she to judge? She'd trusted her own judgment and look what happened to her. Besides, maybe Nicole had found the only true good one left, if there were such a thing.

"I bet you've already shopped for that new dress, haven't you?" Maggie tried to sound as upbeat as she could.

"It's to die for."

It was the first time since her divorce she'd ever heard Nicole actually look forward to a relationship. "You have fun. I'm happy for you, Nicole, I envy you actually. Out of the three of us, with all that you've been through you deserve it the most."

Several weeks later Kyla called her with her own surprising news. "I'm taking a leave of absence," she said.

"Are you having problems with your leg? It's healed now, isn't it?" Maggie was concerned about her leg, thought surely that could be her only reason for a leave of absence.

"It's healing fine. I'm moving to Texas for a little while, we agreed on six months."

"You and Alan?" Maggie said with the shock evident. "Kyla Reeves, I never thought I'd see the day you put your heart ahead of your brain."

"Alan's right. If I don't at least give it a shot, it will be like something that might have been and I can't live with that. I have to know for sure and giving up my career is nothing if I find out it isn't that important to me anyway."

Maggie laughed. "It isn't like people don't get divorced in Texas. So you'd have to commute to the nearest large city, but divorce is everywhere."

"Maybe later. We're taking the six months, and then marriage, then possibly kids right away, neither one of us wants to be walking with a cane when they graduate high school."

Maggie smiled, both of her best friends on the verge of new lives, happy and fulfilled lives. She'd be lying if she didn't say she felt a small pang of jealousy, but then the coldness she'd consumed herself with returned and the feeling was quickly gone. She could only wish the best for them, but her cynical side said she'd be there for her friends when it didn't work out.

"It sounds like you won't even need the six months, sounds like you've already made up your mind."

Kyla smiled to herself. "I think I have. Ever since we came back from the cruise I haven't been able to get Alan out of my mind. All I keep thinking about is someone else ending up with the life that's supposed to be mine. I know if I don't claim it now, I may never get another chance."

"How lucky you are it's yours for the taking."

"Come visit me. I'll be staying with Alan but I know his mother will have me out on the farm feeding chickens, please come save me when you get a chance."

Maggie laughed hysterically at the thought of Kyla on a farm with all the chores that entailed. "Don't worry, I'll be there to visit, I have to see this for myself."

Maggie's behind the scene's article won an award for the magazine. The industry gave them kudos for having the courage to portray the truth in an age where young kids looked at advertisements and lacked confidence at not looking like beautiful icons of society. Maggie's article showed them the nightmare behind the facade. Put silent pain inside the happy exterior of the beautiful faces.

She held the magazine in her hand and looked at the beautiful pictures Jackson took. As if they worked in sync, her words and his pictures went together as if it had been planned that way. He captured a sadness in them that went perfectly with the printed page Maggie so eloquently put together. Gorgeous scenery and gorgeous faces that hid their misery, they were poignant in their beauty and the irony of it all didn't escape her.

There was much she wanted to write about the mysterious photographer, the man who'd been responsible for her torturous pain, and the words wouldn't have been kind. But Maggie was a professional, she'd written in general terms with slight innuendoes scattered about. 'His trickery, with things such as white balance and shutter speed, makes him a sought after photographer who knows how to capture things on film'… 'Jackson Turner seems to take the simple touch of his finger and show us beauty, yet as you read this article you'll find underneath beauty there is deception'.

Only Maggie knew the hidden meaning, and she suspected that if Jackson read the article he would guess she had discovered his fraud. Then again, he wouldn't be the type of person who would care, and Maggie suspected she wasn't something he was thinking of, he'd probably already moved on to his next victim.

Wilma had trusted Maggie's judgment and taken the chance with the article without another argument. Maggie didn't know if her threat to leave was the driving force or not, but she would have stayed true to her statement and walked away, taken her story elsewhere. She owed that to the girls.

But since her hesitation, now Wilma was ecstatic when it paid off but was mindful to give Maggie all the credit.

"You have a whole slew of fan mail to answer. So many letters are coming in from young girls it's unbelievable. And I know you have all control over your next few articles but maybe you could do another like this but without models, the average girl who's struggling with her self confidence."

Maggie would have to admit her own self-confidence so lacked at that stage in her life. Her words were sarcastic with an 'I told you so' attitude. "How many times have you stressed your magazine promotes beauty and poise?"

"Well, apparently there are more ugly people out there who need help than there are beautiful people in the world, and if it sells my magazine then so be it."

"Do I get full control and a bigger spread?" Maggie pushed.

"Have you got another offer from someone?" Wilma asked suspiciously, her voice a little nervous.

"None that I'm seriously considering."

Wilma was quiet for a moment. "How much are they offering?"

"I'm not asking for a raise."

"I'll give you full control, more pages and ten thousand more."

Maggie laughed. Wilma was in her own bidding war with herself for Maggie truly hadn't thought of leaving, but she wasn't going to turn it down. Before she could agree Wilma thought her laughter was because someone else offered her more and she upped her own ante.

"Fifteen thousand more." Wilma shouted out quickly.

"I'm not going to take advantage of you, I'll take the first offer of ten, but along with the bigger spread I also get my choice of stories." She wouldn't take advantage, but she wasn't going to turn down something she fully deserved.

That night it was at least something to smile about, and she hadn't been able to do that lately. She loved her job, now even more so with newfound money and newfound respect for her work that came with the award. It was a shame there would be no one to walk in her door that evening and ask how her day was. She found herself even missing that from Jackson, simple little stupid words. 'How was your day, Maggie?' It was something that began as a joke when she had the conversation with herself, and he asked her that every time he saw her at the end of the day. She didn't want to think about it now, didn't want to think about how much she still hurt.

Maggie called her mother with her good news about both the raise and the award she'd earned.

"That's wonderful, dear." Her mother said with reserved enthusiasm.

"I actually did have a better offer of money, but I like the magazine, and now even better that I have more control."

"So what else is happening in your life? Anything else new?"

Maggie knew what she was asking about, and her enthusiasm waned. "No, Mom, nothing else new."

"I thought maybe..."

Maggie couldn't hear it again, couldn't let her mother finish her sentence. "Just wish the best for me, Mom, stop wishing for something that isn't in the cards." Maggie sighed, her excitement of before now shadowed with the thought that it wasn't enough.

****

When Simone called with an invitation to go out with them it didn't take her long to agree it was a wonderful idea. All of them, Simone, Kelli, Tedi, and Tiffany, they wanted to get together to celebrate the magazine article so Maggie met them at a hip downtown bar.

They had a good time catching up and all of them thanked her. Grateful she'd run the story just as it was and it had changed their lives. Before Maggie left them, she'd given them the number to a good therapist she had interviewed once, never guessing they would actually go but they had, all of them. And though the road ahead wasn't a short one, they felt it was already helping.

Tiffany smiled broadly. "I'm going back to school."

"Back to school?" Maggie questioned.

"I'm getting my GED, I never finished, and I've already enrolled in classes at the University." She smiled mischievously. "And I don't want to jinx myself, but I met the best looking guy when I was signing up, single and poor."

Both Kelli and Simone were working hard on their eating disorders, Maggie noticed Simone looked a little more human, a few more needed pounds on her so thin frame and Kelli was the same only she hadn't been as thin. Tedi had entered a full time facility for drug addiction and was getting the help she needed, she was an outpatient now and knew she had a hard fight before her, but was confident it was one she could conquer.

They asked about her friends, Kyla and Nicole, and she gave them a quick update on their lives. Tiffany mentioned working with John on her last shoot and Simone had seen Jackson a few weeks ago. Maggie quickly changed the subject to something else.

When she left them, they all agreed to a follow up article on their progress. Maggie of course mentioned all the mail she had gotten and all the people they were helping with their stories, the models seemed proud to know that and she assured them she was proud of them.

That evening as Maggie lay in bed it was difficult to do so in the dark night. So many lives changed by one small week. The few days they'd all come together had such an impact on their worlds. Maggie among them, for she knew hers would never be the same.

CHAPTER EIGHTEEN

Maggie had never felt so hurt before. Other men she'd dated hadn't the ability to hurt because they hadn't touched her heart. When she thought about Jackson a searing pain shot through her, one she tried to replace with anger and was successful most times, but even after a month when she lay alone in the dead of night and he crossed her mind, the pain of the wound crept in. The memory of his skin, the way he made her feel inside haunted her.

It was when the lights went out and she was alone that she felt the most vulnerable to his memory. She suffered from a hole in her soul, could almost physically feel the void of emptiness, and when the lights went out there wasn't anything to be but heartbroken.

Maggie knew she'd fallen in much deeper than she'd suspected previously. She wouldn't feel so much pain had it been just a passing fling, merely the sexual release it began as, and she wouldn't go to bed as late as possible and endure the long night with a restlessness she'd never felt before. He'd connived and manipulated his way deep into her soul and she wondered if she would ever be free of his memory.

It amazed her that in such a short period of time he'd managed to pierce her so deeply when she'd been so guarded before him. He'd broken through when she wasn't even looking, affected her in ways she never thought possible. Maggie had to tell herself the obvious, as painful as it was to do, she had to admit to herself that somewhere along the line she'd fallen in love with him. Now she only had to figure out how to stop it.

When she heard his voice on her answering machine one day the sound of his sweetness infuriated her. His voice sounded so sincere it made her ill.

"How was your day, Maggie?" He laughed with hesitation, and then continued. "I ran into John on a shoot and he gave me your number, I hope you don't mind. I wanted to say congratulations on your great article. I was looking forward to seeing it, knew it wouldn't be anything they expected and I wasn't disappointed. I've been in and out of town on assignment so my cell phone is the easiest to get in touch with me. Call when you get a chance, maybe we can meet up sometime."

He left his number and repeated it several times before he hung up, but she certainly didn't pay any attention and deleted the message immediately. Yeah right, she thought, his cell phone was the easiest. In actuality it would prevent her from calling his home where his wife would answer and find out exactly what kind of man he was. And meet up sometime? For what? A secret rendezvous in a sleazy motel? Maggie slammed the button to delete it so hard she knocked the machine on the floor and it broke. She didn't care, was glad the phone was now out of order, she wouldn't be able to receive another message from him.

Several weeks passed before she heard from him again. Unfortunately she'd gotten a new machine and now thought about changing her number to an unlisted one just to avoid his calls.

"I don't know if you got my first message or not, I haven't heard from you. I was wondering if you wanted to get together for coffee or something, maybe catch up a little. I know we agreed on nothing but what we had on the cruise, but I thought," he hesitated, "I thought maybe we could talk."

Again she deleted it immediately, cursed him loudly in the empty room even though he'd never hear her. Maybe she should call him to curse him to his face, put a stop to his calls. She decided to give it a little more time and hoped he'd get the hint when she never called him back.

The next attempt he made was a package that was delivered to her office. Maggie was sitting at her desk and had to sign for the large thin box, and didn't know who it was from as there was no indication on the outside other than a company name on the return address label. She unwrapped the plain brown paper, opened the box, and after she got through all the protective packaging, she sat and stared at the Joshua Canner painting Jackson had purchased for ten thousand dollars on the cruise.

Taped to the back of it was a note in an envelope that read...

'From afar, I watched one day as you admired this painting. I didn't purchase it for myself, I didn't purchase it as an investment as I said, I purchased it because I could sense it made you feel something, you seemed drawn to it and I thought you should have it. Don't misconstrue its meaning as some sort of gift to gain your attention, as you've made it perfectly clear you wish no communication. I understand and that isn't the intent of this painting, the intent is solely as I said, I didn't purchase it for me, it belongs to you, Maggie.'

He didn't sign it, but he didn't need to. It did make Maggie feel something, and before she was drawn into it, drawn into thoughts of Jackson, she quickly packaged it back up and immediately shipped it back to the address on the return label with hefty insurance coverage and a note written to return to sender. She felt better when she received the delivery confirmation and the responsibility of it was out of her hands.

It was another month before her mind cleared a little of him again. Maggie wasn't as angry at him anymore, she was angry with herself.

The signs were there and she just chose to ignore them. Flashing neon signs and she'd chosen to push her doubts away, and she had no one to blame but herself.

****

"Hey, Maggie." Bruce Parks poked his head around the corner to see Maggie sitting at her desk. "Are you ever going to get out of here tonight?"

"I doubt it." She didn't look up as she typed away on her computer. "What are you doing here so late? Normally I'm the only fool."

"I did leave, I just forgot something in my desk, an invitation I needed for a party this evening. Why don't you ditch that for the night and come with me? You haven't been away from your desk since six this morning, you're going to go blind."

She sat back, closed her eyes, and rubbed them with her hands. "You're probably right, but I don't think I need a party, I need sleep."

"Just a quick drink, it's probably almost over anyway."

Maggie looked at him and decided it wasn't a half bad idea. Bruce was safe, he was gay and in between boyfriends for the moment, so he made the perfect date. It was all her intentions to have the quick drink he spoke of then leave, but she ran into John who she hadn't seen since the cruise and ended up talking to him for a few hours. He was doing well and it was good to see him, she worried when she didn't.

"I was going to call you this weekend. I sold my house and there's a new place I'm about to put a contract on, but I wanted to make sure. Think you could give me your opinion?"

"Sure, John, want me to pick you up?"

"It would probably work better if you met me there, the real estate friend I'm working with will just give me the key, and if you like it and think it's okay, I'll just meet her afterwards and sign all the papers and I don't want to take up your whole day."

Maggie promised to do so that weekend and looked forward to it. She'd spoken with him a few times since returning home, he called her after Jackson's first message and told her he hoped she didn't mind but he'd given Jackson her number. Said he thought he wanted to congratulate her on the article. She lied and told him of course she didn't mind, and yes he'd called and congratulated her, which he did say in his message, so that wasn't a lie. John hadn't known anything about their involvement and she certainly wasn't going to confess what a fool she'd been.

It would be a nice break from work to go with him, which she'd taken no break from in weeks, and as she drove just to the outskirts of the city she could feel some of the stress ease away. It was a nice neighborhood, the street lined with brownstones and a cobblestone sidewalk. It wasn't a neighborhood she was familiar with, but it was nice, looked like it belonged deep in the suburbs instead of just on the outskirts of the bustling city.

She parked the car in front of the address he'd given her. "I love the neighborhood already," she said as she stepped out of the car and saw him on the steps waiting for her.

"My realtor gave me all kinds of print outs. The safety of it, the schools, of course I don't need that kind of information, but its very family oriented. I've already met a few neighbors." He hugged her in greeting, kissed her cheek. "You look tired."

"Thanks for the compliment."

"I didn't mean…"

"You don't have to apologize. It's the truth, I am tired, doing nothing but working 24/7 it seems. But it's by choice, lot's to get done." She didn't elaborate on the half truth, there was so much to get done, but it certainly didn't need to get done at the pace she was going. But it was a pace that kept her sane.

"Come in and see. The people have already moved and the Realtor is a friend, she gave me the key to get in myself. I think you'll like it."

Maggie did like it. It was very nicely decorated and he would purchase it furnished. "You could move right in without a care in the world. How easy is that?"

"I felt like I needed some new furniture and everything anyway, and they're moving out of state, didn't want to haul it off with them."

They'd gone upstairs and John decided to open the attic and go up to see it, while Maggie went back downstairs. She was in the kitchen when she heard a familiar voice from the doorway.

"Hey, John? Sorry I'm late, Mia had…" His voice stopped when he saw Maggie.

John joined the two as he walked down the stairs with an immediate guilty look on his face as he looked to Maggie, but tried to play off what seemed to be coincidence. "Oh, I forgot to mention, Jackson would be one of my neighbors."

She didn't want to be mad at him, but certainly he wouldn't want to set her up with a married man, maybe he didn't know either, maybe Jackson had conned him about his life too. She would be sure to call him later and they would have a nice talk, but right then she needed to get out.

She smiled as best she could. "Oh, then he would be a great one to ask an opinion from when it comes to the neighborhood. I think the house is great, looks like all you'll need." Maggie kissed him on the cheek. "I do have to run though, I just got a call on my cell and have to meet someone. You'll call me later?"

Jackson looked just as confused as Maggie, hadn't known John had planned their meeting, and only watched as Maggie bolted from the door.

"Aren't you going to go after her?"

"John, I know you think you're doing well, but…"

"Jackson, I know it's none of my business, but there was something between you and Maggie. And I know you still feel something, you've been moping around since we got back."

"It's the way she wants it."

"And I know that's not right either. I know Maggie, and I know there's something wrong. You're not the only one that's been moping around since that cruise." John could see he still looked hesitant. "I won't be able to figure it out but you can, but only if you face her. So get out there and figure out what's going on."

Jackson stood for a few moments and decided he didn't have anything to lose, he caught up to her just as her hand was about to open her car door.

"Hey, Maggie."

She looked up quickly, eyes cold as steel. "What do you want, Jackson?"

"I thought we could talk a little."

"There's nothing to talk about." She went to open the door and he leaned against it. "What do you want from me now? You got your sex, leave me alone."

He couldn't believe her attitude, it confused him even more. This wasn't the Maggie he'd discovered, knew it wasn't an attitude of sticking to their previous agreement of just sex, there was more to it than that and he was now determined to find out what it was.

"I know we said…"

"Leave me the hell alone," her voice was like a snake's hiss.

"What is this? Where is this coming from?"

"I'm not into married men so go home to your wife."

"Married men?" He was totally confused by her words but it revealed why she was angry.

"I was going to leave you a note in your camera bag the last morning on the ship, I saw the nice little family picture, and my luck even saw the wonderful little homecoming at the airport. I don't blame you, there were rumors I ignored and I had a stupid lapse in judgment but it won't happen again. How easy I made it for you to have an affair. All I wanted was sex and you obliged, under no false pretenses. It worked out perfect for you, didn't it? I feel like an idiot!"

"Maggie, it's not what you think."

"Are you going to tell me you're going through problems? Your marriage is on the brink of divorce? Separated? Oh…" She gasped with pretended surprise. "She doesn't understand you, isn't that the clichéd excuse for your cheating kind."

"Mia always picks out the picture I take with me, and that was my sister, Maggie, my child and my sister, not wife."

She laughed sarcastically. "How stupid do you think I am? You can't even make up a decent lie. No wonder you don't date, guess the wife doesn't allow it. If you sleep with someone you don't consider it a date so it doesn't count? Weird relationship but if it works for you have at it, but I want no parts of it."

"I don't have a wife." Jackson tried to convince her but he could tell she was closed off, her mind wouldn't even open to the possibility.

"Don't try to bullshit now. I've had time to think about it and put it all together. It's why you were so adamant about nothing but sex, that's all you wanted it to be."

"That's all you wanted," he too now shouted in frustration.

"And how wonderful for you to run into a fool like me. It worked out perfectly, you had your little affair and had I known it certainly wouldn't have happened, but don't think I'll continue to be your bed partner."

"It wasn't just sex, Maggie, yes it started out that way but I changed my mind and was going to talk to you that morning over coffee but you disappeared."

She didn't believe anything he said, her mind was stuck in the closed position as she'd listened to him before and had suffered because of it. "What do you want from me? To be your mistress? Your secret lover?" She'd been so hurt and angry, the deceit imbedded so deep she wasn't even listening to what he said. Refused to believe his words, refused to be dragged back in where she was vulnerable and exposed to the pain he caused. "We're not on a cruise ship anymore where reality doesn't matter. This is reality Jackson and you won't find me in your bed again."

"If you'll let me..." He couldn't finish because she quickly cut him off.

"I have to say, you were certainly the best asshole I've ever come across, you certainly know how to blindside somebody. But it doesn't matter, I'm not interested, remember?"

Maggie jerked her arm away from him and reached for her door again but he grabbed her by the shoulders, turned her square to face him and pressed his lips hard on hers. She couldn't pull away, his hand behind her neck held her there and his sensuality and her longing still, made her give in for a few brief seconds before she managed to pull away. She would have slapped him but he must have known that, for he held her arms firm.

"You son of a..."

"I'm in love with you, Maggie, are you interested now?"

"Don't hand me bullshit because you think it will work to seduce me again. Look at me, Jackson, do I look like the fool you met?"

Jackson noticed the hard edge he hadn't seen before. He felt guilty for the pain he was the cause of, the misconception she'd dealt with since they'd been apart. He grabbed her arm and forced her to go with him, practically dragged her down the sidewalk but it was his only option, Jackson wouldn't let her leave until she saw the truth. After that, if she still wanted to leave he'd have to let her, but she was going to know the truth first.

"Come on."

"What the hell do you think you're doing?"

"I'm going to introduce you to my so called wife. If you're really not interested, you're not interested, but I can't sit by and think that any chance we may have is lost because of your false notions."

"Can't you just leave me the hell alone? You can't force me to go with you, this is kidnapping," she huffed.

"No it isn't, you aren't a kid." Jackson commented.

She stubbornly stopped on the sidewalk and he knew she was right, he certainly couldn't actually pull her unwilling along the sidewalk if she didn't want to go, so he stopped. When he looked at her there was a soft pleading in his eyes. "Come with me. Let me prove you wrong about your notions. It's my sister, Maggie, my sister and my daughter you saw in that picture. If you want nothing to do with me after you see I'm telling the truth, I'll accept that. I won't like it, but I'll accept it, I can't let you think like this."

Maggie complained and protested in her anger but went along with him. "Where are we going?"

"My home. My sister doesn't see Mia during the week and comes and stays with us for the weekend sometimes."

Maggie listened to his words and began to think she'd been wrong. All she had to do was look at her and know it was the same woman in the picture, so surely Jackson couldn't try and pull anything over on her. He didn't say anything to her so she had time to try and think things through and so many things ran through her mind. They all mingled together to make a jumbled mess of her thoughts and nothing made sense.

The way it sounded was as if his daughter lived with him, so where was the mother? Divorce? Why didn't she have custody? Or was it joint custody and his sister came on the weekends he had Mia? So many thoughts jumbled her head and the one that stood out the most was his words of love. Hadn't he said he loved her? Or had she only imagined that?

Okay, so there was no wife, there was a child and Jackson was a father. Why hadn't he told her? She wished she could go along without any thoughts but it's the way she was, always questioning everything, always trying to figure everything out.

The neighborhood was nice. Maggie would have suspected Jackson, as a bachelor, to live in the city, a nice little comfortable apartment. But this was Jackson, the father, and he rounded a corner and stopped in front of a lovely townhouse but they didn't go inside as he looked down the street and saw the ice cream truck and knew Mia would still be there.

Before he could say anything else Mia ran up to them, her nutty buddy happily in her hand. She looked up to Maggie and smiled broadly. "Hi, my name's Mia, what's yours?"

From somewhere unknown she found her voice and smile again. "I'm Maggie."

The little girl laughed hard. "Mia and Maggie, that's funny."

As she laughed her arm swung out and the pile of ice cream that rested atop the cone flung off but Maggie's quick reflexes caught it before it hit the ground. "Whoa, a save, here you go. I promise my hands are clean." Maggie placed it back on the cone then wiped her hand on her jeans.

"Hey, Aunt Lori, this is Maggie. She just caught my ice cream, did you see?"

"Hi." The woman smiled pleasantly, with more than a little curiosity in her eyes.

The woman before her was undeniably the same one in the picture with Mia and she now had a name and relation to go with the face, his sister Lori. Who carried a family picture with a sister? Jackson did, he'd said Mia always picked the picture out, and her jumbled thoughts, although still jumbled, began to clear a little as things fell into place.

Maggie reached out and shook her hand. "Nice to meet you."

"Jackson didn't tell me we were having company today."

"I just ran into him down the street."

"Maggie's a friend of John's also, she was at his house." Jackson answered without anymore explanation.

"Are you joining us for dinner?"

Maggie wasn't sure what to answer, she was still half dazed at all that had transpired in what seemed a few short minutes. Jackson again spoke up.

"Let's all go inside, Maggie will be staying for dinner." Jackson put his arm around her as if she needed to be guided and she felt she did.

So many things went through her mind, the main thought being the beautiful little girl Mia. Where had she come from and why hadn't he told her? Just when she thought she knew the kind of man Jackson was he confused her and threw something else into the mix. Her first impression was the mysterious handsome stranger, then her images of him as a married man with a family that haunted her, and now he was a single father with a beautiful home. How many lives did he have? What else was in store?

The house was impeccably decorated, and she would assume by a woman, although it was masculine and homey. A decorator? The sister Lori? The ex-wife? Had it been their home when they were married? Was he separated? Fully divorced? Was it his weekend with Mia?

She'd fallen in love with a man she truly knew nothing about. It was overwhelming to confess to herself that she had fallen in love with him but couldn't process any more information other than that. Who was this man? Who was this stranger she knew nothing about? Details she couldn't process, information that was overpowering, so Maggie fell into being Maggie, her true self she'd always shown, unlike Jackson, there was no secret side.

"I'll check the lasagna. Mia, come on in the kitchen with me to finish your ice cream or it will be all over the floor." Lori went into the kitchen and Mia followed.

"Lori makes the best lasagna. You will stay for dinner, won't you?"

"I... I guess..." She still found it hard to speak to him.

"I just needed you to see the truth, I couldn't let you hate me, couldn't let any chance we might have slip away."

"A chance for?" Maggie raised her eyebrows, was he offering more than what they agreed to? Did he now want more than to be her bed partner? Had she heard the words of love correctly? They still reverberated in her mind.

"A relationship Maggie, I want more than what we had on the cruise, much more, but I'll take as much as you're willing to give. It's up to you."

"This isn't you. It is, but it isn't the you I pictured." Maggie looked around. "When I first met you, I pictured a bachelor condo in the city, maybe a nice little one bedroom number within walking distance to a good Chinese restaurant."

"I hate Chinese."

"See? That's the point. I have this picture in my mind, I end up at your doorstep and it's nothing that I imagined. Everything is twisted and turned and I can't even begin to think about what I think about all of it. Does that make any sense?"

Jackson took her hand in his and kissed the back of it. "It makes perfect sense, and I'm sorry I didn't tell you any of it. I'll explain anything and everything you want to know."

"Oh, you will explain. Now that I'm here I'm not leaving until you do." Maggie began to walk away from him then turned back. "You did say you loved me, right?"

"I love you, Maggie Pace," he said with the smile that twisted her heart.

She saw the truth in his eyes, it was the one piece of information that continued to come through above all else. "It's a good thing you have that to back you up or you'd be in trouble. I'm going to go help with dinner, you can go tell John not to worry about us, because I know he feels bad, and I know he's worrying."

He laughed as she walked to the kitchen.

"Can I help with something?" She asked Lori who was about to cut the vegetables for salad.

"I don't think so, relax and visit, you're a guest."

"I don't feel a very good guest if I'm not helping out. It's a habit that came with birth, when I go home to my parents we all sit in the kitchen and do something for dinner, of course half of it is gone by the time we're done because we're all picking." Out of the habit she spoke of, Maggie plopped a piece of cucumber in her mouth but grabbed a knife from the knife block and began to cut the next one.

"How about some wine? I always keep a few bottles here for when I visit, Jackson never has anything but milk in the fridge."

"I'd love some."

"I like milk." Mia commented then approached Maggie with the vegetables. "Can I help cut?"

Maggie would have guessed Mia to be around five or six, and thought that was a little young to wield around a sharp knife. "I'll cut and you can do the most important thing."

"What's that?" The little girl asked with anticipation.

"You can assemble it in the bowl, but it has to be just right."

Maggie helped her layer the salad, it didn't need to be of course, but it gave her something to help with. They laughed together as she coaxed Mia into making a face on top, using the cherry tomatoes for eyes, nose and mouth and cucumbers resembled hair.

When Jackson returned, he told them he'd invited John to dinner but he went to the realtors to sign the contract to become his neighbor. Then after doing the garlic bread, Lori took the opportunity when she had it to motion him secretly into the other room.

"She caught the ice cream cone in her hands, wiped it on her pants and didn't think another thing about it. I love her, Jackson, where did you ever find her?"

"The cruise trip I took."

"I knew it!" She exclaimed. "I knew there was something wrong with you, you're in love, aren't you?"

"And that's a 'wrong' thing?" He laughed.

"Not when it's right," she said softly. "And her? How does she feel?"

"I don't know, this is the first time I've seen her since the cruise." Jackson didn't explain the misunderstanding Maggie made of Lori being his wife.

She looked over to Maggie through the opening into the kitchen where Mia giggled and Maggie laughed as they created with vegetables. "She's the genuine article. When you used to date, I could tell the ones that were nice to Mia just because they were trying to impress you, but she's not doing that, she's the real thing."

"Maggie knows no other way to be."

They all laughed at dinner and carried on as if they enjoyed meals together every evening. Mia told them tales and giggled and Maggie thought her delightful. She was a happy and outgoing child. Her opinion was she must have more of her mother's personality, whoever she was, as opposed to Jackson's silent, strong masculinity. But the softness she'd broken through in Jackson on the cruise, was nothing compared to now as he playfully teased his daughter. The two of them were bonded in a relationship like one she'd never witnessed between a father and a daughter. She'd never seen this part of him before.

Maggie didn't know much, didn't know where the mother was, or if she was still in the picture at all. Jackson said it was his and Mia's house, and Mia never once mentioned her mother. Not one word uttered about the mystery woman who gave birth to her, but as she watched the two of them interact, they didn't need any more than what they had.

Lori was a nurse and had an early shift at the hospital the next day so after dinner she left to go home and Maggie joined Jackson and Mia for an evening bike ride, using one of Jackson's old bikes. This was his life. It wasn't something one would expect, and yet now that she was in it, it fit him well. A role he'd taken with great pride and she could see it gave him much satisfaction.

At one point, Maggie put Mia on the seat of her bike and told her to hold on tight, to use the belt loops of her jeans as makeshift handles. Then she stood and peddled while the little girl giggled behind her as they raced Jackson and of course won, even though he appeared to be putting up a good fight.

They were out until almost dark and Maggie enjoyed another glass of wine while Mia bathed and Jackson put her to bed. Before she left for her room, Mia threw her arms around Maggie to tell her goodnight. She smelled of fresh soap and her soft youthful skin against her cheek was still damp. It was no wonder Jackson had gladly given up any other kind of life he could have had for her.

"Is Miss Maggie coming for dinner tomorrow, daddy?"

He pulled the covers up tight to her neck. "I don't know, honey, I'm sure she has to work tomorrow, but we'll see."

"Maybe the next night then."

Jackson moved her hair from her eyes. "We'll see. She's just a friend of mine, Mia, I worked with her once, don't read anything into it."

"But she's prettier than your friend Ricky."

He laughed, "Yes, she is."

It was why he'd given up dating. Jackson didn't want Mia to think that every woman that came through the door was a possible mother, didn't want her becoming attached to someone who wouldn't be in his life but for a short time. With Maggie, he knew he wanted much longer than a short time, but he would have to wait and see what would come. She didn't know his real life, he'd never had the chance to explain it, he could only hope now that after he did she would want to be a part of it.

Maggie wandered around, found a den with the walls lined with stunning pictures, but she redefined them as photography pieces, pictures seemed too menial a word. There were no models, no high fashion shots that splattered the covers of magazines and advertisements, instead they were of far off distant places and other things.

Many of Mia were displayed in different ways. Some were black and white, others with an aged effect, some digitally enhanced in several ways but all a beautiful display of her lifeline. Pictures from her as a small newborn baby up until recent and her black curly hair framed her face as big doe brown eyes peered mischievously, sweetly, the perfect picture of innocence.

She found not one that contained anyone who would appear to be her mother. No family pictures and no mother and child pictures, nothing. Later she would find out the only picture of her mother was in a lone frame in Mia's room.

As she made her way around the room, she came to some that looked familiar. They were the islands they'd just recently visited and among them she saw herself as she played on the beach with some children. The colors of the sunset golden, and the faces and details of the figures couldn't be seen, merely dark silhouettes against the Belize beauty of the shore, but she remembered that day, that place in time.

"Mia loves those. She wanted to know why she wasn't there." Jackson watched her silently from the doorway for a few minutes and she turned to see him.

"They're beautiful, all of these."

"You didn't think I spent my whole life taking pictures of skinny women with big boobs, did you? It pays the bills well, but all of this is my true obsession."

"How was I to know? I've discovered there's not much I do know about you." Maggie said quietly.

He continued to lean against the door jamb in silence as she looked at the others. Beautiful scenery captured in various forms of sunrises, sunsets, even a picture of nothing but water that seemed amazing. And there were so many more she knew were taken on their trip, things captured on film when she hadn't even realized he'd been around.

Several while they were at the orphanage in Roatan, happy smiling children receiving gifts they accepted graciously. A couple of the models, looking disheveled and out of sorts, as they sat on the ground with several children and no one would ever suspect they were some of the most beautiful faces on the covers of magazines. Then her hand reached up and touched one, Jackson had captured the moment Katera had given her a hug, the moment the little girl had trusted her enough to get that close.

"That's one of my favorites," he said.

"I thought about trying to adopt her once, but that was being unfair. She's happy where she is, and taking her out of that environment would devastate her. So I try to do what I can."

"You do more than try, you actually accomplish more than several people together would ever think to even attempt. It's easy for people to feel sorry for those kids, but there are few who do anything about it." He walked over to her, found it difficult not to touch her, so he stood behind her and wrapped her in his arms. "Do you know how difficult you make it for someone not to love you? Not only are you beautiful, but there's a substance to you that is rare."

"Oh," she teased sarcastically. "And I guess the great sex never crossed your mind?"

He laughed as he took her hand and led her back to the quiet comfort of the living room and its overstuffed sofa and poured her another glass of wine. They settled in and he explained his situation.

Mia's mother was a model he dated and thought he'd fallen in love with but when she became pregnant and he thought their lives would be fantastic, it turned into his worst nightmare. She didn't want to get married. Instead, it seemed the worst thing that could happen to her, so vain she was about her body and looks to the point that her bulimia got out of control even when she knew she had an unborn child that needed to be nourished.

Jackson tried desperately to get her help, not only for her, but also for the child he knew she must have been killing inside. There was nothing or no one she would listen to, ignored doctor's warnings, medical advice, therapists, he did everything but for nine months she seemed to waste away instead of becoming the healthy glowing mother he prayed for. But her vanity came at high cost and she paid the price of her life in childbirth. The stress too much for her body to handle and her vital organs ceased to function as they shut down one by one. Mia was premature, less than two pounds and her outlook was not good but with the expertise of skilled doctors and staff and the tiny little girl who fought for her life, they managed to save her and give him the greatest gift he'd ever known.

"You could have told me," Maggie said quietly.

"I could have," he didn't disagree with her. "But I made a promise to myself long ago that I don't bring people into my personal life. There's only been a handful of times when Mia was younger that she ever saw any woman I was dating, but as she got old enough to understand a little more, I didn't want her to have any sort of connection to one, only to have it break off and go through the process over and over."

"That's admirable, most men wouldn't think of such things." She curled her legs underneath her. "But you're not like most men."

"There were so many times I thought of telling you more, but our relationship had become one of sexual satisfaction, remember? You didn't want anything from me, and I pretended I didn't want anything from you. So I took it for what it was, something we both wanted and needed, but nothing more. I was determined to tell you everything that last morning on the ship but when I came back to the room you were gone, and I assumed it was the way you wanted to leave it."

"Then you called a couple of times."

Jackson smiled. "I couldn't stand it. I tried not to, but I couldn't stop thinking about you."

"And then the painting."

"I'd bought it with the intention of it being yours all along, it didn't belong to me."

"I'm glad you forced me to come," Maggie said quietly as she snuggled closer into the couch.

"You don't make it easy on a man, do you? I'd given up, thought you were involved with someone else and wouldn't be interested in anything I might have to offer."

Maggie knew him bringing her into his home, meeting his daughter, was evidence how he felt about her. It was his personal domain he shared with no outsider and she felt privileged to be able to share it with him now and she knew how important the meaning was.

"And what is it you're offering?" She smiled coyly.

"I need you outside of the bedroom, I want you fully in my life. I don't know how you feel, you may not even be thrilled with the fact of this is how my life is. Maybe you prefer the single bachelor pad in the city with the Chinese restaurant down the street, but this is who I am. My life is not glamorous and free and I can't take off on a whim for a dinner date or waste time on romantic weekends away for two. Or anything else women want..."

"My life is filled with messy ice cream cones. Toys, crayons, and arguing for thirty minutes with a five year old girl when I try to explain why she can't wear her Snow White outfit to school. Rainy days are spent piling up on this big couch and watching a Disney movie with popcorn. If I'm lucky, Mia will fall asleep in my lap instead of on the other side of the couch..."

Jackson took her hand in his. "So I don't know if that kind of life appeals to you but it's the way it is, and I want you to be part of it. I've been going out of my mind thinking about you, and I love you, Maggie. I want you in my life, but I'll understand if it's not something you expected and decide it isn't what you want."

"How can you even question that?" Maggie touched his face softly. The man she'd fallen in love with along tropical shores edged in turquoise sea was a stranger to her, one who only shared his sexual intensity. She loved this man in front of her even more, for he was willing to share his life.

CHAPTER NINETEEN
ONE YEAR LATER

"What time does your flight come in?" Nicole asked excitedly.

"Six o'clock. Kyla and Alan get in at the same time so we're renting a car together to save you the trip to the airport."

"We can pick you up." Nicole began to protest.

"You have an entire list of last minute wedding details to take care of, we're not adding to it. We'll see you at your house when we get in," Maggie insisted. "You've other things to do, don't give us another thought."

Mia was excited for her first plane ride. She sat in the middle between Maggie and Jackson and held each of their hands with the look of wonder in her eye when the plane engines roared, they took off down the runway, then it lifted from the ground.

"Wow, can we do that again?"

"Not now." Jackson laughed. "When we leave California."

When she was a little more comfortable she wanted to sit next to the window so Jackson switched with her but she still had requests. "Can mama sit next to me, daddy?"

Maggie's heart leaped from her chest, she'd never called her that and Maggie had never given it any thought that she would. When Jackson moved aside and they switched, Mia looked up to her with the sweetest eyes she'd come to know so well and Maggie saw concern there.

"Can I call you mama?"

"Of course you can, Mia." Maggie's voice almost cracked on the tears that threatened to sting her eyes.

"I thought since there would be other kids there it would make us look like a family, just like them, but if you don't want me to..."

Maggie took her hand and squeezed tight. "Mia, it makes me proud you want to call me that. We are a family, not official yet, but we are."

"And we'll have a wedding too, right?"

"Grandma Lee is planning most of it as we speak, all we'll have to do is show up." Maggie laughed.

"With flowers and pretty dresses and cake? A big cake. The biggest cake."

"The biggest cake you've ever seen, all that and more," Maggie promised.

Jackson proposed marriage to her several weeks after her first visit to his home. He'd planned a special evening out when Lori came for the weekend but plans were canceled when Mia came down with a fever and they decided to stay home. He proposed to her on the comfy couch after they watched a movie and the little girl had fallen asleep between them.

Mia's head rested on Maggie's leg, her feet and legs stretched over Jackson, and as they finished watching a popular cartoon movie, even after she'd fallen asleep and they could have changed it, he asked her to be his wife. Jackson reached underneath a cushion and produced a small, beautifully wrapped box with a bow that once was a crowning glory, now it was squished almost flat.

"I warned you ahead of time this was what my life was like. I'm sorry about dinner, and if I wait for another night to do this while we're alone, I might have to wait until Mia's in college, so I might as well do it now." Jackson handed her the box and Maggie opened it to find a perfect brilliant diamond. "I can't promise much more than this, but I'm hoping it'll be enough to coerce you into a life with me."

"Much more than this? There is no more than this." Tears sprang to Maggie's eyes when he placed the diamond on her finger.

"So the answer is yes?"

"Of course its yes, what other man comes with a bonus like Mia?"

"I have no shame, if my daughter is what it takes to seal the deal, I am one lucky man." Jackson then looked a little guilty as he leaned over easily to kiss her, tried not to wake Mia. "I'm glad the answer is yes, I've already hung your painting in the bedroom."

"You did? Well you were confident, weren't you?"

"Hopeful is a better word, I would have taken it down had you said no, it doesn't belong here without you."

She looked at him as her eyes filled with the love she felt. "I would have gone through all the bullshit again to get here, all of the early searching, all of the failed relationships, I'd do it all again if I knew it would bring me to this place."

"But you're here now, that's all that matters."

They toasted the engagement event with warm chocolate milk.

Her mother had been more than pleased when she and Jackson went to visit, with Mia of course, and they announced their plans to marry. Not only the news that her only daughter would finally wed, Mia pleased her even more and she insisted she call her Grandma. Mia also came to call the others Aunts and Uncles.

All of her brother's and their families welcomed both, transformed the two from the solitary life they lived and threw them into the rambunctious and plentiful Pace family. Both Jackson and Mia fell in as if they'd always belonged there. Maggie often thought of it in terms as they'd always meant to belong there, only now just found their way.

Of course Jackson had to survive the interrogation from every last one of her brothers, which he did with comfortable and confident ease. He'd gone from one to the other as they bombarded him with questions, followed by more questions, and then a test of his athletic skills in a game of football and her father tested him with chess. He went along with all of it, and not once did his smile waver. They were a possessive and protective family but there was not a one who didn't agree that he was the one they'd all waited for.

Unlike Nicole's quiet affair at the courthouse, or Kyla's small affair less than six months after her move to Texas, Maggie's mother insisted on a huge wedding. It was a first for both, and encouraged by Mia, they couldn't argue and agreed.

Mia attended Kyla's wedding with them, and now Nicole's, and her excitement only added to what she felt was in store for them. She often talked of nothing else and bragged to her friends and anyone else that would listen about 'their' big wedding that would come soon.

As pre planned, they met Kyla and Alan in luggage claim when their plane landed and Mia was very familiar by now, felt comfortable running to them in greeting. Maggie laughed, everyone to Mia had become her family, part of a large family she'd never experienced until now, but flourished in the presence of it.

"Look how big you're getting." Maggie beamed at the sight of a very pregnant Kyla.

Kyla whispered in her ear. "Alan and I haven't told anyone yet, but you can tell Jackson. It's twins."

Maggie held Kyla's face in her hands. "You are glowing. That's unbelievably fantastic."

"Shhhhh, I don't want to make a big deal of it, its Nicole's day, I won't tell her till after the wedding."

As they left the airport Maggie noticed that Alan was glowing just as well. When Mia was a few feet away and couldn't overhear she told Jackson the news and congratulated Alan.

"Twins? Well you two aren't wasting any time. Congratulations." Jackson shook Alan's hand and then they hugged.

Alan beamed proud, an expectant father who felt so blessed. "Getting a late start we don't have time to waste. I guess it won't be long for you two either."

Jackson sighed deep. "I have to make an honest woman of her first, her brothers would take turns killing me, I have this picture of one of them killing me and just reviving me so another can do the same."

Maggie laughed. "It isn't that bad, they love you."

"Yeah, and they'd kill me too."

Alan added. "I know your brothers, Maggie, a formidable group to say the least. Jackson knows what he's doing."

Nicole and Derek had purchased a new home, a bigger one than either previously had since they would have four kids between them. Even though Derek's kids would only be there on the weekends during the school year, they spent much more time in the summer, they would have their own room when they came, always to feel an integral and important part of the now larger family.

Their neighbors surprised them, told them not to worry about a thing after the ceremony and beautifully decorated their large backyard that overlooked a lake with white tents and white lights in the trees. A dance floor was made and green vines and lights hung from corner posts and candles in luminaries lit the edge of the water. It was a soft fairytale vision created for two special people.

Music played and champagne flowed as Maggie stood quietly and watched from the sideline. Kyla and Alan danced and she laughed at the distance between them caused by the protruding stomach of their unborn twins. Nicole and Derek looked beautiful together, serene, content, and in love as they swayed in each other's arms as close as they possibly could. Derek whispered something close to her ear and the smile on Nicole's face was radiant and fulfilled. Maggie had never seen her so beautiful.

The older kids had taken Mia under their wing as they always did. Even the older boys were always so kind and Nicole's son let her stand on his feet and they too danced. When Mia saw her watching she beamed and waved.

"Look, mama, I'm dancing."

Maggie waved back with eyes that watered as Jackson put his arm around her.

"Look at you all sentimental," he held her tightly to him and kissed the top of her head.

"It's my hormones." Maggie leaned into him with tears that streamed down her face now. "I'm pregnant, Jackson."

"Maggie," he whispered softly and lovingly as he wrapped her in his arms.

"It's a good thing the wedding's soon, maybe everyone will think it happened on the honeymoon."

"I'm not worried about everyone, I'm worried about your brothers," he kissed her then, his lips soft against hers in the tender moment as his hand cupped her face. "But I think I've proven my love for you, maybe they'll be lenient."

"Maybe, but you'll have to get me ice cream and pickles when I crave them. And not laugh at me when I look like a whale or can't put my shoes on. If you can put up with me when my hormones are even more out of whack, I'll do what I can to save you."

Jackson felt she'd already saved him. He would have spent his whole life loving Mia and no one else, was prepared to do so until Maggie came along and showed him all he would have missed. She completed the both of them, neither he nor Mia were really whole before, it took Maggie to fit into their lives so perfectly to show him that.

Maggie stood in the safe, loving haven she'd found in his strong arms, was pregnant with his child, felt a mother to a child who had stolen her heart as if she'd given birth to her and who now called her mama as if she had. If she hadn't been part of it, she would have thought it an illusion, a distant fairytale dream she'd had as a young girl. The kind the three of them, Maggie, Kyla and Nicole had dreamed of often and given up hope on. So much joy and happiness surrounded all of them now.

One year previous they were three lonely women, each lost and alone amidst an empty horizon they saw before them. Now the house and yard overflowed with joy that could be heard in the laughter of many. Many things had changed for them, and many things remained to change ahead, but each of them found their future. The same vast horizon they looked at as empty before, had given them everything.

Printed in the United States
57717LVS00003B/81